P. G.
County

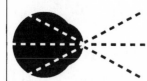

This Large Print Book carries the
Seal of Approval of N.A.V.H.

P. G. County

Connie Briscoe

Thorndike Press • **Waterville, Maine**

Published in 2003 by arrangement with Doubleday, a division of the Doubleday Broadway Publishing Group, a division of Random House, Inc.

Thorndike Press Large Print Basic Series.

The tree indicium is a trademark of Thorndike Press.

The text of this Large Print edition is unabridged. Other aspects of the book may vary from the original edition.

Set in 16 pt. Plantin by Al Chase.

Printed in the United States on permanent paper.

Library of Congress Cataloging-in-Publication Data
Briscoe, Connie.
    P. G. County / Connie Briscoe.
      p. cm.
    ISBN 0-7862-4931-5 (lg. print : hc : alk. paper)
    1. Prince George's County (Md.) — Fiction. 2. African American families — Fiction. 3. Mistresses — Fiction.
4. Adultery — Fiction. 5. Large type books. I. Title: PG County. II. Title.
PS3552.R4894 P18 2003
813'.54—dc21   125- 4337   2002190769

For Roderick,
my wonderful husband,
for your support, encouragement, and love

Acknowledgments

I have to thank Janet Hill, vice president and executive editor at Doubleday Broadway, for her enthusiasm, patience, and dedication, and most of all, for being a joy to work with. Shelby Tuck-Horton, event planner extraordinaire, took time out from her busy schedule to help me with some of the details in the wedding reception scenes. I also want to thank publicist Felicia Polk for working so hard on my behalf and asking for so little in return.

Thanks to Brandon and Jasmine for enriching my life.

And thanks to my agent, Victoria Sanders, for her support and friendship.

Chapter 1

Barbara Bentley was sweating profusely and it wasn't the shakes this time. She hadn't had a drink in years. This time it was that philandering husband of hers, Bradford Bentley III, slipping out of bed at the crack of dawn to run to his mistress.

She listened to him moving around in the bathroom — the toilet flushing, water running — and fumed under the bedcovers. Only seconds ago, she'd been tucked contentedly between her Egyptian cotton sheets, dreaming of the exquisite preparations for her daughter's upcoming wedding — of beluga caviar and smoked salmon, of starched white tablecloths and lilacs and lilies. Then came the familiar bed tremor as her husband jolted her awake. Honestly. The man had no shame when it came to his uncontrollable sexual urges.

But she didn't utter a word. She simply adjusted the silken mask over her eyes and turned to face away from the bathroom door.

She had long since learned not to question the man who slept next to her each night about these things unless she wanted to be thoroughly dressed down. And lied to. He'd give her his "how dare you question me" look and tell her to quit whining. He was only going to play golf, to hang out with his buddies for a few hours, and hadn't he given her everything a woman could possibly want? They had a big beautiful house, a condo at Wintergreen ski resort and another in Nassau, a Jaguar and two Benzes in the driveway, a forty-foot boat sitting on the Potomac and country club membership.

But at fifty years of age, she now knew better than to be deceived by his sly diversions. She wasn't some wide-eyed young bride anymore, and he wasn't running off to hit any balls into little holes in green grass. No indeed. He was off to put his little pecker into a certain brown hole down the block.

She threw the bedcovers off. She needed to cool down. Normally she would have shrugged it off, he'd done this for so long. But this was their daughter's wedding day. Didn't the man have even a shred of decency? Propriety? Sympathy? Even when it came to his daughter?

The bathroom door opened, and she fumed as she mentally ticked off the myriad tasks she had to complete — without benefit of her husband's help — before the guests arrived at their home that afternoon for the reception. She had a wedding planner to help out, of course, but Barbara trusted no one to completely handle this very important affair.

Only after she heard the bedroom door shut and her husband's footsteps on the stairs did she yank the silken mask from her eyes. Then she swung her feet over the edge of the bed and reached for the pack of Benson & Hedges sitting on her nightstand.

"Men," she hissed under her breath as she lit up. Her husband was fifty-six years old. She wished he'd grow up and act it. She took a deep puff, then blew it out.

She went to the window, pulled the drapes open and looked out over the estate. It was a perfect June day with a beautiful blue sky. The edges of the white tent that had been erected on the lawn the previous day blew gently in the breeze. She smiled. At least the weather was cooperating.

She glanced at the clock on the wall and decided to let Rebecca sleep a little longer. The wedding didn't start until two, and the future bride had probably been up late last night talking on the phone to her fiancé. Rebecca needed her beauty rest for this special day.

Barbara had to admit to herself that she

preferred it when Bradford wasn't around. As long as he handed over the green stuff whenever she needed it, she could get along just fine, thank you. Although lately he had started to nag her about how much the wedding was costing them. How much was this? And why do we need that?

Honestly, what did he expect? A proper wedding with three hundred guests took money, piles of it. As he often reminded her, they were the Bentleys of Silver Lake, one of the finest families in one of Prince George's County's grandest neighborhoods. He was founder and president of a multimillion-dollar technology company, one of the most successful black-owned firms in the area, hell, in the United States of America. To quote him, they had an image to uphold. Well, Mister Big Shot ought to know that they couldn't get away with a two-bit piddling wedding for their daughter.

The day Bradford struck it rich fifteen years ago when his firm landed that twenty-million-dollar software development contract, she'd promised herself that their two daughters would always have the finest of everything. Private schools, music lessons, beautiful dresses. And on their wedding days they would get a lot more than a little rinky-dink cafeteria-style reception in the church hall. That was all her aunt could afford for her, but now Barbara could afford the world for her daughters. And they would have it.

When she was twelve, her daddy took off for good — flat out disappeared. Her mother tried hard to raise her only child on her own. But it was tough for a single black woman in rural Virginia back in the 1960s. Her mother lost job after job, and pretty soon she took to drinking and welfare. Within a couple of years after her daddy left, they lost the house, then the car, and Barbara became the poorest girl in school. "Barbara the bag lady," they called her, as her dresses became more tattered by the day.

You so po', yo' mama make you wish sandwiches for lunch, two slices of bread and wish you had some meat.

Ha, ha, ha.

Where your daddy, bastard child?

That was how she learned her parents were never married. And in the sixties it was still something to be ashamed of, especially in Smithfield, Virginia.

She would never forget how frightened she was the day she came home from school and walked into their tiny one-bedroom apartment to find her mama dead on the couch. An empty bottle of Boone's Farm lay nearby on the floor. It was her fifteenth birthday.

Her mother's sister whisked her off, and her living standards jumped up a notch or two. But Aunt Gladys took every chance she got to trash Barbara's "no-good daddy." Aunt Glady's favorite saying was "Most men are dogs, the rest are boring as hell." Uncle Marvin mostly sat in the living room watching TV when he came home from work. He was considered one of the boring ones.

Bradford was one of the dogs, and Aunt Gladys was dead set against their marriage. She suspected that beneath all the Southern charm oozing from the pores of Bradford Bentley III was a cold and distant man. Barbara had long since come to realize that her aunt's opinions about Bradford weren't entirely unfair. He *was* a dog at times.

But he could also be kind and generous with her and the girls. He rarely denied them anything. And she and Bradford had a lot more in common than many people realized. Everyone seemed to think that Bradford came from a prestigious Southern family, that he was born into money because he was so polished and charming. But he was from Smithfield, and his folks were pure country just like hers.

His parents had stayed together, and that made Bradford's life a little easier. And instead of fleeing as her daddy had, Bradford's dad had stayed in Smithfield. But he worked in the factories all his life and died penniless and mad at the world.

To this very day, Bradford's mother still lived in the same house with one of Bradford's sisters. But Bradford rarely visited them or talked about them. He seemed to have this need to run as far and fast as he could from his humble beginnings, and he had done a good job of leaving all signs of his past behind. They both had. Although she still visited her aunt regularly, she didn't keep in touch with anyone else from Smithfield.

If those snotty-nosed country kids down there could see her now, in her fine stone-and-stucco, Spanish-tile-roofed, seven-bedroom, eight-bathroom house, they'd be shocked. She had a housekeeper who came every damn day except Sunday. She got manicures and pedicures weekly. She was a long, long way from being "Barbara the bag lady."

She put her cigarette out. That enough daydreaming. She had a busy day ahead of her. The aroma of fresh Jamaican coffee drifted up the stairs, and that meant Phyllis, her housekeeper, had arrived. Thank goodness. A hit of caffeine was just what she needed to charge her fifty-year-old batteries for this long day.

Not that she looked her age. No way. She took care of herself. She gardened, in a climate-controlled greenhouse, of course. She exercised. She was still a slim size 8, one size bigger than she was the day she got married. People often thought she was in her late thirties. No bag lady, this. Not Barbara Anne Bentley.

She looked down at the ashtray. If only she could get rid of that nasty habit. Her complexion was starting to dry out from the cigarettes. But dammit, considering all that Bradford had put her through over the years, she was entitled to a crutch.

She opened the nightstand drawer for a fresh pack to go with her morning coffee, then paused and stared at the bottle of Belvedere vodka in back of the drawer. It looked so tempting, she nearly smacked her lips. The bottle had been sitting there for two years now as a pointed reminder of the dark days behind her, and she normally opened this drawer several times a day without even noticing it. With the big day ahead and Bradford acting the usual horny, selfish fool, she couldn't be blamed for being tempted. But she was beyond that now. She slammed the drawer shut.

She tossed her silk floor-length bathrobe across her shoulders, lit up with her eighteen-karat gold cigarette lighter, and followed the scent of coffee down a long hallway to the stairs. Thank God for Jamaica Blue Mountain and housekeepers.

Chapter 2

"Oh yeah . . . baby, that's it. Ooh. Oh yes!"

Jolene had trouble believing that was her own voice making those lewd noises, especially after she promised herself never to let this man touch her again unless he left his wife. After all, she was ready to leave her husband for him.

Now here she was, leaning up against a stud in the frame of her unfinished house, with her denim Versace skirt hiked up above her ass and her Manolo Blahnik mules strewn across the wood subfloor, while Terrence rammed it up. She dug her three-inch red nails into his back. "Oh . . . yes, yes, yes!"

So much for promises.

Terrence moaned, stiffened, relaxed, then let her go. They both huffed and puffed as they sank down to the subfloor to catch their breath. It was the middle of June and the house had no air-conditioning, didn't even have a roof yet to protect them from the sun. She sighed contentedly and watched as Terrence stretched his tall, perfect body out on the floor.

You silly girl. Letting him get away with this crap again. Not even this rich hunk of an architect was worth getting your heart broken over. This was it, the absolute last time until he agreed to leave his wife. She was worth more than an occasional screw on the fly.

She shifted onto her knees and crawled across the floor toward her shoes while thinking how best to tell him. She was tempted to give it to him straight — me or her, now or never.

"Not bad for a thirty-six-year-old broad," Terrence teased, smacking her on the buttock playfully. Jolene slapped his hand away, a little harder than intended.

"Whoa. I'm only kidding, baby," he said. "You have a beautiful body. That ass, those boobs, those legs. Mmm-umph!" He touched his lips with the tips of his fingers and made a kissing sound. "You do it to me every time we get together."

"I could do it every night if you'd leave your wife," she retorted. "Every morning, too." She looked at him pointedly as he nodded without comment and reached across the floor for his undershirt. That's right, she thought. You know where this conversation is heading, don't you, sweetie? And now you're gonna duck and run.

Her eyes followed him as he stood and zipped his fly. The sight of him standing there above her, his honey-toned muscles gleaming against a sleeveless white undershirt, was enough to tempt her to say the hell with this crap about his wife and pull him back down on top of her. Terrence Turner was the sexiest man she'd ever slept with. And as part owner of an architectural firm, he was also the most successful. She loved a take-charge, go-get-'em kind of guy. So unlike her husband. But she wanted *all* of this hunk, not just these quickies on the sly. She wanted to be the architect's wife.

She stood up, moved within inches of him, placed her hands on her hips and turned on her sexiest smile. "Don't you want to be with me, sweetie?" she purred.

He squeezed her arms gently. "You know I do, baby. But you also know how I feel about leaving my wife before my boys grow up. I have to put them first."

Jolene sighed. "I know your boys are important to you. But it'll be three more years before your youngest goes to college. Kids are stronger about these things than you realize. Hell. You think I'd take Juliette away from her dad if I thought she couldn't handle it?"

He stepped back. "Your situation is different from mine. My —"

"How?" Jolene interrupted. "We're both

married with teenagers. Both in rotten marriages, I should add. But we love each other, sweetie. Right?"

He sighed. "Yeah, baby, but —"

"Then what's stopping us? Huh?" She knew she was pouting, whining even, but she couldn't help it. She just didn't understand why Terrence wouldn't leave that lame wife of his if he wasn't in love with her. The woman was all wrong for him. She had supposedly attended Spelman College in Atlanta and her father was a doctor. But from what Jolene had heard, she was a mealymouthed, plain-ass Jane who took little interest in her husband's career. Terrence was a top-flight architect and a business owner. He needed a strong woman to help him shine. He needed *her*.

"We've been seeing each other for almost six months now, Terrence."

He let go of her arms and shook his head. "I told you, it's simple. I can't leave my kids now. OK? Laura's not strong like you. She'll fall apart if I split while the boys are growing up, and I can't do that to the mother of my boys. They need her. I was the first man Laura was ever with, and —"

Jolene smacked her lips. "Oh, please, give me a break. What about *me?* What about *my* feelings? I don't want to have to wait that long for us to be together. You said this house will be finished in another six months, right?"

He nodded and frowned at the same time, clearly wondering what was coming next.

"When it is finished, I want us to move in here together and be a family and —"

He pointed to the floor. "Here?"

"What's wrong with that? Patrick won't want to have anything to do with this house if I ask him for a divorce. He barely wants anything to do with it now." She chuckled wryly. "He thinks I get carried away and that it's much too big and expensive. You and I had more to do with building this house than he did. We're good together, sweetie, and you know it."

Terrence smiled with pride as he looked around what was the future great room, with its soaring two-story-high ceiling and a spiral staircase leading up to a second-story balcony. "It is going to be one hell of a showpiece when it's done. One of the nicest homes in Silver Lake."

"Damn right it is," she said. Better than just about anyone else's in Silver Lake, including the white folks'. Unlike the house she lived in now on the southern edge of Silver Lake, this one was being built on the north side, where the Bentleys and all the other big-money folks in Prince George's County lived. If she'd had her way, their new house would have been even bigger than the Bentleys'. But Patrick could be so tight with a buck she sometimes thought she could see blood dripping out of his damn wallet.

Terrence smiled at her. "Look, don't you have a wedding to attend this afternoon? Isn't Bradford Bentley's daughter getting married?"

Jolene turned her back to him and folded her arms. She knew that he was changing the subject on her, just as he always did when she brought this up. Well, he wasn't going to get away with it this time.

"I can't do this anymore, Terrence. I'm tired of having to sneak off to meet you and . . . and screwing in the backseats of our cars and in hotel rooms and now here. If you love me as much as I love you, you'd leave her."

"I keep telling you, sugar, it's not that simple. I —" He reached for her but she stepped out of his grasp.

"It *is* that simple. It's me or her. And I mean it this time." She bit her bottom lip.

He bent down and snatched his shirt off the floor. "Fine. If that's how you want to be. Fuck it."

"Fine with me, too," she shouted at his back as he walked toward the doorway. "Go on, then. Run away. Just like you always do. And don't expect me to call you this time. I'll find me another damn architect."

He waved his arm nonchalantly. "Whatever." He took the stairs two at a time.

"Shit!" She kicked a Budweiser can left by the construction workers across the floorboards. Bastard. Why did she have such rotten luck with men? First Patrick, now Terrence. No. The first was that Jonathan Parker. She shook her head. She'd been married to that asshole Patrick for so damn long, she'd almost forgotten about that prick Jonathan. But not quite. She could never forget someone who had caused her and her family so much pain and humiliation. She was only seventeen when it all came down, and to this moment, that had to have been one of the worst days of her life.

"Tell me who the father is, Jolene," Daddy had demanded after church on that Sunday long ago, his voice booming across his big mahogany desk. He was wearing a navy suit with a patterned gold tie, and Jolene thought his brown face looked so handsome.

But she nearly choked trying to get the boy's name out, she was so scared of what her daddy might do. Especially in that dark den. It was Daddy's favorite room, with its thick Persian carpet and leather-bound books lining the walls. But the room always gave her the creeps.

"Answer me, Jolene," Daddy scolded. "Who is the father?"

"Um . . . um . . . Jonathan," she murmured.

Daddy narrowed his eyes the way he often did from the bench of his courtroom when questioning an attorney or a witness. "Jonathan Parker? Isn't his father an attorney?"

She nodded.

Daddy walked around the desk and paced across the carpet. "What's the matter with you two? What the devil were you thinking? Jonathan Parker comes from a fine, respectable family of lawyers. And so do you. You're a Cooke. You two should know better than this."

He turned toward Mama, sitting in an upholstered armchair. A wide-brimmed burgundy hat with black trim framed her ivory-colored face. Jolene had told Mama the news first, and Mama marched her right into Daddy's den.

"Didn't you talk to her about this, Camilla?" Daddy asked. "About boys and . . . and all that?"

"Of course I did, Charles. But she's always been willful. You've spoiled her so. Her sister, too."

Daddy grunted. "Well, they'll have to get married right away. That's all there is to it."

"I agree," Mama said. "We won't have time to plan much of a wedding, but I'll do the best I can."

Jolene felt her cheeks go hot. She looked down at the floor. "Um . . ."

"Well, what is it, Jolene?" Daddy asked impatiently.

"Have you told the boy yet?" Mama asked.

Jolene nodded slowly.

"And?"

"And he . . . well . . . he . . . he doesn't want to marry me." There. She'd said it. She swallowed hard as a look of sorrow crossed Mama's eyes. She wanted to run and bury her face in Mama's lap and apologize. She never meant to shame the family like this. She knew how hard her mama and daddy worked to get all their nice things. They lived in a big Tudor-style house on upper Sixteenth Street, an area in Washington, D.C., that was so prominent it was called the gold coast. They had two Buicks and a cottage in Oak Bluffs, on Martha's Vineyard. And her parents wanted their two daughters to marry into nice respectable families. But she was too big to run to Mama now. She was wearing two-inch pumps and pink lipstick.

"He said that?" Daddy asked. "He actually told you he won't marry you?"

Jolene nodded. Jonathan told her that and a whole lot more that she would never repeat to anyone. Not ever. He said that he didn't believe he was the father and for her to get lost. He called her a liar whenever she reminded him that he was the only boy she'd ever slept with. How could he say such mean things to her after he had made love to her only weeks ago?

Daddy scoffed. "Well, we'll certainly see about that," he said, going back around his desk. He flipped the cards in his Rolodex.

"What are you doing, Daddy?" Jolene cried. "Who are you calling?"

"The Parkers. That's who. We'll see what that boy's parents have to say about this."

Jolene ran up to his desk. "No, Daddy, don't," she pleaded.

"What do you mean, no? This is his responsibility, too. I'm not going to let him get away with this."

"I . . . I don't want to be married to someone who doesn't want to be married to me. And . . . and" — she stomped the floor

— "he said he would deny it if I said he was the father."

"I don't give a damn what he said," Daddy said gruffly. "If he's the father, then his parents need to talk some sense into his silly little head."

Mama stood up. "Jolene, if you don't marry Jonathan, no decent man will ever want to marry you once you have a child."

"Did you think about that, Jolene, or anything else before you got yourself into this . . . this . . . situation?" Daddy sighed in exasperation.

Jolene blinked and looked down at the floor. No, she hadn't thought about that.

"And college," Daddy continued. "That will have to be put on hold, maybe forever. College is difficult enough without having a child to worry about. You don't have to take our word for it. Ask your sister. Jackie would never have gotten herself in trouble like this before finishing at Spelman."

Jolene clenched her jaw. Why did they always have to throw her older sister in her face? She wasn't anything like Jackie. She didn't get all A's in school. She didn't have long, wavy hair or a flawless near-white complexion like their mama. Her father had a little more color, but he was still fair enough to pass the brown paper bag rule. Jolene wasn't.

"Charles. Maybe we should wait and discuss this later. There are other options we can look into. But you, well, we're all too upset to think straight now."

Daddy shoved his hands in his pockets. "Of course I'm upset. This could ruin her life. And how does it look for a judge's seventeen-year-old daughter to be pregnant and unmarried." He waved his arm at Jolene. "Go on. I don't need to see your face now. But don't you leave this house without our permission."

With a little arm-twisting, Daddy had finally persuaded Jonathan Parker to agree to marry her. Jonathan even brought her flowers the following week, and Mama began to fuss over wedding details. Soon Jolene allowed herself to believe that things might work out, and visions of a pretty house with a white picket fence danced through her head.

But the day before the wedding, Jonathan backed out, and no amount of persuasion or even threats would change his mind. By that time she was almost six months pregnant, too far gone for an abortion. Daddy would barely look at her when he came home from work.

She had spent a week in bed crying over

Jonathan when Patrick Brown came along. He was two years older than she and had just finished junior college and started work as an electrician when her daddy hired him to upgrade the wiring in their big old house. She hardly noticed Patrick as he moved from room to room, but when she did, he always smiled at her and asked after the baby.

Then one Saturday afternoon he caught her huddled in the laundry room crying over a pile of dirty clothes. He offered her a handkerchief, and after she calmed down some asked her if she wanted to go and see *Trading Places*, a new comedy with Eddie Murphy and Dan Aykroyd. He thought it would cheer her up.

He seemed surprised when she accepted, probably because she was the judge's daughter and he was only an electrician. But she was brokenhearted, unmarried and very pregnant. Her daddy barely spoke to her. Attention from a young man was just what she needed. A month later he proposed.

He wasn't nearly as cute as Jonathan, but she agreed to marry him to give the baby a father and erase some of the shame she'd brought on the family. But she soon realized that even though her folks went along with the marriage, it was without enthusiasm.

After all, Patrick was not a doctor or a lawyer, never would be, and his daddy was a mail-room clerk. Patrick wasn't even the father of her baby. And the wedding was arranged hastily in the parlor with only the immediate family present.

Daddy was certain Patrick was scheming to get his claws on the family money, but her folks had come to believe that this was the best they could expect of poor Jolene. A couple of vows, a little champagne and she was Mrs. Jolene Cooke Brown, much to the family's dismay.

A few weeks later she delivered a stillborn baby and fell into another crying spell.

Mama thought that bragging about Jackie when she came to the hospital to visit would lift Jolene's spirits. Jackie had pledged Alpha Kappa Alpha at Spelman College in Atlanta. Jackie was dating a Morehouse Man. Jackie this, Jackie that. Yak, yak, yak. Jolene thought she had never been so fucking miserable in all her life.

She returned to their tiny apartment and stayed in bed for weeks. She cried and smoked a lot of marijuana. After a few months of trying to be patient, Patrick told her to stop feeling sorry for herself, to get up off her butt and get on with her life. Besides, all this grass was burning a hole in his wallet.

She knew he was right. At the rate she was smoking, she'd turn into a dried-up weed right between the sheets. And no amount of crying would bring her baby back or her earlier charmed life. As soon as she was strong enough, she hit the pavement and quickly landed a job as a secretary at HUD. She enrolled in night classes at the University of D.C. It wasn't exactly Spelman College, but it would do.

She even managed to put a smile on her face when Jackie marched down the aisle to marry her precious Morehouse Man. Daddy spent thousands of dollars on the wedding. He kept saying that if he was only going to have to do this once, he might as well do it right.

Jolene had given up marijuana by then, so she knocked back a couple of screwdrivers before the ceremony. She was so tipsy that she tripped and nearly fell over her long bridesmaid's gown on her way down the aisle and had fits of giggles throughout the ceremony. Mama and Daddy fixed her with steely looks of disapproval between their radiant smiles at Jackie, but Jolene didn't care. She was used to it.

She picked her bag up off the subfloor of her unfinished house and took out her compact. She powdered her brown nose, flipped her shoulder-length auburn hair, courtesy of Imani Silken Hair Weaves, and brushed the sawdust off her skirt. No point dwelling on all that ancient history. That's all it was. History. The past.

She was now the boss at work, a god-damned GS-15, Step 10 at HUD, the highest level one could reach in the federal government without going through a special selection process or getting a presidential appointment. A dozen people jumped when she barked.

She worked out three days a week and was a shapely size 6. And she had a big, bad-ass, custom-designed house in the works in Silver Lake, North, where all the executive homes were located. Not even her sister Jackie, with her cattle-sized hips and little-ass colonial down there in Atlanta could top that.

And she would get her handsome, successful man sooner or later, one way or another. Jolene wasn't about to let this little setback stop her. She took her cell phone from her bag and hit the memory buttons for Terrence's number. It was time for them to make up.

Chapter 3

"Humph." Pearl grunted again as she tried to wiggle into her black polyester skirt. She had gained so much weight, she couldn't even get the thing over her hips. She had worn this skirt to a wedding just last summer. How on earth did this happen? *When* did it happen?

She knew exactly how and when — too many bags of Utz potato chips and Hershey candy bars keeping her company late at night after her son left home for college, that's what. She yanked the skirt off and threw it on the bed.

She hated having to get dressed up and face this depressing joke of a closet crammed with cheap, ill-fitting polyester knits. But Barbara Bentley was one of her top clients. She came into Pearl's hair salon every week and she tipped most generously. Pearl was flattered to have been invited to the Bentley home for the wedding reception.

Barbara was also filthy rich and lived in a beautiful house, and Pearl didn't want to go to this affair looking shabby. A lot of rich black folks would be there. And if there was one thing rich black folks liked to throw their dough away on, it was clothes. They'll be prancing around with Armani and Versace adorning their perfect, lean bodies, courtesy of private health clubs that she certainly couldn't afford. They'll be driving up in Benzes and Jaguars and Lexuses, and bragging about their Carribean vacations like they were auditioning for a production of *Lifestyles of the Rich and Famous.*

Pearl would have bet her bottom dollar that half of them didn't have a nickel to spit on after they paid their hefty mortgages and fat car notes at the end of the month. Some of them probably had credit card balances bigger than her annual salary. Still, they managed to walk the walk and talk the talk as good as anyone.

She stared in the closet and smacked her lips with utter disgust. She had way too much black and brown and could find only two skirts decent enough to be seen in. She usually just threw on a pair of slacks to work at the salon since they would be covered by a smock anyway. She made decent enough money, but over the years she had spent most of it on her son, making sure he was raised right — not easy when you had to do it all by your lonesome self. There were music lessons, clothes for school and sports, doctor and dental bills. And don't even mention college.

She even bought this town house for his sake. She had struggled for years, working twelve-hour days at hair salons and catering to save up for the down payment so they could move to Silver Lake and be near the right schools and playmates. Some of the folks in Silver Lake had tried to stop the developer from even putting up the town houses. They seemed to think that anything less than a mini-mansion would mess up their property values. Folks could be so snooty when they thought they had a little something. But that was OK. She could put up with snobbery and a whole lot more for the welfare of her son.

She reached into the back of the closet and finally found a loose-fitting beige polyester dress. At least it had fit loosely the last time she wore it a few years ago, and it wasn't black or brown. She pulled it over her head and tugged it down over her hips. She just managed to squeeze into it.

She frowned at her reflection in the mirror above her dresser. It was getting so she hated to even pass by one of the contraptions for fear of what she'd see staring back at her. She could remember being a size 8 just before Kenyatta went away to college five years ago. Now she was bursting out of a 14. She'd better do something about all these extra pounds she was putting on or she was going to find her fat butt on the doorstep of Lane Bryant.

She sighed, picked up a compact of bronze-colored blush, and leaned over the Maybelline and Revlon bottles lined up on her dresser to dust her cheeks. Then she rubbed a dab of her homemade hair oil into her short natural hair. She spent so much time fixing other women's hair, the last thing she wanted to do when she came home was fuss with her own.

The only thing she did was cut and color it a rich brown. Cut and color were the key, as she always told her clients. And long hair pulled the face — a no-no for most women once they hit their late forties and fifties. This short do suited her forty-seven-year-old caramel-colored face just fine.

She walked to Kenyatta's room and knocked. He opened the door holding a navy suit jacket in his hand.

"Does this fit OK?" Pearl lifted her arms and turned around in the hallway.

"Damn, Ma!" he exclaimed with a glint in his eye. "You done put on a lot of weight down south there."

She smacked his arm playfully. "I told you about cursing and using that Ebonics. I didn't sweat all those years to send you to college to hear that garbage. And never mind my hips. Does the dress look all right?"

Kenyatta grinned as he slipped into his suit jacket. "You crack me up, Ma. Yeah, it's fine. You look real nice. But you really need to do something about all that weight you're gaining. It's not healthy."

Pearl put her hands on her hips. "Don't you think I know that?"

"Hey, don't shoot the messenger. I'm just trying to keep it real here, 'cause I want you to live to a hundred. But how do you expect to find yourself a man unless you slim down?"

Pearl scoffed. "Oh shoot. That's the last thing I need. Some man to worry about. You're plenty. Believe me."

"I won't be around forever, you know. I been hanging around here for a year now, but don't get used to that."

Pearl reached up and pinched both of his cheeks. "I know, I know. You can't sit still for a minute." She looked at her watch. "Speaking of which, you'd better hurry up if you're going to pick up that girl and get to the wedding on time."

"Yeah, yeah. And that *woman's* name is Ashley."

"Excuse me. Woman, then." Pearl reached up to straighten his necktie. "You just make sure you introduce her to me at the wedding. And tell me, what does she think about this hairstyle?" Pearl touched Kenyatta's shoulder-length dreadlocks.

"She likes it just fine, Ma. She's very open-minded."

Pearl shook her head. "Humph. For the life of me, I just plain don't understand why you want to wear your hair like that. I spent all those years trying to get the kinks out of your hair, and here you spend all your time putting them back in."

Kenyatta chuckled, sounding just like his daddy. He had his daddy's hair, too — thick and kinky, not wavy like hers. In fact, he was his daddy all over — tall, dark-complexioned and handsome as the devil. Trouble was, his daddy *was* the devil incarnate, with his arrogant Uncle Tom self. He had left Pearl for a white woman twenty years earlier, and Pearl's heart still ticked like a time bomb whenever she thought about him.

"We need to talk, Pearl."

A chill ran through her gut. There was something about the tone of her husband's voice, the expression on his face. It was sad and happy all at once, and Pearl didn't like the way it made her feel one bit. She stepped back, holding the picture she was hanging in the foyer of their apartment in her hands.

"I've met someone."

Pearl gripped the picture frame tighter. Met someone? What was that supposed to mean? He worked in the mayor's office. He met people every day.

And why couldn't he look her in the eyes? Why was he staring at the floor? The ceiling. The air. At everything but her.

"It's a woman."

Pearl gripped the frame tighter. She stared at him. Look at me when you tell me this, Gregory Jackson. Show me some respect when you tell me about your little fling. Can't you at least do that?

". . . name is Holly, from the office."

Holly? Holly? Your assistant? But that girl is white. And she's only nineteen. She's a blond nineteen-year-old child. She's . . .

Pearl threw the picture at him. "You bastard," she screamed with clenched fists as he ducked and walked away. She had left her family behind in Washington, D.C., as a young woman of nineteen and moved to Detroit to be with him. She dropped out of college to work full-time and help him get through vet school. Then she quit her job to stay home with the baby when he asked her to. She supported him when he decided to get into politics. She had made him the center of her life for years. And now this.

"How could you do this to me?" she screamed after him.

The next day she was packing her bags.

She had wanted nothing to do with him after that. She didn't want his help, his money or anything else. It was bad enough when a husband cheated on his wife, but with a white woman? That was unforgivable in her book.

Her mama and most of her girlfriends thought she was insane walking away from a man with a good job without insisting on a big alimony payment and child support. Never mind who he was fooling around with. She had a child to support.

But Pearl had made up her mind. She would raise her son alone. She left Detroit when Kenyatta was seven years old and never looked back.

"I gotta run, Ma." Kenyatta kissed her on the forehead and dashed down the stairs.

She smiled and shook her head. Despite the hair and occasional sloppy grammar, Kenyatta had turned out to be a fine young man. She had done a pretty decent job with him, no thanks to his daddy.

The sound of the television floated out of

Kenyatta's room, and she opened the door to turn it off. She stopped in her tracks and gasped at the mess that confronted her — clothes and shoes all over the floor, bed unmade, books and CDs piled everywhere. She had just put the books away on the shelves two days ago and even took the time to alphabetize them.

She shook her head. OK, so it was more than the wild hair and sloppy grammar that bothered her. Sometimes she worried that Kenyatta wasn't responsible enough. He was twenty-seven years old and had been out of Morehouse College for five years now. So far he'd held a half dozen jobs and lived in three states. Now he was back home. He claimed he was trying to find himself. Humph. What in the world was he doing all that time in college?

And the girls, or *women*, as he insisted she call them. It seemed he had a different one every time she turned around — Glenda, Juanita, Keisha, Davida. The list went on. They came and went so fast that Pearl hardly ever got a chance to know them.

Sometimes she thought it was her fault. She'd spoiled him by giving him everything. Other times she thought she just worried too much. He was still young, and she supposed he had lots of time to "find himself" and still make something of himself.

She started on the unmade bed first. She had just enough time to make a dent in this mess before she was due at Barbara's to fix Rebecca's hair.

Chapter 4

"Mom, I need to talk to you for a minute."

Candice lowered the wet towel from her head and stared into her daughter's green eyes. Ashley was standing in the doorway of her bedroom, twisting a lock of her long brown hair between her fingers. What was this all about? Whenever one of her daughters used that dreaded tone of voice and twisted her hair like that, it meant one of two things. They either wanted something or had news they knew she wouldn't like.

But it was a surprise to hear it coming from Ashley. Caitlin, at fifteen and still boy crazy and a little rebellious, yes. But Ashley had always been the levelheaded one of the two, and she was going on twenty now. She had done a lot of growing up since starting college.

"Does it have to be right now?" Candice asked. "I just stepped out of the shower."

"It will only take a minute," Ashley assured her. "It's important."

Candice draped the towel around her wet hair and pulled the belt to her white terry cloth robe tighter. "OK, I'm listening. What is it?"

Ashley smiled nervously. "Um. It's about the guy who's coming to pick me up to take me to the wedding."

Ashley paused, and Candice nodded slowly, warily. With two teenage daughters, she had already seen and heard just about everything when it came to guys — long hair, spiked hair, pierced noses and tongues, baggy jeans, drugs and booze. You name it. She'd seen it.

She always tried to remember her own hippie teenage years growing up in the seventies. It was a wild time, and she had tried a thing or two herself. But in the end, she had come out all right, and her daughters would, too. She prided herself on being an understanding mother — tolerant and patient.

"What about him, Ashley? Yesterday you said his name is Kenny."

"Um, yes. But he's . . . he's not white." Ashley shifted her weight from one foot to the other and folded her arms across her chest.

Candice frowned. Then it hit her. Ashley was dating someone outside their race. So much for thinking she'd seen it all. This was totally unexpected, especially coming from Ashley. Patience, patience, she told herself. "Ah. I see. Well, what is he? Latino?"

"Nooo . . . He's black."

"Oh. Really?" Candice tried to keep her voice steady, but it felt as if someone had just sucked the final, dying breath from her gut. She glanced at the door to the master bathroom. She wished Jim would hurry out of the damn shower. Where was that man when she needed him? They had only been married for a year, but he was good at handling stuff like this. He was always so much calmer when it came to the girls. He —

"Mom? *Hello?*" Ashley snapped her fingers in her mother's face.

Candice blinked. "Yes?"

"Um, you down with that?"

"What?"

"You OK with what I just said?"

Candice pulled the belt to her robe tighter. "Well . . . I . . . I'm just surprised, that's all. This is a first."

Ashley shrugged. "But you always told us that people are just people. Right? And that what counts is what's in their hearts."

Candice stared at her daughter, at her white, long-haired, green-eyed daughter. She coughed. She supposed she had said something like that. It certainly sounded harmless enough. But if she *had* said that, she was thinking along the lines of friends, neighbors and coworkers, not lovers. Most of the families in Silver Lake were black, and Ashley and Caitlin both had black friends. Hell, she'd worked as a web designer for Bradford Bentley for seven years now. But this was different. This could involve romance, sex, love.

But how do you go about explaining all this to your nineteen-year-old daughter without sounding like a damn hypocrite? Or worse, a bigot? You, the patient mother. The understanding mother. She twisted the belt to her robe around her fingers. "Um, I probably did say something like that."

Ashley smiled with relief. "Then I'm going to go and finish dressing. He's picking me up in ten minutes."

"Um. Just a minute, honey." Not so fast. She had a million questions about this young man. Where did she meet him? Was he in school? What did his family think of all this? And heaven forbid, had they slept together? But if there was one thing daughters hated, it was prying mothers. She had to tread carefully.

She sat on the edge of the bed and attempted a smile. "Come here. Let's talk a bit before you run off."

Ashley looked reluctant. "I really do need to finish getting dressed, Mom. He'll be here any minute."

Candice frowned. "But the wedding doesn't start for a couple more hours."

"We're going into D.C. to pick up some of his friends."

"This will only take a minute, Ashley," Candice said in an I'm-your-mother-do-as-I-say tone of voice.

Ashley smacked her lips and entered the room as Candice patted the bed. Ashley flopped down.

"So. Does he live in Prince George's County?"

Ashley nodded.

"Well, tell me about him. Does he have a last name?"

Ashley sighed. "Yeah. Jackson."

Candice cocked her head. "Jackson? Jackson? The name sounds familiar. Are they the ones who live in that big Tudor-style house on the north side of Silver Lake?"

Ashley rolled her eyes to the ceiling and shook her head. "No. Not exactly."

Candice frowned at her daughter's strange choice of words. Then it hit her. Oh hell. Don't tell me he lives in *that* part of Prince George's, the rough part inside the beltway. Visions of her lily-white daughter walking around in the ghetto flashed through her head. Her frown grew deeper.

"He and his mom live in the town houses at the southern edge of Silver Lake, Mom."

Candice nodded with some relief. A different class of people lived in the town houses than in the rest of Silver Lake, but at least it wasn't the ghetto. "Just he and his mom?"

Ashley nodded.

"Where's his father?"

Ashley shrugged.

"Does he go to Maryland University with you?"

"No, Mom. He's older."

Oh great. All she needed to hear was that this guy was in his thirties or forties. Then what? That he was a drug dealer? That he had just gotten out of prison? This might be Silver Lake, but they were only fifteen miles outside of Washington, D.C.

"How much older is he?" Candice knew she was pushing, but she couldn't help it. This was her daughter. She had every right to be pushy.

"Kenyatta's twenty-seven, Mom. Not that much older."

Candice raised an eyebrow. Kenyatta? What the hell kind of name was that? "Isn't that the name of a country in Africa?"

"It's a derivative of Kenya, Mom," Ashley said with strained patience.

"It sounds so militant."

Ashley looked to the ceiling with annoyance. "I am so not believing you're acting like this, Mom. There's nothing militant about Kenyatta, I assure you. You're probably more militant than he is. Didn't you protest the Vietnam War in college?"

"I beg your pardon?" Candice asked cynically. "That was thirty years ago. I was just a child during that war."

"Whatever," Ashley said nonchalantly. "You're still into that whole hippie scene. The way you dress, the crystals and the candles."

"It's not rebellious. I just happen to like the look. And stop changing the subject. There's a big difference between nineteen and twenty-seven. What does he do? Does he have a —"

Ashley jumped up and faced her mother. "Jim is fifty, for crissakes, nine whole years older than you are."

"You don't have to shout," Candice reminded her. "I'm sitting right here. And that's different. The years don't mean as much when you get to be our age."

"You mean it's different because Kenyatta is black," Ashley accused. "And before you ask, yes, he has a job. I met him when his firm sent him to Maryland U. to recruit. What's going on with you? You sound like a racist with all these insinuating questions."

Candice jumped back as if she'd been slapped in the face. "That's not true."

"Pfft. You usually only start getting curious after I've been out with a guy a few times."

Candice licked her lips. If it was true, it was only because after the first couple of boyfriends she had come to realize that most of them hung around for only a few months or so before they were replaced by the latest craze — the quarterback, the drummer, the one with a brand-new sports car. The this or that. And that was just fine with mom. At fifteen and nineteen, Caitlin and Ashley were both too young to get serious about boys or men, in her opinion.

She took a deep breath. Maybe she was jumping the gun here. Why should this one be any different? It was probably only one more date with one more guy. And she knew how these things worked. If mom protested, daughter would rebel. Like that time she tried to get Caitlin to stop hanging around some of her friends who smoked cigarettes. The friends she later picked up were into smoking a lot more than just cigarettes. It was probably best not to make waves with

Ashley about this guy. At least not yet.

Candice stood up. "OK. Fair enough, Ashley. No more questions. I just hope you know what you're doing."

"I'm fine, Mom." Ashley looked at her watch impatiently. "I'm going now. I'm really running late."

Candice nodded. "You be sure to introduce him to us when he arrives."

"I can't. I promised him I would come out when he honks since we're running late."

"Then you'll just have to be late," Candice insisted. "I . . ." She paused at the sound of a car horn outside.

"Oh, darn," Ashley said. "There he is. And look, you're not even dressed. I'll introduce you at the wedding, I promise. I gotta run now."

Candice nodded reluctantly.

"Don't worry, Mom. You'll like him." She kissed Candice on the cheek and darted out the door.

Candice lit a candle and placed it on the windowsill. It was scented with lavender to soothe the nerves, and boy, did she need that just now. She closed her eyes as she removed the towel from her head and shook out her brown shoulder-length hair.

There was nothing like a teenage daughter to keep you on your toes. And she had two. Her youngest liked fooling around with reefer. Her oldest was going to show up at Barbara Bentley's house with a black man on her arm in front of her neighbors and co-workers. What the hell was everyone going to think? She let out a deep breath.

No need to panic, Candice Jones, even if this wasn't exactly what she had in mind when she preached open-mindedness and fairness to her daughters. This was the twenty-first century, and Prince George's County had a lot of black and brown citizens. Hopefully, if the past was any guide, this new interest of Ashley's would be gone soon, just like all the rest.

She walked into the master bath and was greeted with the sound of Jim singing "I'm in the Mood for Love" at the very top of his baritone voice. She chuckled. So she wasn't losing her mind. The world wasn't falling apart. Jim sounded just as horrible as he always had.

She knocked on the glass shower door, and he stopped singing and slid the door open a crack. He was covered with suds from head to toe, and Candice thought he looked so cuddly. He might be fifty but he was in good shape and had a head full of dark wavy hair, with a little gray around the ears and a salt-and-pepper beard.

After divorcing the girls' father twelve years ago, she thought she'd be spending the rest of her life as a single mom, since it was tough for a woman with kids to find a man. And after what she'd been through with her two-timing ex-husband, she didn't think she *wanted* to find another one.

Sometimes she still found it hard to believe that she'd lucked up and met Jim when she was nearing forty and that they were married within a year. Everyone thought she was nuts to marry him so soon and that it would never last. But they had made it for a year now, and still counting.

She smiled at him. "Haven't you been in there long enough? Something has come up with Ashley, and I need to talk to you about it."

He nodded. "I'll be there in a sec, babe."

He closed the door, and she turned toward the bedroom. That's what she loved about Jim. She could always count on him. He was so . . . She heard the shower door sliding open and turned just as he reached out and grabbed her. Before she knew what was happening, she was standing under the shower nozzle with him.

She didn't know whether to laugh or scream as she cupped her hand and wiped away the water streaming down her face.

"Have you lost your mind? My robe is getting soaked."

"I'll fix that." He reached for the belt.

She grabbed his hands between fits of giggles. "Wait a minute, Jim. Down, boy. We'll be late for the wedding. And I —"

He wrapped his arms around her and planted wet kisses down her neck, and all the tension drained from her body. What the hell. She opened the belt to her robe and let it drop to the tile floor.

Chapter 5

The blast from the gun scared her so bad, she could have eaten her heart for lunch. But *he* scared her so much more, coming after her with those big, foul hands.

Lee lowered the gun and pointed it at him as he crawled across the floor. She squeezed the trigger again. And again.

Take that, she whispered between clenched teeth. *Take that, punk-ass.* Always messing with her. She could hardly walk for days whenever he came after her. He was the nastiest man in all of P. G. County.

You won't do that no more now, will you, Uncle Clive? Will you, huh?

She stood across the living room floor with both hands wrapped around the gun and watched until he stopped moving. She inched closer, looked down and cocked her head to the side to listen. He was still breathing, his breath coming fast and heavy, when suddenly one of his hands reached out for her foot. She shot him again.

His body went limp.

She gasped. Oh shit. She stood there and stared at him as he lay in a heap, and her shoulders began to shake. What did she do now? Call her mama? The police?

No. No fucking police. She didn't want to end up in juvee. She was only fifteen. Run. She had to run.

She dropped the gun on the couch and ran into the kitchen. She grabbed the black shoulder bag sitting on the table next to her history book and threw her things out, one by one. Lipstick, hairbrush, mirror, tissue. She finally found her wallet and fished through it, practically pulling it apart in her haste. Damn. She had two lousy dollars and some change. That wouldn't get her very far. She needed more.

She ran back into the living room and stared at his body. The punk. Even now, lying there lifeless, he made her sick to her stomach. But he always had lots of cash on him.

She sucked in a deep gust of air, then crept up to the pool of blood surrounding him. She thought she heard a sound come from him but couldn't be sure. So she kicked one of his legs lightly, then jumped back and eyed his hands closely. Knowing him, he could be trying to fake her out, waiting for her to get close enough so he could pounce. But he didn't move.

She covered her mouth with her fist. Oh shit. He was *really* dead. *See what you've done, Lee, you fool. You killed him.* She didn't mean to kill him. She just wanted him to leave her alone. To stop doing those nasty things to her.

She swallowed her tears and gritted her teeth. There was no time to feel sorry for him now. She had to get her ass out of there before Mama came home.

She reached down and touched his back jean pocket. She felt something hard, so she held her breath, stuck her fingers in and grabbed the wallet. Inside were several ten-dollar bills and some singles, about a hundred bucks. She took it all and shoved it into the pocket of her blue jeans.

She was about to turn and flee when she thought about the keys to his car. She had her learner's permit, and Mama had taken her out to practice driving a few times. That would be way better than the bus.

She glanced at his hands to make sure they had no more life in them. Then she dug around in his front pocket until she came up with a ring of keys. She remembered the gun on the couch and decided to take that, too.

She grabbed her bag off the kitchen table and ran out the front door and down to the corner. Uncle Clive's old BMW was parked at the curb, just as usual. She jumped in, started the engine and pulled away.

She had no idea where she was going. But she had just wasted her mama's man. She had to get the hell out of P. G. County.

Chapter 6

Barbara stepped back and smiled at her daughter. Rebecca looked regal in her beaded ivory satin gown, and for a moment Barbara forgot the utter chaos on the lawn. She forgot about the tent being decorated with flowers, the tables and chairs being arranged, the band, the buffet, the bar.

Rebecca stood in front of the mirror above her dresser and picked at her upswept do. "Does it need more hair spray, Mama?"

Barbara glanced at Pearl.

"No indeed," Pearl replied as she reached up and fussed with a tiny stray hair on Rebecca's forehead.

From all that Barbara could see, Rebecca's hair looked absolutely smashing. Pearl had done a fantastic job, as always.

"Another drop of spray and it will be sitting up there looking like a rock, child," Pearl continued. "Your hair looks beautiful just the way it is."

"I've never seen you look prettier, sweetheart." Barbara kissed her daughter gently on the forehead, being careful not to muss her makeup, then she turned to Pearl. "Let's get the veil on her now. It's already twelve-fifteen, and the photographers are due at twelve-thirty."

Pearl reached for the floor-length veil sprawled across the bed as Barbara took a quick glimpse out the bedroom window onto the lawn. The wedding planner, a petite black woman named Darlene Dunn, was leading the florist around the grounds as they placed brightly colored centerpieces and other doodads on the tables inside and outside of a large white tent. The caterer and his staff were running back and forth between the four-car garage, where they had set up a temporary kitchen with food warmers, and the buffet being set up under the tent.

Despite the busy atmosphere, everything seemed to be falling into place, Barbara thought thankfully. Well, almost everything. The only exception was that husband of hers. She checked her watch. The photographers would arrive soon to take pictures and video before the family left for the church, and the father of the bride was still out banging his mistress. Unbelievable.

She needed a cigarette badly. But she had promised Rebecca that she wouldn't smoke on this day. She sighed and turned to help Pearl lift the veil just as something outdoors caught her eye. She looked out the window to see a black car turning onto their driveway. Now who on earth could that be? Rebecca's godmother had offered to come by and ride to the church with them so she would be there to supervise the procession of the wedding party and Barbara could take her place in the front pew and relax. But Marilyn drove a tan Lexus.

Barbara frowned with disapproval as the car approached the house. Anyone arriving at this early hour was either extremely rude or just plain ignorant. Her frown deepened as the sporty little car ran right up over the edge of the asphalt onto the freshly mowed lawn.

What the devil? Barbara blinked hard. Her eyes must be playing a horrible trick on her. She had been awfully busy planning this wedding lately and sometimes she didn't know if she was coming or going. It was entirely possible that her eyes were giving out.

Barbara blinked again as the little black sports car kept coming across the lawn. This was no illusion. Some idiot had lost control and now the car was plowing straight toward the reception tent.

"Oh my God!" she screamed just as the car smashed headlong into the tent frame. Pearl dropped the veil on the bed and followed Rebecca to the window. Barbara could have sworn the whole tent would come crashing down, but mercifully it didn't. The car, which by now Barbara realized was a small late-model BMW being driven by a woman, backed up. Thank goodness. What an idiot.

But before Barbara could catch her breath, the engine revved and the car jerked forward. Barbara gasped as it picked up speed and rammed into the tent frame. This time the tent sagged on one end.

This woman wasn't drunk. She was doing this deliberately. Barbara covered her open mouth with her hand as Darlene, the florist, the caterer, and the waiters all ran to and fro. It looked like a fire had broken out under a circus tent.

"Lord have mercy," Pearl whispered, clutching her breasts.

Rebecca shrieked. "Who is that?"

"I have no idea," Barbara said, turning toward the bedroom door. "But I'd better get down there."

"That woman is crazy," Pearl said.

"Mama!" Rebecca cried. "Daddy just pulled up."

Barbara turned back to the window to see Bradford's silver Jaguar convertible come to a screeching halt. He jumped out, ran

61

toward the BMW and yanked the driver's-side door open.

Slowly it dawned on Barbara that she recognized the little black car. It belonged to Sabrina, that hussy mistress of Bradford's. Barbara twisted her lips with disgust. This was utterly ridiculous. She snatched her cell phone off Rebecca's dresser.

"I'll be right back," Barbara said hurriedly. "Pearl, can you stay here and help Rebecca finish getting dressed? I know I'm only paying you to do her hair, but —"

Pearl put her forefinger to her lips. "Shh. Don't worry about a thing. Of course I will."

"Thank you so much," Barbara said as she raced to the door.

"Mama, wait!" Rebecca shouted. "Oh my God. She's getting out of the car and yelling and screaming and waving her fists at Daddy." Rebecca lifted her gown and followed Barbara to the door. "I'm going down there with you."

Barbara held her hand out. "Oh no you aren't," she said firmly. "Your father and I will handle this. I don't want you getting involved."

"But Mama, she's —"

"No buts."

Rebecca sighed and ran back to the

window and stood next to Pearl. Barbara walked out the bedroom door so fast she nearly bumped into Robin, Rebecca's older sister.

"What's going on? Who is that crazy woman outside?" Robin asked. She was wearing her lavender maid-of-honor dress and fastening pearl earrings.

"I'm going down there now," Barbara replied.

"Do you want me to come with you?" Robin asked.

"Absolutely not. Go help your sister get ready."

Robin blinked, clearly puzzled by her mother's harsh reaction. Barbara didn't like the tone of her own voice. Certainly none of this was Robin's fault. But she couldn't help it, not when Bradford had allowed his whore to pull such hysterical antics on their daughter's wedding day.

She took the back stairs in her satin Ferragamo pumps two at a time, threw the back door open and marched out onto the lawn. Sabrina was still in the driveway screaming at the top of her lungs as Bradford, dressed in a navy running suit, held his hands out and tried to calm her down.

Darlene Dunn and the others stood around in a small cluster nearby, listening and watching like it was the latest installment of their favorite soap opera. Barbara was so embarrassed but determined to stay calm. She had to get this mess straightened out before Marilyn arrived, not to mention the photographer and the three hundred guests expected later that afternoon.

"You bastard," Sabrina screamed. "I can't believe you didn't invite me to the wedding. How could you do this to me, Bradford?"

Barbara couldn't help but notice how young and thin Sabrina was — and how beautiful. The woman couldn't be more than thirty and had one of those size 4 figures with forty-inch boobs. Barbara also noticed how the spaghetti straps to her black negligee kept slipping off her honey-colored shoulders. The skinny little whore hadn't even taken the time to get dressed after her little tryst with Bradford.

"You're going to have to calm down, Sabrina," Bradford said in a firm tone of voice. "Look at the mess you're making here. You're going to ruin Rebecca's wedding, and I won't have that."

"Like I give a fucking shit," Sabrina retorted, oblivious to the black mascara streaming down her cheeks. She ran toward a cluster of tables on the lawn outside the tent and grabbed a chair by the back. She flipped it over, then ran inside the tent and knocked another chair down.

Barbara was appalled. She ought to grab that whore and throw her off their property. But she was wearing a two-thousand-dollar silk suit, and Sabrina looked downright dangerous. Barbara was not about to get into a public fight over a man, even her husband. Better to let Bradford handle it. She wished he'd hurry up and get rid of her. Marilyn would be arriving any minute, and it would be horrible for Rebecca's godmother to see this.

She followed Bradford as he rushed inside the tent.

"After all I've done for you the past year, Bradford Bentley," Sabrina wailed as she stopped in front of the buffet table. "And this is the thanks I get. A whole fucking year I wasted on you. I do everything for you. I cook for you. I listen to you talk about your problems with your wife. I give you every fucking thing you want in bed."

Bradford stole a glance at Barbara. She glared back at him, eyes smoldering. It was about time he noticed her. And yes, she had heard it. Every word.

"Sabrina, don't make me have to force you to leave. It'll be better for everybody concerned if you just go and get in the car quietly."

"Fuck you, Bradford Bentley," Sabrina yelled. She grabbed a carving knife off the buffet table and held it out in front of her.

Bradford clenched his fists and circled Sabrina silently and cautiously just as Marilyn's Lexus pulled into the driveway.

Damn, Barbara thought, as if all this wasn't enough. Marilyn turned off the engine but stayed inside her car. She looked over the scene with a puzzled expression on her face and rolled down the window.

"What's going on here, Barbara?" she called out.

Barbara waved toward the house. "Go on inside and wait for me there."

Marilyn got out slowly, then ran to the front door and disappeared inside the house.

"Bradford, do I need to call the police?" Barbara was damned if she was going to let this woman ruin Rebecca's wedding day. She lifted her cell phone to dial.

"No," Bradford responded without taking his eyes off Sabrina. "Just stay back."

"Bradford, you'd better tell that bitch to put that phone away," Sabrina shouted. Then she swung the knife in Barbara's direction and lunged.

Barbara screamed as Bradford grabbed Sabrina from behind just in time and they both fell to the ground. They tussled for a moment until Bradford wrestled the knife away. He stood up quickly and stared down at Sabrina with such fury that she began to crawl away in fear.

Barbara put her hand to her breast. She was huffing and puffing like she'd just run a marathon. She couldn't believe that woman had come after her with a knife. On her own property. The woman was clearly out of her mind and needed to be locked up. She punched the buttons on her cell phone and marched toward the house.

Bradford took his eyes off Sabrina, who by now was sprawled out on the grass and crying like a baby, and looked at Barbara. "Who are you calling?" he asked gruffly.

"The police. Who else?"

"You don't need to call the cops," he said tersely. "I'll take care of this."

Barbara turned and glared at him. Take care of it? You call this taking care of it? Letting her put all your dirty business out in the street? She'd had enough embarrassment as a child to last a lifetime. *Barbara the bag lady.* She didn't need this, especially on her daughter's wedding day.

That was what she wanted to say, but she

didn't care to argue with Bradford now. Rebecca was standing at her bedroom window watching her wedding day go down the drain. Not to mention Pearl and Marilyn.

Barbara hung up the phone. "Well, you'd better get her out of here now. We leave for the church in less than an hour and the photographers are coming. You're not even dressed yet."

"I said I'll handle it," he snapped. "The best thing you can do is go on back in the house. You're obviously just making her angrier."

Barbara squeezed the phone until her fingers ached. How dare he make it sound as if this were *her* fault. The bastard. But this was not the time to get into an argument with him, not in front of all these people. She took a deep breath and signaled for Darlene to follow her as Bradford reached down and pulled a still-sobbing Sabrina up from the ground.

"Are you all right?" Darlene asked as they stepped outside the tent.

Barbara nodded. She had to remain calm and somehow get through this. First, she had to deal with the tent. "How much damage did she do?"

Darlene shook her head anxiously. "It

doesn't look good. It's going to need some repairs. Give me a minute and I'll make a few calls to try to get it fixed in time."

While Darlene made her calls, Barbara picked up the chairs that Sabrina had knocked over. Bradford was now talking to Sabrina as she sat in the car, and she looked much calmer. Sabrina finally backed out of the driveway and screeched off down the street.

Darlene covered the mouthpiece. "I'm trying to get the rental company back out here to repair it. But they're giving me some crap about being booked all afternoon."

Barbara threw her hands in the air as Bradford walked across the driveway and back toward the lawn. This was all his fault, but she had to stay calm in front of the help. "Bradford, they can't get out here to fix the tent in time for the reception. What are we going to do?"

He walked up to the tent and examined the damaged area. It was all Barbara could do to keep from yelling at him in front of everyone.

Bradford turned to Darlene. "Tell them we'll double their normal fee to get out here and fix it before the reception," he ordered. "Whatever it takes, just get them out here now."

Darlene's eyes lit up. "Whatever you say, sir." Within a minute she was snapping the phone antenna back into place and smiling in victory. "They're sending someone right away. The reception doesn't start until three, so that gives us two and a half hours. In the meantime, we can finish setting things up. I don't think it will topple over."

"Nah," Bradford said. "It should hold up fine until they get out here to fix it."

Barbara sighed with relief. She had to hand it to her husband. He was always so good in a crisis, even one of his own making. "So you think everything will be ready on time, Darlene?"

Darlene nodded. "Yes. I think we'll make it."

Barbara smiled. "Thank goodness. Do your best."

Darlene nodded and walked off with the phone at her ear as she directed the other workers to get back to their jobs. Just when Barbara thought she could relax a bit, she noticed a young man walking around on the patio near the house, snapping away with a 35-millimeter camera. "Oh my God," she exclaimed in horror. "Bradford, it's Peter, the photographer."

Bradford followed her gaze. He let out a

deep breath. "I'll handle this."

Barbara didn't say a word. She was too stunned to speak. When did he get here? How much had he caught on film? God forbid she should wake up tomorrow morning to photos in the style section of the *Washington Post* or on the Internet of Bradford's mistress wrecking Rebecca's wedding reception tent.

Bradford walked briskly across the lawn to the patio and spoke to Peter for a minute. Barbara let out a sigh of relief as the photographer fiddled with his camera, then handed something over to Bradford. The photographer disappeared into the house, and Bradford turned toward Barbara. "It's OK. I got the film from him."

"This is your fault, Bradford," Barbara snapped. "What the devil was that all about?"

Bradford shook his head with regret, but he didn't say anything. There was no apology and Barbara didn't expect one. The women came and went so often that Bradford seemed to realize that apologizing when he got caught was getting stale.

"Never mind," Barbara said. "We don't have time to get into it now, anyway."

"Where is Rebecca?" Bradford asked. "Did she see any of this?"

"Of course she saw it," Barbara snapped. "How could she miss it? Not to mention Marilyn and Pearl and God knows who else. I'm sure we're the laughingstock of Silver Lake now."

"Barbara, please," Bradford said tiredly. "Don't be so melodramatic. I'm going to go get into my tux."

"Fine," Barbara said crisply. "We'll discuss it tomorrow."

"There's nothing to discuss."

"Nothing to discuss? Your mistress just drove up onto our property and . . . and practically ruined our daughter's wedding. Or didn't you notice?"

"You mean ex-mistress. The reason she was so upset was because I called it off."

Barbara scoffed. "You told me last month that you called it off."

"Well, it's true. But she's having problems accepting it."

This was why she tried to avoid these arguments with Bradford. It was impossible to win any of them. He had an excuse for everything. "So that's why you ran over there first thing this morning, I suppose?" she said sarcastically.

"She called last night crying, so I —"

"Bradford, please," Barbara said. "Spare me."

72

"Look, I didn't want to get into this, but you —"

"Daddy?"

They both turned to see Rebecca and Robin standing in the doorway leading to the patio with frustrated expressions on their faces.

"Yes?" Bradford smiled and moved toward them.

"Who was that woman?" Rebecca asked, her eyes narrowed with suspicion.

Bradford shoved his hands in his jacket pocket. "Nobody for you to worry about."

Rebecca looked from Bradford to Barbara with doubt. "She looked like plenty to worry about to me. Look at what she did to the tent."

"Your father is right. And the tent will be repaired in plenty of time," Barbara said. No doubt Rebecca and Robin had long ago come to realize that their parents' marriage was a rocky one, but she never discussed Bradford's philandering with them, or anyone else for that matter. The dirt between her and Bradford would stay between her and Bradford.

"What on earth was she so upset about?" Robin asked.

Bradford shrugged. "She works for a friend of mine, and, uh, she was mad because we didn't invite her to the wedding."

"You've got to be kidding," Robin said.

"What if she comes back?" Rebecca asked, a look of horror on her face.

Bradford smiled and put his arm around Rebecca's shoulder. "She won't. I promise you that. And did I tell you you look stunning? Ralph is one lucky guy."

Rebecca tried to smile. "Thanks, Daddy. But you're not even dressed yet."

"I will be, in fifteen minutes sharp. I've already shaved and showered."

No doubt after you screwed your whore, Barbara thought. Because he certainly didn't shower here this morning. And all that talk about Sabrina losing control because he broke up with her was bull. Bradford could keep a hundred employees in check. He could manage millions of dollars. But he couldn't keep his mistress in her place? Mister Big Shot? Please.

"By the way," Bradford said. "The lieutenant governor called at the last minute and said she was accepting her invitation to the reception."

Rebecca's eyes widened. "You mean Kathleen Kennedy Townsend? Oh my gosh."

"And you waited all this time to tell us, Bradford?" Barbara said. "Honestly."

Bradford shrugged. "She called just this morning."

"She probably sees the reception as an opportunity to line up votes in her campaign for governor," Robin said.

Barbara sighed with impatience.

"What's the big deal?" Bradford asked. "She and the governor have both been here before."

"That was for political receptions, Bradford, not our daughter's wedding. She'll need special seating."

"I'm sure you'll carry it off without a hitch," Bradford said. He kissed Rebecca's forehead and walked into the house.

"I can't believe all this is happening," Rebecca said.

"How could Daddy let that woman in here today of all days," Robin said with annoyance.

"You can't blame him," Barbara said. "He tried to stop her."

Robin shook her head with frustration. "You always defend him."

Barbara grimaced and touched her forehead. So much to do, so little time. She was going to have to get herself together. And fast. She put her arms around both her daughters and forced a smile. "Come on, girls. Let's forget about this. We have a big day ahead of us. The lieutenant governor is coming, not to mention half of Silver Lake and our family and friends. We have to look and behave our best."

Barbara held her head high and led her daughters back into the house.

Chapter 7

Jolene smiled at her reflection in the full-length mirror. Everything on her was designer, from the black Victoria's Secret thong and bra to the dark blue St. John suit. She loved the way the suits flattered her curves. They cost more than a thousand bucks a pop but were worth every last penny.

Not that she needed much help with her curves. Not her. With the exception of a teensy-weensy midriff bulge that she could hide by sucking her breath in, her figure was damn near perfect. Her derriere was a bit ample, and the skirt to the suit fit like a second skin. But black men liked for their women to have a little extra meat on their bones.

She chuckled. It was a downright scandal the way she could sometimes get so giddy about herself. But hell. Nothing wrong with liking yourself. Too many women didn't have enough confidence. She certainly wasn't one of them.

She picked out one of the four pairs of Manolo Blahnik shoes sitting on the shelves that lined the walls of her closet and slipped them onto her feet. This skimpy-ass walk-in closet was one of so many reasons why they needed a bigger house. The closet, no, make that dressing room, in the master bedroom of the house they were building was as big as the whole bedroom in their current house. She could hardly wait the six months until they could move in and invite her parents over. And her sister Jackie. Hell, it was going to be big enough to have the whole neighborhood over.

If it had been up to her, they would have put a hot tub on the deck outside the bedroom and enclosed it with glass walls on three sides. That way they could sit back and look over their two-acre estate in style. But Patrick was such a penny-pincher. She would have to settle for lawn chairs instead. At least for now.

Every time she got a good idea he'd knock it down. Too expensive. Too showy. Too pretentious. Yak, yak, yak. Didn't he understand? That was the whole frigging idea. They both busted their butts working all the time. They deserved to show off a bit.

He almost had a fit when she insisted they hire an architect to design the house. He wanted to use a design out of one of those plan books you get at the supermarket and be his own general contractor. Puh-leeze. She had to put her foot down on that one.

She was finally getting to build her dream house in Silver Lake, North. This wasn't the time to start acting like the Beverly Hillbillies.

She stood in front of the full-length mirror and fluffed up her reddish brown hair weave, then she placed her long acrylic nails on her hips and posed Marilyn Monroe style. She'd changed herself from a babe in denim to a queen in silk in record time. No wonder Terrence couldn't resist her. When she'd called him from the construction site, they were cooing on the phone in no time and making plans for a tryst the following afternoon, promptly after church.

Now for the crowning touch of her ensemble. She opened her dresser drawer and removed a small package wrapped carefully in silk. She opened it and held up a Judith Leiber clutch. She loved the way it glittered in the light. She knew she had to have one of these bags the minute she first laid eyes on them at Neiman Marcus.

Barbara Bentley didn't have much of a fashion sense, but she had the kind of bucks that made it damn near impossible to look cheap. The woman probably considered Saks bargain-basement shopping. She could afford to have her rags tailor-made. A wedding and reception at Barbara's estate was the perfect excuse to pull out all the fashion stops.

Jolene held the glittery bag up and smiled. And to think, here she was building one of the biggest houses in the community and just a few doors down from the Bentleys'. Eat your heart out, Silver Lake.

"Mom!"

Jolene jumped at the sound of her daughter's voice in the bedroom doorway. "Oh, precious. You scared the living daylights out of me."

"Sorry, Mother," Juliette said, "but is that a new Judith Leiber bag in your hand?"

Jolene pressed her finger to her lips. "Not so loud, sweetie. Where's your father?"

"He's downstairs getting the car out of the garage. He sent me up to get you."

Jolene held the bag up proudly. "How do you like it?"

"Oh, I love it!" Juliette exclaimed. "Can I take one of your other ones to the wedding? Please?"

"You're too young for this kind of thing just yet, precious."

"I'm fourteen," Juliette said tartly. "And it's only a purse."

"It's a grown-up's purse. So the answer is no."

Juliette stuck out her bottom lip, and Jolene smiled with amusement. Her daughter was such a pretty young thing, even when she pouted. And so poised and well groomed. Every strand of her hair weave was always in place, just like her mama's. And even though Juliette had just started wearing blush and lipstick, it was always applied perfectly. "Now, now, precious. Is that any way to act? You just got those diamond earrings that you're wearing for your birthday. Isn't that enough?"

Juliette put her arm around her mother's waist. "I love them, Mama, but Caitlin next door has half karats."

Jolene lifted a brow. "She does, does she?" Jolene didn't want her daughter to feel second best to anyone ever. She knew from her own experiences with her older sister Jackie that it was not a good feeling. "Well, we'll have to see about getting yours upgraded then, won't we?"

They both giggled.

"Do you think the Joneses will be at the wedding, Mom?"

"When I talked to Candice a few weeks ago, she said they were going. I'm sure they will since Candice works for Bradford Bentley, just like your father."

"Is Mrs. Jones a programmer like Dad?"

"No, she's a web designer."

"Oh. Does she make more money than you? Or Daddy?"

"I doubt it. Why do you ask?"

" 'Cause Caitlin has all this fancy jewelry and she said she was getting a car next year when she turns sixteen. Everybody is going to want to hang around her if she does."

"Caitlin is a year older than you are," Jolene explained. "And remember, we're building a brand-new house in North Silver Lake. All the houses over there are custom-built, unlike the ones here on the south side. And as far as I know, the Joneses plan to stay over here. And you can have a car, too, when you turn sixteen."

Juliette scoffed. "Dad will never go for that."

"We'll see. I have some say in it too, you know."

"Still, that's not for two more years."

"There's nothing we can do about that, Juliette. The law is the law. Aren't you the most popular girl in school now?"

Juliette shrugged and admired herself in her mother's full-length mirror. "Depends on who you ask, I guess."

"Well, people like you for your personality, anyway, not what you wear or drive." That sounded like the right kind of thing to tell your fourteen-year-old daughter, even though Jolene didn't really believe it — not entirely. Personality was a start, but having a car and other nice things could definitely improve a teenager's popularity. And she wanted Juliette to be popular, especially with the right boys. She didn't want any Jonathan Parkers breaking her daughter's heart.

"So what do you think, Jim? Am I jumping the gun here, worrying about this?" Candice looked at Jim as he backed their Ford Taurus out of the driveway.

Jim nodded. "Probably. Ashley's only going out on a date with this guy, not marrying him."

Candice sighed and leaned her head back. "You're right." She smiled and waved at the Browns. Patrick was sitting in the driveway behind the wheel of their Mercedes as Jolene and Juliette climbed in. The Browns smiled and waved back.

"Even if she was marrying him, so what?" Caitlin asked from the backseat. "It wouldn't be the end of the world. You always told us not to judge other people by what they look like or how much money they have. Right?"

"Yes, but —"

"But what? Isn't that what you're doing now, Mom?"

"It's not that simple, Caitlin," Candice explained. "I was thinking of friends and co-workers when we said those things. I never thought it would come to this. Dating and marriage are . . . well, that's different."

"My friend Sue Ellen is seeing a black guy. What's so different about it?"

"Marriage and even dating are a lot more complicated than most other relation-ships," Jim said.

Thank you, Candice thought. This was so difficult to explain. She didn't even really understand her own feelings about it. "Mar-riage is hard even between two people of the same race. You saw what I went through with your father."

"Mom, what happened with you and Dad was . . . was worse to me than two people of different races getting together. Daddy couldn't keep his dick in his pants."

"Caitlin!" Candice glanced at Jim out of the corner of her eye. He seemed to be fighting real hard to keep a smile off his face.

"Sorry, Mom. Just telling it like I see it."

"And I'm sorry you had to go through that with your father and me. But can you imagine how much harder it would have been if your father and I were of different races? It would have meant one more thing to deal with on top of everything else that comes up. 'Cause even if the two of you accept it, others won't, and they can make your life pretty miserable."

"But if two people love each other, who cares what everyone else thinks?" Caitlin protested.

"It's a lot easier to just find someone of the same race." Candice shrugged. "Well, Ashley is only nineteen. Like Jim said, it may be premature to worry about it now."

"Knowing Ashley, she'll be swooning over someone else next month," Jim said.

"I wouldn't be so sure," Caitlin said smugly. "Do you see the look on her face when she talks about this guy? I think she's in love."

"Come on," Jim said incredulously. "She just met him."

Candice didn't say anything. She just prayed that her smart-mouthed daughter was mistaken. She had finally found a wonderful man in Jim, and aside from the occasional minidrama with Caitlin, her life was good. So good in fact that at times she thought something bad would surely happen just to even things out.

Chapter 8

OK, OK. She was handling her position at the head of the receiving line just fine. She was smiling graciously — the perfect picture of the mother of the bride greeting her guests with her husband at her side.

Something black moved in the corner of her eye, and her head jerked toward the driveway. Mercifully, it was only one of the valet parkers backing a Cadillac up. Not Sabrina's BMW.

Barbara sighed with relief and stole a sideways glance at Bradford as they greeted one guest after another. Look at him. Mister Big Shot. Nothing fazed him. The lieutenant governor was here and his mistress could show up any second, but he was cool and confident as always, working that Southern accent like a charm. Over the years he had trained himself to be able to turn the accent on and off at will. It would instantly become deeper whenever he thought it would work to his advantage, whether to charm the ladies or disarm a business adversary.

She focused back on her guests. She smiled broadly. Even though she had no doubt they knew. Every last one of them.

Oh, they pretended not to, but they were laughing at her, pitying her. Barbara the scorned wife. Her husband cheated on her. He even allowed his mistress to crash their daughter's wedding. And still Barbara stayed with him. Why?

There was a time when she could have explained her reasons for staying. All one needed to do was look around, she would have said. Check out the husband and the lifestyle he provided. He was smart, successful, handsome.

A man like Bradford landed in a black woman's grasp about as often as a million-dollar lottery ticket did. And if he slipped up now and then, she was first in the pecking order. She was his wife, the one and only Barbara Bentley.

That was what she would have told someone before today, if they dared to ask. But in all her life she'd never been so humiliated as she was earlier that afternoon. Certainly Bradford's fooling around was nothing new, but he used to be discreet. He used to care how it would affect his family. There was a time when he would have had that woman arrested before she got anywhere near their property, especially on his daughter's wedding day. He was either getting sloppy or far too brazen to suit Barbara.

And that worried her more than anything.

She smiled as Patrick Brown approached with his wife and daughter. Patrick was a programmer for Bradford. But for the life of her, Barbara couldn't remember his wife's name. Or the daughter's. Barbara had seen the Browns at the Christmas party she and Bradford threw every year for his employees and their families. But lately she had become so forgetful. That was what middle age and menopause did to you.

She extended a hand. "Patrick. So nice of you to come." She smiled at his wife, willing the name to come back to her. Oh come on, Barbara Bentley. Think. How could anyone forget this woman's name, with that ridiculous hair weave and those mile-long fingernails? Barbara couldn't understand why Patrick's wife was so over the top. She was a naturally pretty woman and didn't need to wear all that fake nonsense.

Barbara held her hand out. "Hello, it's good to see you again."

The wife extended her hand. "And you, too, Barbara. Congratulations."

Barbara smiled. "Thank you."

How rude, Jolene thought. How insulting. It was so obvious that Barbara Bentley had forgotten her name. She started to remind Barbara — Jolene and Juliette, you rich idiot — but never mind. Let the woman suffer. Jolene smiled tightly. "You look lovely, Barbara. And so does Rebecca."

Bradford reached for Jolene's hand and cupped it between his own. He smiled. "Real nice of you all to come, Jolene, Juliette."

Well, at least Bradford remembered their names, Jolene thought wryly. He was still trés sexy, too. Maybe he was a little grayer around the ears since she'd last seen him at the annual Digitech Christmas bash, but he was just as poised and polished as ever. He radiated money. And to her, nothing was sexier than a man with money. Wasn't Barbara the lucky one? The woman had everything a girl could want — a good-looking man who earned a pile of money. Jolene smiled seductively at Bradford.

Barbara narrowed her eyes. So that was her name. Jolene. Well, it looked like Miss Jolene was flirting with Bradford. Honestly. It seemed all women wanted her husband. It wouldn't be so embarrassing if Bradford didn't have to flirt right back. She wanted to smack him on the spot.

Instead she dabbed her forehead with her handkerchief. What she needed more than anything was a cigarette. She could get through all this a lot easier if she could break away and sneak a few puffs. But judging from the size of this receiving line, that wouldn't be anytime soon. They probably had a hundred more guests to greet. Barbara sighed. At least in that sense the wedding was a smashing success.

The Browns moved on to greet the bride and groom and Candice Jones and her family approached Barbara. "Candice, thank you for coming. It's so good to see you again."

"It's good to see you too, Barbara," Candice said. "And you, Bradford. You both remember my husband, Jim, don't you? You met him at our wedding last summer."

"Good to see you both again," Jim said, smiling stiffly.

Barbara shook Jim's hand. "Why, yes, of course, I remember." Barbara thought Jim looked a bit jumpy. He probably wasn't used to being around so many black folks and no doubt felt out of place. Barbara patted his hand reassuringly. "How are you, Jim?"

"Just fine, thank you."

"And you remember Caitlin?" Candice asked.

Barbara nodded. "Hi, Caitlin. You've really grown."

Caitlin smiled and shifted on her feet the way teenagers often do around adults.

Barbara thought Candice looked remarkably happy, although she still dressed like a hippie, in long flowered skirts and corny-looking ballet-type shoes. And she always had a crystal around her neck. Honestly. The least she could do was put on pumps at a wedding.

But there was no denying that she looked so much better these days — her cheeks were rosy and she smiled more readily. And it was no wonder. Jim was a pretty good-looking man. He reminded her of that actor, the first one to play James Bond. She couldn't think of his real name. This was getting ridiculous. She couldn't remember much at all these days.

From what she'd heard, anything was probably an improvement over Candice's first husband, Ben. Supposedly he was a very successful dentist — and a cheat just like Bradford. Barbara had heard that Candice finally got fed up and kicked him out, and now she seemed to be doing just fine, thank you. That was encouraging. "You're looking good, Candice."

"Thank you," Candice said. "It's a lovely wedding, Barbara."

"It's been fun planning it and seeing how

happy Rebecca and Ralph are, hasn't it, Bradford?"

"Oh yeah," Bradford replied. "But I have to confess that I keep thinking. One down, one more to go."

Candice and Jim laughed.

"I know exactly what you mean," Jim said as he nodded with understanding. "I went through this with my daughter about two years ago. My ex-wife and I are still paying the bills."

"Aw shoot," Bradford said. He slapped Patrick on the back and chuckled. "Don't even go there."

"You have an older daughter, don't you, Candice?" Barbara asked.

Candice nodded. "Yes, Ashley. She's nineteen now. She'll be coming later with a friend." And when she does get here, what on earth will Bradford and Barbara think? Candice wondered. What will everyone think of her white daughter arriving with a black man?

"So you'll be doing this yourself someday soon," Bradford teased.

Candice forced a smile. "Hopefully, not too soon."

Bradford leaned over and whispered something in Candice's ear, and Candice tossed her head back and laughed.

Barbara fumed. Why did her husband have to flirt so shamelessly with every woman coming through the receiving line? Honestly. She stole a quick glance at Jim. He didn't seem to be bothered at all by Bradford's behavior. No doubt he too had been wowed by Bradford's charms.

The Jones family moved on through the receiving line and sat at an empty table under the tent. "Not too many other folks here look like us," Jim said softly.

Candice frowned for a moment, not understanding, then she nodded. What he really meant was that there weren't many other white folks here. Jim was from Chicago and no stranger to black people, but this was probably his first time attending a function where whites were in the minority.

Candice had gotten used to being one of only a handful of whites. Sort of, anyway. She doubted one ever got completely used to it, but she was comfortable with it. She had worked for Bradford for several years now, and probably seventy-five percent of his employees were black. She would never be as comfortable around them as she was around her own kind. But she had come to know that they all wanted the same things in life — to live with their families in peace and prosperity — and she could relate to that.

She smiled sympathetically at Jim. "You'll get used to it, honey, sooner or later."

Caitlin laughed. "Now you see how they feel when they're around a bunch of white people."

Jim rubbed his hands together in anticipation. "Well, I see something that will help me get accustomed to it right quick," he said, trying to sound Southern. A big grin spread across his face as he stood and nodded in the direction of the bar. "The great equalizer. Can I get something for y'all beautiful ladies?"

Caitlin giggled, and Candice rolled her eyes skyward. She had told Jim a million times that people living in the D.C. suburbs did not think of themselves as Southerners, and that they did not have Southern accents, at least not what she considered a Southern accent. Still, she had to smile at Jim's poor imitation. It was worse than his singing in the shower. "A glass of red wine would be nice, honey."

"Yeah, that sounds good," Caitlin chimed in. "I'll take one, too."

"Not in this lifetime," Candice said crisply. "At least not around me. A Coke for her, Jim."

Caitlin smacked her lips as Jim walked off

toward the bar. "It's just a glass of wine. I'm fifteen."

"That's what I know," Candice said.

"I'm going to have to learn to drink sooner or later. Wouldn't you rather I do it around you?"

"Oh, so now I'm supposed to believe that you've never touched alcohol in your life."

Caitlin smiled guiltily and cast her eyes down.

"Uh-huh." Teenagers. They all seemed to try as hard as they could to keep their parents off-balance. Candice stretched her neck and scanned the crowd for Ashley.

For the life of her, Jolene couldn't figure out which designer Barbara was wearing. Knowing Barbara, it was just some expensive off-the-rack rag. Barbara could damn well afford to wear custom-made Armani or anything she pleased on special occasions like this. After all, the lieutenant governor was here, and she had spotted D.C. mayor Anthony Williams in his customary bow tie just outside the tent.

The Bentleys had really done it up for this affair, gone all out, Jolene thought as she crossed the carpeted tent with Patrick and Juliette, noting one prominent face after another. She wouldn't be surprised if they had dropped five figures on this classy shindig. Hell, they even had valet parking in front of the house and waiters serving drinks on trays. None of those cheap chrome fountains here.

Even her folks would have approved. And the judge and his wife were not easy to please. They had definite ideas about what was proper and what wasn't. This was how you entertained, Jolene thought as she looked across their linen-covered table. She hoped Patrick was soaking it all in so he'd be prepared when Juliette's time came. Just to be sure, she tugged at his arm the minute they were seated.

"Did you see the spread at that buffet?" she asked. "And that's only hors d'oeuvres. Dinner will be served at the tables at five."

"I saw this huge bowl of caviar," Juliette said with delight. "I'm out of here. See you all later." She picked up her purse and walked off toward the buffet.

Jolene chuckled. Her daughter was a girl after her own heart. Patrick was another story. No amount of coaching and needling would ever get him out of his working-class frame of mind.

Patrick shook his head. He was obviously stunned by all the wealth on display. "Man, they spent a damn fortune."

Jolene smacked her lips. "The Bentleys have class. I'm loving every minute of it."

"Yeah, you would," he said sarcastically. "Anyway, Bradford can afford all this. He owns the store."

"Well, you work for him," Jolene retorted. "Listen and learn. You could do the same thing."

"Do you know how long it took him to get all this, Jo?"

She shrugged. "So? You're still young. You're only thirty-eight. He's got to be in his fifties."

Patrick shook his head in disbelief.

Jolene nodded toward the house in the distance. "What do you think of the Spanish-tile roof? We could —"

Patrick held up his hand to stop her before she got started. "I think they can afford it, and we can't. That's what I think."

"We could if you weren't so damn cheap," she snapped.

"Spanish tile is out of the question. You saw the last bill from the contractor. Shit. The foundation was way over what Terrence told us to expect. Some architect he's turning out to be. I told you to let me handle it. But no, you had to go hire some fancy architect to meddle with things. All he does is drive up the cost."

If Patrick knew what else the architect was meddling with, he'd be really pissed. "Terrence can only give us estimates as to what the builder is going to charge," she said coolly. "Not a solid figure."

"Yeah, especially if you keep changing the floor plans at the last minute. You seem to forget that I'm just a programmer at Digitech, not a VP or even a director. And you work for the government."

Jolene rolled her eyes skyward. "Puh-leeze, Patrick. We're not exactly poverty-stricken either. Which reminds me. You're way overdue for a promotion, you know. Bradford's company is obviously pulling in big bucks."

"I just got a raise."

"That's not the same as a promotion. We could use the money. Why don't you invite the Bentleys over for dinner? Butter them up some."

"Give it a rest, Jo. I'll ask for a promotion when I think the time is right."

She sighed. This was all so Patrick. Always so damn reasonable and practical. That was what she needed in a man when she was young and pregnant and alone. And stupid. Now she wanted to get ahead, to climb out of the box.

Marrying Patrick was the biggest mistake

of her life, no doubt about it. He was a decent enough man, just not right for her anymore. The only good thing she'd gotten out of this marriage was Juliette. Her daughter was precious. But Jolene wanted so much more.

Pearl glanced up from her plate of spiced shrimp at the sound of her son's voice.

"Ma." Kenyatta cleared his throat. "I want you to meet someone."

Pearl turned to see Kenyatta standing behind her. She was about to smile and stand up herself when she realized that he was holding the hand of a white woman. Pearl grabbed her napkin and covered her mouth. She had nearly lost her food.

"Ma, this is Ashley. Ashley, this is my ma."

Ashley extended her hand, and Pearl stood up. "It's nice to meet you, Mrs. Jackson. Kenyatta talks about you all the time."

"Oh?" Pearl shook Ashley's hand and smiled feebly. "Um, Kenyatta mentioned that he was bringing someone." Only not that she was white. Pearl blinked. Was she dreaming? No, no. This white girl was real.

Kenyatta had dated a couple of white girls in college, so it wasn't like this had never happened. But every time it did, Pearl was so sure it would be the last. She was always careful to say nice, positive things about the black women he dated. She hadn't raised her son to do things like this. She clasped her hands together at her waist.

"Ashley lives here in Silver Lake, too, Ma," Kenyatta explained as he reached over and took a shrimp from Pearl's plate.

"Oh really?" Pearl looked at the other guests seated at her table and smiled. She had been talking to them before Kenyatta showed up. They were employees of Bradford's, and Pearl had been bragging about how smart and well rounded her son was. And then he shows up with this white girl. Pearl was sure the others at the table were sucking in every ounce of this. She would be on her best behavior if it killed her, but Kenyatta would get an earful in the morning. "Did you all go through the receiving line yet?"

"No, not yet, Ma. We just got here. I wanted to hook you up with Ashley first."

Pearl looked at the girl and attempted a smile. She was pretty enough, with gorgeous green eyes and long brown hair. At least she didn't have *blond* hair. But she was still white as a sheet. What was the matter with that boy of hers? Couldn't he find himself a pretty black girl?

Kenyatta reached down to her plate for another shrimp and Pearl smacked his hand away. She regretted it the moment she did it, but he was annoying her.

"Kenyatta tells me that you own a beauty shop, Mrs. Jackson," Ashley said.

"Hmm. Yes," Pearl said. "A hair salon." *Please, now don't tell me you're going to ask me to do* your *hair. Lordy.*

"How long have you been in business?" Ashley asked.

"Oh. I've been doing hair since Kenyatta was a baby. But I always worked for other people before. I ran a catering business on the side back then. I opened my own salon after he graduated from college. So it's been about five years now."

"That's amazing," Ashley said. "Kenyatta, you never told me all that."

What was so amazing? That a black woman could run a business? Heck, did this child know who Madame C. J. Walker was? Most likely not. Pearl folded her arms across her chest.

Kenyatta cleared his throat. "Well, Ma, I guess we'll go get some grits."

Pearl nodded. "You be sure to say hi to Mrs. Bentley."

"We will."

"It was nice to meet you, Mrs. Jackson."

"You too, Ashley."

Kenyatta took Ashley's hand, and they walked toward the receiving line. Pearl sat back down and stared at her plate.

"He seems like a nice young man," someone at the table said.

"Yes," Pearl said. But she didn't want to talk about him anymore.

Chapter 9

"I heard that a woman drove right up onto the lawn and wrecked the tent," Candice said in a loud whisper.

Jolene gasped. "You're kidding."

"And that Barbara was right here when it happened."

They were standing just outside the tent as the sun dropped below the horizon. Candice was working on her second glass of red wine, Jolene on her third flute of champagne, as music from the live band drifted out from the dance floor and fashion designer–clad bodies pulsated to the beat of "Booty Call."

"When did all this happen?" Jolene couldn't believe something like that had taken place here at the Bentley residence, of all places.

"This afternoon," Candice said. "Supposedly the woman was upset 'cause Bradford didn't invite her to the wedding. So she crashed it."

"Literally," Jolene added with a chuckle. Candice said all this with a straight face, but Jolene thought it was hilarious. She could barely keep from laughing out loud. Maybe it was all the champagne. "Do you know who she was?"

"Bradford's mistress probably. Who else would do something silly like that but a mistress?"

Jolene raised an eyebrow. "Bradford has a mistress?"

"You mean mistresses," Candice corrected. "They come and go so often, they're like the flavors of the month. Although Sabrina has been around longer than any of them. She's even showed up at the office once or twice. Everyone at Digitech knows about her. But you didn't hear any of this from me."

Jolene took a big sip of champagne. This was getting more interesting by the minute. So Barbara's seemingly perfect life wasn't anything of the sort. In fact, it looked like the girl had some real competition. Lots of it. The invisible wall of decorum she'd erected around herself was full of leaky holes.

If everybody at the office knew about Bradford's mistresses, Jolene wondered why Patrick had never mentioned it to her. Although maybe that shouldn't be a surprise since they didn't talk much. Sometimes they would go for weeks without speaking to each other.

"My heart goes out to Barbara," Candice said with sympathy. "Bradford can be so charming, but sometimes I want to clobber him for the way he treats his wife."

Jolene felt sympathy, but not for Barbara. Not really. Why should anyone feel sorry for Barbara? She had everything. No, Jolene felt sorry for the mistresses. Getting so close to a man like Bradford, with all he had to offer, but not being able to snare him must be pure torture. "You can't blame Sabrina. It sounds like he got serious with her, and she thought she was entitled to come to his daughter's wedding."

"I couldn't agree with you less," Candice said. "I know what Barbara is going through. My ex was a lot like him. And he —"

"Shh," Jolene hissed. "She's coming up right behind you." Jolene smiled broadly. "Barbara, how are you?"

"Hello, ladies," Barbara said cheerfully. "I'm just fine. Anything I can get for you?"

"Oh, no," Candice replied. "This is really a beautiful reception, Barbara."

"Yes, it's fantastic," Jolene added. "And dinner was wonderful. You must be exhausted, though." Jolene had to hand it to Barbara. You'd never suspect that Barbara had spent the morning dealing with her husband's angry mistress. She looked like a proud and happy mother of the bride.

Barbara let out a deep breath. "Oh, I'm holding up. I had a lot of help. Do either of you know Darlene Dunn, the wedding planner?"

Candice and Jolene shook their heads in unison.

"Well, when it's your turn, come and see me. You must use Darlene. She's a lifesaver. I could never have pulled this off without her."

Candice was all ears. With two teenage daughters, she was going to have to go through this twice, although hopefully no time soon. She had always figured that wedding planners were way beyond her budget. "Aren't they expensive?"

"Mmm. Probably not as expensive as you think, especially if you're planning a big wedding. What you save in aggravation is priceless." Barbara leaned in close. "Bradford handled all the bills for this, but I think we paid Darlene something in the low five figures. That's not bad for a wedding that ran into six figures."

Candice gasped, and red wine sloshed over the edges of her glass. Fortunately it just missed her skirt. She was right, a wedding planner was definitely out of the question for her. "Hmm. Sounds like I'll be doing it myself, with a little help from

Martha Stewart."

Barbara laughed.

Jolene blinked. Did Barbara say they spent six figures on this wedding? *Six* figures? Damn. It was obvious that the Bentleys were well off, but Jolene had no idea Bradford was pulling in that kind of dough.

"Actually, that doesn't sound bad at all," Jolene said coolly. She looked across the lawn at Bradford. Her admiration for the man had just shot up tenfold.

Barbara didn't miss the seductive glance toward her husband. She would have to keep an eye on this Jolene Brown. She might be married to Patrick, but it was obvious the woman was a major flirt. Look at all the cleavage she had on display. Her suit jacket was open practically down to her navel. Jolene was exactly the kind of woman Bradford went for. She was a little browner in complexion than the usual maybe. But truth be told, Bradford went for just about every kind of woman.

"How's the house coming, Jolene?" Barbara asked, more to get the attention away from her husband than anything.

Jolene's eyes lit up. "Oh, it's wonderful. I'm so excited about it."

Candice spotted Ashley coming toward

them from the dance floor and holding hands with Kenyatta. Oh, hell. Ashley would have to approach as she was talking to Barbara and Jolene. Candice drained her glass of wine and smiled stiffly. "Ashley, have you introduced Barbara Bentley to your friend?"

"Hi, Mom. Yes, we were in the receiving line earlier."

"It looks like you two are having fun," Barbara said.

Ashley smiled. "Kenyatta is teaching me how to do the electric slide."

"You mean the booty call," Kenyatta said, laughing.

"*Hello*, Ashley," Jolene said, trying to keep her voice steady. Who on earth was this with Ashley? Jolene stole a look at Candice. Come to think of it, Candice did look uncomfortable the way she was clutching that crystal around her neck.

Candice cleared her throat. "Um, so, Kenny, do you know Jolene Brown, our next-door neighbor?"

Ashley licked her lips. "Um, he goes by Kenyatta, Mom. Not Kenny."

Candice blinked. "Oh. Sorry." Candice distinctly remembered Ashley referring to him as "Kenny" when she first mentioned him. Of course, that was before Ashley was ready for her mom to know that he was black.

Kenyatta shook Jolene's hand, then they all stood around and smiled awkwardly at one another. Candice thought she should say something since it was Ashley and her date who had disrupted the conversation. But she couldn't even get the guy's name right. Anything she said would probably be taken the wrong way. If she asked about where he lived, normally a harmless enough question, Ashley might think her mom was trying to embarrass her date since he lived in a town house and many Silver Lake residents frowned on them.

"Kenyatta," Barbara said, finally breaking the silence. "That's such an unusual name. You must be Pearl Jackson's son."

He nodded. "Yes, she does your hair. You're one of her favorite clients."

Barbara smiled. "She always talks about you when I go to the salon."

"I met Rebecca once or twice," Kenyatta said. "We're around the same age."

"Oh really?" Barbara said. "Did you go to school together?"

"Nope. When we lived in D.C., I went to a private elementary school, but after we moved out here I had to go to public school. My mother couldn't afford to pay the mortgage on our town house and for private school at the same time."

"Oh, I see," Barbara replied.

Jolene blinked. This was too much. Dreadlocks, public schools, and he lived in the town houses. She had done everything she could to stop those things from being built. She had formed committees, organized demonstrations at the construction site, and written countless letters. Building town houses so near million-dollar mansions was absurd. They would never dare try something like that in an exclusive white neighborhood.

"Your mother is around here somewhere, Kenyatta," Barbara said.

"I saw her earlier and introduced Ashley to her," Kenyatta said.

Hmm, I wonder how that went, Candice thought wryly.

"Well, I need to mingle," Barbara said. "Enjoy yourselves, everyone." She waved and walked off.

"It was nice meeting you, Mrs. Brown," Kenyatta said as he took Ashley's hand and they headed for the dance floor.

"How on earth did Ashley meet *him?*" Jolene demanded to know as soon as they had all split.

Candice shrugged. "I'm not sure. I just

met him for the first time today."

"You're kidding? And?"

"And what?"

"Are you down with it?"

"Oh God, Jolene. You sound just like Ashley. Is that some new black slang?"

Jolene chuckled. "I think it's more like old teen slang. It's been around for a while, Candice. Some of Juliette's white friends talk like that, too."

"Oh."

"But are you OK with her dating him?"

Candice shrugged nonchalantly. "It's just a date. I haven't really thought about it much." What a lie. She hadn't been able to think of much else since Ashley slapped her with the news. But she wouldn't feel right saying that.

Jolene narrowed her eyes. "Well, you're taking it better than I would if it was Juliette."

Candice was puzzled. She didn't see why Jolene would object to her daughter dating Kenyatta since they were of the same race. "What do you mean?"

"I would go nuts if Juliette wanted to go out with some guy wearing dreadlocks. And he lives in the town houses. Did you know that Pearl and some other town house owners tried to get the homeowners' associ-

111

ation to put up a basketball court near the country club last summer?"

"I heard about that. They thought the boys in the neighborhood needed something to occupy their time."

Jolene waved her hand. "Puh-leeze. We put a stop to that. Let them join the country club or take those dreadlocks and baggy clothes elsewhere. At least Kenyatta dresses halfway decent. But that hair . . ."

As Jolene rattled on, Candice's eyes drifted to Ashley and Kenyatta dancing under the tent. Why was a black man, any black man, interested in her green-eyed daughter? And why was her daughter interested in him?

Chapter 10

Barbara lounged on the butterscotch-colored sofa in her silk pajamas and robe with her feet propped up on a dainty hand-stitched foot-rest. She held a coffee cup in one hand, a cigarette in the other, and watched from the solarium as workers dismantled the tent on the lawn.

She was exhausted. All the weeks leading up to the wedding had absolutely drained her. If she had to lift even one fingernail . . . well, she simply couldn't. But at least it was over, and except for the scene with Sabrina, it had been a smashing success. And now her younger daughter was married and off honeymooning in Jamaica.

She glanced at her older daughter Robin, sitting at the other end of the couch sipping coffee and reading the *Washington Post*. Robin and Rebecca were like night and day when it came to men and marriage. Rebecca had wanted to marry and have a family from the time she was just a young thing. Robin, on the other hand, had coasted through her twenties without even coming close to "that dreaded state," as she so often put it. Her daughter was now twenty-nine years old and still single. Happily so.

Until a year ago, Robin had been a hot young programmer at Digitech and lived in a luxury high-rise apartment building nearby. She had decided to cut her work hours and move back home while attending graduate school but expected to do even better once she got her master's degree. She was now hunting for a condo. Although Barbara would have loved nothing more than to see her elder daughter happily married off, she was proud of Robin's accomplishments.

"How do you think everything turned out yesterday?" Barbara asked as she stubbed out her cigarette.

Robin glanced up from her newspaper and fanned the smoky air with mock exaggeration. Barbara smiled with guilt. She wanted to quit so badly, but she had already given up the bottle and needed something to fall back on with a husband like Bradford.

"It was beautiful, Mama. Just perfect except for one thing." Robin wrinkled her nose and cocked her head in a way that accentuated her short natural hairstyle. "That little episode just before the ceremony was a disaster."

"Oh, *that*." Barbara twisted her lips in disgust. "Honestly, that silly woman had me worried to death. I was so afraid she would come back and ruin everything."

"I know, I know. But she didn't, thank goodness. And the important thing is that Rebecca was so happy. She was beaming."

Barbara nodded and smiled. "One down, one to go?"

"Please, Mama. That's not me. I'm focusing on my career now."

"Yes, I know. That's what you always say. And I'm all for having a career, sweetheart. I'm just not sure I understand why you have to wait so long to get married."

"A husband would just get in my way at this point," Robin said. "And if I get married now, I'd be stuck with the guy for fifty years or more. I can't even imagine that. I don't see getting married before forty."

"Forty? You'll be too old to have children by that time."

"Who said anything about waiting until I'm forty to have children, huh? This is the twenty-first century. I don't need to be married for that."

"You don't need to be, but you should be. Children need a father as much as a mother."

Robin shook her head. "Not if the mother and father don't get along. I think they're better off with one parent in a peaceful, loving home."

Barbara sighed. Who was she to argue that point? She couldn't exactly hold up her own marriage as a good example. Her bad relationship with Bradford could very well be one of the reasons Robin was down on marriage.

As if to mock her thoughts, Bradford strolled into the solarium wearing a white dress shirt and navy blazer and set his briefcase down on the floor next to the glass serving cart. Sunday was Phyllis's day off, and she always set up the coffeemaker and placed it in the solarium on Saturday evenings. All Barbara had to do in the morning was get up and turn the pot on.

"Good morning, ladies," Bradford said as he poured himself a cup.

"Morning," Barbara said.

"Where are you running off to so early, Daddy?"

"I have to go into the office for a few hours."

Barbara frowned. Into the office on a Sunday? The day after his daughter's wedding? That was ridiculous.

Of course, Bradford had always put in a lot of hours over the years. That was how he had built a multimillion-dollar technology firm from scratch, as he would so quickly remind her whenever she dared question or complain about his hours. It paid for the roof over their heads and had allowed her to stop working as a teacher's aide in the D.C. public schools shortly after they were married.

"Show some appreciation, Barbara" was one of his favorite sayings whenever she complained.

But his mistress had shown up uninvited just the day before at about the worst possible moment. Barbara thought she had the right to question him about anything and everything.

"You're going to work at nine-thirty on a Sunday morning?" she asked, her voice full of doubt.

Bradford shrugged. "I couldn't schedule a meeting Friday because of preparations for the wedding, so that left today."

He had so many excuses, so many reasons. "Can't it wait until tomorrow?" she inquired crisply.

"No, it can't," he responded just as crisply.

Barbara twisted her lips. Or *she* can't. Barbara would have bet her last dollar that he was off to see that whore who almost ruined the wedding. Unless he was already screwing someone else. But this was not the time to get into it with Robin sitting there.

"Well, we need to talk at some point, Bradford."

"About what? If you mean about what happened yesterday afternoon, I told you, there's nothing to talk about."

Barbara smacked her lips impatiently. "You always have excuses, Bradford." She glanced at Robin. "Can you excuse us for a minute, sweetheart?"

Robin held her mug up. "But I'm having my coffee now. And I like it here in the sunroom. It's not like I've never heard you two argue before."

Barbara bit her bottom lip. She had never discussed Bradford's indiscretions with the girls, but they had seen and heard a lot over the years. Too much. Even though she had tried to shield them from Bradford's philandering, it was impossible to conceal it completely — as the scene just before the wedding made all too painfully clear. "We're not arguing, Robin. And it will only take a minute."

"Do as your mother says," Bradford said impatiently. "But we won't be long. I need to get going."

"Oh, all right." Robin reluctantly took her mug and the business-section of the paper and left the room, and Barbara banged her coffee mug down on the table, ready to confront him. But before she could utter a word, he spoke up.

"Look, Barbara," he said tersely. "I don't know what you want from me. I've already explained it once. She's having a hard time accepting the breakup. So I went over there yesterday morning to try to calm her down. Obviously, that didn't work."

"No kidding," she said sarcastically. "You left here before the sun came up. Are you trying to tell me that it took all morning to calm her down?"

"I went to the golf course first, hit a few balls. Then I stopped by the office. I didn't get to her place until almost noon. We argued, and it didn't look like I was getting through to her so I started to leave. But she ran ahead of me and jumped into her car. I had no idea where she was going, but something told me to follow her." He shrugged. "What more can I say?"

Barbara lit another cigarette. He always made it seem like she was foolish for questioning him about these things. And so she would drop it. But she wasn't going to give in so easily this time. Things had gone too far with Sabrina. "All I know, Bradford, is that I can't take any more of this."

Bradford rolled his eyes skyward, walked into the kitchen and dumped the rest of his coffee down the sink.

How dare he turn his back to her in the middle of their conversation. She stood up so quickly she bumped into the coffee table. Her cup rattled and coffee spilled out. She set her cigarette in the ashtray, grabbed a napkin and dabbed at the spilled coffee.

"I mean it, Bradford. I'm not some pawn in a chess match that you can jerk around at will. You might get away with that at work, but I'll . . . I'll walk if this keeps up." There. She bet she had his attention now.

He returned and stood in the doorway between the kitchen and solarium, his face contorted with anger. The change in his expression was so abrupt that she forgot about the spilled coffee and stood up straight. She'd seen this many times before, but it always startled her. He would be calm and then his mood would change suddenly.

"Walk?" he said, sneering. "Where the hell to? You don't have any damn place to go. Your father was dead before I met you. Your mother drank herself to death. And your aunt is senile."

He waved an arm in the air. "You're lucky I married you and took you away from all that. So, tell me, Barbara. Just where the hell do you think you're going to go?"

She picked up her cigarette and noticed

that her hand was shaking. That always happened when he used that nasty tone of voice with her. He could be so harsh. "I . . . I can get my own place."

"Ha! You've never been out on your own. You don't have any skills, you've never bought a car by yourself, never handled taxes or paid bills. You don't do anything around here except supervise all the help I pay for — a housekeeper who comes almost daily, a weekly gardener, lawn maintenance. You'd be completely lost in no time at all, Barbara, even with my money. Shit, you'd have your head back in the bottle before your feet hit the pavement."

She stubbed the cigarette out. "I don't have to listen to this. You weren't exactly born with a silver spoon in your mouth."

His face softened a bit. "Look. You're the one who started this, Barbara. No, my childhood wasn't a hell of a lot better than yours. Why do you think I work so damn hard all the time? So you and the girls can have nice things. The least you could do is show some appreciation."

"I do appreciate everything you've done, Bradford. But yesterday with that woman here was too —"

"I said it was over with her, but you can't accept that. No, you want to start a fucking interrogation. So if you want to leave, fine. Go right ahead. But I promise you, I'll fight you on every dime in court. This house, the cars, the boat and condos. Everything. You think you're so miserable now? Hell, you don't know miserable." He snatched his briefcase off the floor. "I won't be home for dinner." And with that, he calmly walked off.

Barbara paced back and forth in front of the sofa. She could barely catch her breath. How could he throw the drinking in her face like that? She hadn't had a drink in two years. Bradford had never been the warmest man, but lately he seemed downright cold, cruel even. How did this happen? *When* did it happen? With all the drinking, she had been in a fog through so much of their marriage and had never seen this coming.

The scary part was that he was right about so much of it. He handled everything, made all the major decisions. That was fine with her in the beginning. When they met, she was only eighteen and was a lowly sales clerk in a department store. He was twenty-four, had just gotten his M.B.A and even then was talking big. He was going to get them out of Smithfield, Virginia, and start his own business. They would live in a big house and drive nice cars. They would have all the things money could buy.

He eventually did everything he said he would do and more, with one conquest after another. She began to think he was a god and they were living in paradise. When it slowly dawned on her that he had to conquer beautiful women, too, she took to the bottle rather than face up to it.

She sank back down on the couch and stared at the ceiling. Now she was older, wiser and sober. And she didn't like what she saw around her. Her children were grown, and "all the things money could buy" weren't enough anymore. She wanted love and kindness. She wanted respect.

She picked up her cigarette case, opened it and stuck a Benson & Hedges in her mouth. Her life would change drastically if she left him. She would probably be able to keep the house, but what about everything else? What about the condos in Nassau and Wintergreen? The boat and cars? It wouldn't be easy to walk away from all of that.

And their friends. Most of them would side with him, of that she was certain. They were politicians and businessmen and their wives. They needed Bradford and his business. They didn't need her.

She couldn't even count on Marilyn, even

though they had been friends for nearly thirty years. Marilyn's husband James owned a small technology firm, and Bradford had thrown a lot of contract work in his direction over the years. James worshiped Bradford.

But that didn't mean things couldn't change. Marilyn was a top-selling real estate agent in Prince George's County, and was always bragging about her latest million-dollar sale. Barbara often thought she could do that. She knew about sales, and she and Bradford had built this house from the ground up. What was to stop her from going for her license?

And immediately she knew. She had just turned fifty. That's what would stop her. A fifty-year-old in school, just starting out on her own — what a joke. Bradford was right. She was nothing without him.

Her hand trembled violently as she picked up her gold lighter and tried to light her cigarette. She soon gave up and threw the lighter on the floor. She wrapped her arms tightly around her waist. In the old days, she would have headed to the kitchen cabinet for a shot of vodka right about now. That would soothe her rattled nerves almost instantly. There wasn't any liquor in the kitchen cabinet now, but her secret stash was still in her nightstand.

She stood up and smashed the unlit cigarette out in the ashtray. She didn't know what she was going to do about her marriage, but she was not going to take a drink. That wouldn't solve anything.

She squinted and looked out over the lawn. Emilio, the gardener, wasn't coming until tomorrow, and she needed fresh flowers for the solarium. She would change into her sweats and do some gardening. That always calmed her. The garden was the perfect place to think — quiet and cheerful — just what she needed to clear her head.

Chapter 11

Jolene walked faster. She was up to four miles per hour and had been at it for forty minutes. Her body was sweating from head to toe. She could feel herself getting stronger, tougher. God, she loved this power-walking stuff.

A morning at the health club always did wonders for her mind and body. It was just what she needed, especially after fussing with that cheap, penny-pinching husband of hers. Since they had started building the new house, there was always something to argue about. This morning it was the roof. After spending time at the Bentley house the day before, she wanted tile so badly — it was different, exciting, expensive. Patrick wanted dry old asphalt shingles for one lousy reason only. Money. They were cheap and boring, just like him. Hell, Patrick would put straw up if he thought it could withstand the cold Maryland winters.

"Probably ninety-nine percent of the population has a plain old asphalt shingle roof," Patrick had pointed out to her earlier. "But nah, you can't be happy with that. You gotta go find the most expensive roof material known to mankind to be happy. Well, guess what? We can't afford it."

Yak, yak, yak! The man was so frigging cheap she could scream. She pressed a few buttons on the treadmill and upped the incline.

Sometimes she wondered why she had stayed with him for so long. There were days when she felt like pulling out every single strand of the weave on her head. He was too damn much aggravation.

Come on, girl, she told herself, breathing deeply as she walked. You know why you stay. The main reason could be summed up in one word: Juliette. Even though the child behaved like her mother, she worshiped her daddy. Juliette would often go to her father to talk about things like boys and music. They had the kind of close relationship that Jolene always wished she'd had with her own father. And she didn't want to break that up.

Besides, if they separated now, Patrick would have to find another place to live and that would mean additional rent. They couldn't possibly afford that along with the mortgage for their house and the note for the construction loan on the house they were building. Separation would most likely mean giving up the new house or at least postponing building it for a while, and she couldn't have that. That big baby shaping up on the hillside in Silver Lake, North, was her dream come true.

She was going to have to put up with Patrick for the time being. Living with him wasn't all bad. He didn't beat her or anything like that, or she would have been gone a long time ago. He didn't even cheat with other women, at least not to her knowledge. He came home by seven every night. Hell, she wished he would put in more hours at work. They could certainly use the money.

Patrick just wasn't the right man for her, and she had known it for a while. They had learned to tolerate each other by staying away from each other much of the time, coming together only when needed, such as for the Bentley wedding and for some dry, quick sex about once a month.

She had gotten used to their boring life together, but that didn't mean she planned to live this way forever. No way. She was only thirty-six years old. Much too young to be stuck in this dull, predictable life.

Terrence was exactly what she needed to spice things up. But she wasn't going to waste a whole lot more time on him, period. She was starting to feel like she was being jerked about, and she hated that.

She would give Terrence a few more

months to come around and that was all. If he was still making sorry excuses, she would have to move on. She hoped it wouldn't come to that. She really thought Terrence was the perfect man for her. He had so much going for him.

She remembered the first time she visited his office on a trendy block near Dupont Circle in D.C. like it was just yesterday. Patrick was being his usual cheap-ass self. He thought hiring an architect was a ridiculous waste of money and had refused to even go into town to meet with Terrence. Fine, she told him. Be that way.

So she went alone on her lunch hour and almost flipped when Terrence Turner strolled into the waiting room to greet her. He was tall and handsome enough to be a movie star. When they sat down in his office, she kept asking him questions so she could stay longer and just look at him.

Their second meeting went straight from cold salads at lunch to a steamy tryst at the Hyatt hotel. She had to tear herself away late that night and come up with an excuse for getting home past midnight.

She smiled. Damn. She was getting horny just thinking about the man. She punched some buttons on the treadmill, and it slowed to a stroll as she patted her face dry with the towel draped around her neck. She reached for her cell phone and dialed the Hyatt.

Terrence always went to church with the wife and kids on Sunday morning. But they were due to hook up that afternoon for one of their little escapades, and she wanted to have a bottle of Veuve Clicquot, her favorite champagne, chilling at the bedside when they arrived. A bit of bubbly would help Terrence loosen up, and she'd have better luck convincing him that she was the best woman for him.

Pearl removed her black wide-brimmed hat and patted her short natural hairdo in place. Then she cocked her ear toward the stairs and listened for the sound of rap music that would tell her that Kenyatta was home. Sometimes Pearl could coax him into going to church with her, although most mornings it was impossible to get him out of bed after he had spent a late Saturday night partying or visiting friends. She didn't even try this morning. After the wedding reception, he and that new girl went to Blues Alley in D.C. to listen to some jazz. Now what was her name? Oh, right, Ashley. Humph! The child's *name* even sounded white.

Pearl didn't hear music. That meant he was either out or still dozing, even though it was now after eleven in the morning. Chances were that he was still in, since he knew she always fixed a big brunch on Sundays after church — bacon and sausage, grits and fried potatoes, and scrambled eggs. But she wanted to check before she got started. Kenyatta could eat enough for two, and she wanted to be sure to fix plenty if he was in.

She climbed the stairs and walked to her bedroom. She tossed her hat on the bedspread and slipped out of her black dress and heels and into a long cotton shift and slippers. Then she went to Kenyatta's door and knocked softly.

"Yeah," came his sleepy voice from the other side.

She cracked the door open. He was sitting on the edge of the bed and wiping his eyes with his fists. Pearl smiled. He looked just like he did when he was about six years old, rubbing his face like that. It was so good to have her boy back at home, even if only for a short while.

"Late night, huh?" she asked.

He yawned. "Tell me about it. We got back, like, three a.m. I was beat."

Too beat to hang up his clothes, obviously, she thought, eyeing yesterday's wrinkled suit and shirt lying across the back of a chair. She entered the room and picked the clothes up one by one, slinging them over her arm. She didn't know how he had ever managed living away from home by himself. "You worked late every day last week. That's why you're so tired."

He shrugged. "I need the money so I can get my own place and be out of your hair."

She waved a hand at him. "Oh pish. You can stay here as long as you like, you know that."

"Thanks, Ma. But no thanks. I need to get my own place." He stood in his briefs and stretched leisurely. "So what time will breakfast be ready?"

"Sooner than you will, judging from the look of things around here," she teased as she placed his shoes in the closet.

He chuckled and sat back down. "Good, 'cause I'm starving, and I got a big day ahead. Ashley and I are going to a cookout in Northwest, and then to a concert out in Columbia, Maryland, tonight."

A chill went up Pearl's spine. He was seeing that girl again? So soon? "I see," she said slowly. "This sounds like it's getting serious."

"You mean with Ashley?"

Pearl nodded.

He smiled broadly. "Yeah, I really like her."

"Mm-hmm." Pearl paused. She knew she had better approach this gingerly. "Are you sure you know what you're doing, Kenyatta, getting involved with this girl?"

"What do you mean exactly, Ma?"

"Well, I only met her for a minute, and she seems fine as far as I can tell. It's just that, well . . . you know, she . . . she's . . ."

"She's white?"

Pearl caught her breath. "Well, yes."

"And your point is?"

"I mean, life will be much easier for you if you stick with your own kind."

Kenyatta grunted. "Easier? How?"

"With society. With other people. You —"

"Ma, I go for the person, not their skin color. Ashley's sweet and down to earth. I couldn't care less what others think."

Pearls lips tightened. "Maybe you *should* care. I mean, black men have been killed for messing with white women."

Kenyatta waved his arm in exasperation. "C'mon, Ma. Not these days. Not around here. Why are you tripping?"

Pearl smacked her lips with impatience. Kenyatta was too young to remember such things. With all the fancy homes going up, it was hard to see that Prince George's was once Hicksville — pure redneck country. Some parts of it still were.

"Oh, it still happens. Maybe not as much as when I was your age, but it still happens. Believe me."

"It's so rare, Ma. She's the one who catches all the flak, mainly from black chicks. Sometimes I think you just never got over Daddy and Holly."

Pearl felt her body go tense. She hadn't heard that woman's name in years and she preferred it that way. She placed her hands firmly on her hips. "Boy, don't you throw that up in my face. This has nothing to do with your father or that white woman. It's not that I don't like Ashley. I just don't think she's right for you. Is she going to stand up for you when you're butting heads with white society? I don't think so."

"How can you be so sure?" he protested. "You hardly know her. You never like it when I date outside our race. You always wanted me to take advantage of their schools, their recreational facilities, but —"

"Excuse me," she interrupted. "If you think of those things as *their* things, or as white things, then you have a problem, young man. We have just as much right to them as anybody. I pay my taxes just like they do."

"You know what I mean, Ma. You think it's OK to mix with them up to a point, even to be friends with them. But when it comes to getting involved romantically, it's like, hey, stay away. Not *my* son. I don't get that."

"Blacks and whites don't mix romantically without trouble."

Kenyatta scoffed impatiently. "I give up."

She shook a finger at him. "Listen, I'm going to tell you exactly how I feel when I think you're making a mistake."

"Don't I know it. We've always been up front with each other, Ma, and I value that. But you don't have to worry about me all the time."

"You're my son. I'm always going to worry about you. And I'm not —"

He held up a hand. "Look, Ma, can we finish this discussion some other time? I need to get cleaned up now."

"Fine. I'll go fix you some breakfast before you go." She reached for the clothes on the bed. "I'll take these and throw them in the washing machine."

Kenyatta grabbed the clothes before she could get to them. "I'll do it."

"But I'm going down. I might as well take them."

"Ma, I said I'll do it."

Something in his voice told Pearl not to push him. "Fine. I'll see you in the kitchen in a bit."

She shut his door and walked to the stairs. A lot of this was her fault. She sent him to majority-white schools and praised him when he made friends with white children. She told herself that he was learning how to deal with white people and that would help him get ahead in life.

But this white girlfriend stuff was going too far. When he came home in the evening after dealing with white folks all day at the office, he needed a nice black woman to greet him, someone who understood what it meant to be black in this world.

Chapter 12

Candice parted the living room curtains and watched as Ashley ran down the walkway to an old tan Volvo that supposedly belonged to Kenyatta's mother. Candice couldn't believe that Ashley was seeing him again so soon. She had been through a lot with her daughters, but never anything like this.

The Volvo pulled off, and Candice let the curtain fall. She lifted her cup of Chinese green tea to her nose and inhaled deeply. She needed something to soothe her frayed nerves. The night before, she had dreamed that she was falling off a cliff into a dark void, helpless to save herself.

She took a sip of tea, sat in a stuffed armchair and stared at the drapes. Why was she so bothered by this? If anything was more puzzling than Ashley's behavior, it was her own reaction to it. She had worked around black people at Digitech for seven years now. She had black friends and neighbors.

Back in the sixties and seventies, when blacks started moving in droves from Washington, D.C., to the suburbs of Prince George's County, many whites fled. She was ten years old when the first black family moved onto their block, and her dad wanted to leave right away. "The niggers will ruin property values," he muttered as he got a real estate agent on the phone. But her mom didn't want to move. Mom didn't think one black family would cause much harm and she convinced him to stay.

Then another black family moved to the block six weeks later. Within a month her dad was packing the family into the station wagon and driving north to upper Montgomery County, where he crowded them into a new housing development on a measly quarter of an acre. All the houses were carbon copies of one another, and there was barely a tree in sight. There were barely any black people either, and that seemed to suit her dad just fine.

In Prince George's, where land was cheaper, the family had lived on several wooded acres, and Candice fondly remembered running and playing in the woods and wide-open fields as a young girl. So when she got her divorce, she moved back to the county and had been here ever since.

Their house was small compared with others in Silver Lake, but they had a half acre of land. They would never have been able to afford that in Montgomery County. True, Prince George's lacked the sophistication of Montgomery County in Maryland and Fairfax County in Virginia. You could count the number of decent restaurants and shopping malls on one hand. And some areas in Prince George's County were downright rough, especially inside the beltway as you got closer to D.C.

But Silver Lake was special — the jewel of Prince George's County. All the folks here wanted the same things she did — a prosperous, safe place to raise their children. They were no different from middle- and upper-income families anywhere. And unlike her parents, she had wanted her children to attend schools with children of other races. The country was full of black and brown people with more arriving every day, and she wanted her daughters to feel comfortable around them.

So why was this thing between Ashley and Kenyatta bothering her so? From what Ashley had told her, Kenyatta was bright and full of promise. He seemed to treat her well and was very polite. That was more than she could have said about some of Ashley's white boyfriends.

Still, she wanted to know more about this one. She *had* to know more. She jumped up and rushed through the living room into the kitchen, where Jim was reading the Sunday paper at the breakfast bar. "I'm going to call around and find out more about this guy, Jim."

Jim looked up from his paper. "I wouldn't do that just yet, hon," he cautioned. "If Ashley finds out, she won't be happy about it."

"She won't find out about it," Candice said firmly.

Jim sighed. "Who are you thinking of calling?"

Candice set her teacup on the bar and sat down on a stool. "Jolene next door to start. I talked to her briefly at the wedding. She doesn't know much about this guy, but I'll bet she could find out some things if I ask her to. And maybe Barbara Bentley, since Kenyatta's mother does her hair."

He shook his head in doubt. "I wouldn't do that, but it's your call. Just be ready when Ashley finds out that you've been snooping around."

Candice stood up with determination. "I'll take my chances. I'm her mother, and I have to protect her, even if she is nineteen now. I don't think she really understands what she's getting herself into. *I* don't even understand it. I mean, he could be a great guy, but a lot of people will judge her negatively because of her association with him."

"You don't have to convince me. Call around if that's what you want to do." He went back to his newspaper.

Candice headed toward the door, then paused. "Jim?"

"Yes?" he responded without looking up.

"Tell me the truth." She paused and fingered the charm around her neck. "Am I being racist?"

Jim looked up with a puzzled expression on his face.

"I know my dad can be old-fashioned when it comes to race, and that's putting it mildly, but I've always tried not to —"

"No, no. Hell, no. I think you're being a concerned parent living in a racist world. You should feel good that you raised a daughter who's obviously color blind. But then" — he paused and exhaled — "you wound up with something like this to deal with. I wouldn't be surprised if this fellow's parents have some reservations about it, too. They may think she'll make his life more difficult than it needs to be."

She leaned over and kissed him. "Thanks, honey. I needed to hear that. I'll be in the bedroom on the phone. Caitlin is upstairs, so I'm going to close the door so she won't hear me. No point getting her riled up. Wish me luck."

Candice walked up the stairs and tiptoed quietly past Caitlin's bedroom, although with the way rock music was blasting from the CD player she could have stomped all the way down the hall and never been noticed. Candice didn't like all this sneaking around her own family, but Caitlin was likely to give her a harder time about this than Ashley would.

"Oh hell," she mumbled after she had closed her bedroom door. She felt like a spy in her own house. It was only a phone call. And she had every right to do this.

She cracked the door open, sat on the bed and flipped through her phone book to the B's for Jolene Brown's number.

Chapter 13

Lee rubbed her eyes with her fist and sat up. She looked out the rear car window to see a big empty parking lot. Where the hell was she? She struggled to sit up in the backseat, then she remembered. Last night she had left P. G. County and pointed the car north until she reached Baltimore and pulled into a shopping center on Reistertown Road.

She blinked against the early morning light and rubbed her stomach. God, she was hungry. And funky. She hadn't had a real bath in a week, just a couple of birdbaths in public rest rooms with paper towels. And here it was the middle of summer. But the worst of it was that her money was running low. She reached up to the front passenger seat of the car for her shoulder bag and pulled out her wallet. She was down to her last six dollars and had only a half tank of gas left.

Damn. She had tried to be careful with the money. She pulled into parking lots at night and slept in the car. She ate at McDonald's and Burger King. But food and gas cost too damn much when you were living on just a few lousy bucks.

She threw the bag on the floor and uttered a string of profanities. She had been too damn greedy, splurging on Big Macs and large fries. At this rate, her ass wouldn't last out here more than a couple more days, max, even eating once a day at McDonald's.

She pulled a photo of her mama and daddy out of the bag and ran her fingers across the surface. It was a cheap snapshot they had taken in a photo booth on the street years ago. Mama had said it was taken on their second and last date as they were coming from a bar in downtown D.C., and that it was the last time she ever saw Lee's daddy.

She stared at her mama's pretty round face. She missed her so much. No doubt Mama and her brother were worried sick about her. But she couldn't go back there, she couldn't even call. She had killed a man and she was scared the cops would find her and haul her ass off to juvee.

Why did Mama have to make them move into that rat-infested stink hole in Seat Pleasant with Uncle Clive? It had to be one of the toughest parts of P. G. County. Fat-ass rats marched around that apartment building bold as you please, acting like they owned the place.

The roaches were even worse. They ruled the kitchen. It was so bad she was scared to open the cupboards. Once she finished a glass of iced tea and found one floating at the bottom. They ran around in the bedroom and sometimes even crawled into the sofa bed where she slept with her six-year-old brother. She'd wake up in a fit and throw off all the covers.

They didn't have much before they moved in with Uncle Clive. Just a little one-room apartment in Landover, Maryland, and she and her baby brother, Vernon, slept in the bed with Mama. But it was clean and there was no Uncle Clive.

Mama said it was all on account of her losing her government job. The only work she could find was cleaning office buildings part-time at night, and she couldn't make the rent at their old place anymore. So they had to put up with the rats and roaches at Uncle Clive's until Mama got back on her feet. Mama said they should be thankful Uncle Clive let them stay there. At least they weren't living in a cardboard box in an alley somewhere like some folks.

Maybe it wouldn't have been so bad if Uncle Clive was their real uncle and he could have kept his foul hands to himself. But he wasn't and he didn't. He was some creep Mama met a few months before they moved in with him. And for all Lee could see, he was just a low-life punk drug dealer.

But Mama said Uncle Clive was gonna help them get out of the hood. Uncle Clive might be a drug dealer now, but he had ideas. Uncle Clive might have a hot temper, but he had cash to keep a roof over their heads. Uncle Clive might be skinny, but he had a car. He was going places and he would take them with him if they were nice to him. So said Mama.

Lee held up the photo and ran her fingers over her daddy's face. He was so handsome and had the nicest smile she'd ever seen. She wished she could find him. He could help her out of this mess. But all she knew about him was that he went by the name Smokey and lived in Maryland when Mama knew him. Every time she tried to get more information about him from Mama, she got herself scolded.

"But what about my real daddy, Mama? Or what about Vernon's daddy? Can't one of them help us? I hate Uncle Clive."

"Shut up, child. You don't know what you talkin' 'bout. Your real daddy? Shoot. He don't even know you alive. I told you that. I met him in a bar one night. Saw him twice and that was it. He took off before I even got a

chance to tell him about you. Hell, before I even knew I was carrying you. That's the honest-to-God truth. Shoot. Forgot what that man even looked like until you was born. Cuz you the spitting image of that man, I swear. And I don't know where Vernon's daddy is neither. He was a young thing when I knew him and he made it clear he didn't want nothing to do with us."

"But you can try and find my daddy, Mama. Can't you find him and tell him about me? He might come and take us away from all of this. You know what I'm saying?" The rats and roaches. And Uncle Clive.

"Didn't I tell you to hush? That was a long time ago. 'Sides, he probably don't have much of nothing to be giving to us, anyway. Probably got a family of his own somewhere and not a dime to his name. Just like the rest of these sorry-ass men out here."

Lee hugged the photo to her chest. She didn't believe that. Her pops wasn't like other men. She could tell just by looking at the way he smiled in the photo. He looked just like Cliff Huxtable. *The Cosby Show* was her favorite TV program ever. She would bet her last dollar that her pops was rich, lived in a big fancy house and had plenty of money, just like the Huxtables.

Chapter 14

Barbara waved at the gatekeeper as she glided her Mercedes sedan through the entrance at Silver Lake. Her shopping trip had been an utter disappointment. She had driven all the way out to Annapolis, Maryland, and back and had one tiny bag of cosmetics to show for her trouble. Twenty long miles there and back.

It was ridiculous to have to go so far out of the way to find decent shopping. But most of the malls near Silver Lake were so shabby, with Target or Kmart being the usual anchors. She wouldn't be caught dead anywhere near one of those cheap discount stores. Planning a trip to a Nordstrom or Saks or Neiman Marcus was like planning a trip to the moon.

It simply made no sense in a community full of half-million-dollar-plus estates, her own included. In Montgomery and Fairfax Counties, you could practically trip over the Bloomingdale's and Nordstrom stores. The only explanation was that many of the estate homes in Prince George's were owned by African-Americans. For some reason, upscale department store owners were scared of African-American money.

She sighed as she drove slowly past the shimmering man-made lake that flowed through the community. She had planned to do a lot more shopping on this trip, but she had gotten so frustrated thinking about Sabrina as she tried on swimsuits that she left the mall after being there less than an hour.

None of Bradford's other mistresses had put such a big strain on her marriage. In the weeks since the wedding, Sabrina had called the house at least half a dozen times and hung up when Barbara answered the phone. Barbara knew it was her. Who else would do such a thing? But she didn't even mention it to Bradford. They were barely speaking, and he would simply deny it was Sabrina.

She turned into their driveway and pressed a button in the roof of the Benz to open one of the three garage doors. She was surprised to see both the SUV and the Jaguar convertible parked as she pulled in. Before she left this morning, Bradford said he was going to be out on the golf course all afternoon with some of his buddies since it was such a beautiful summer day. And nothing could drag Bradford away from the golf course when he had his mind set on hitting those balls. She wouldn't have expected him back before dinnertime and here it was just after noon.

She entered the kitchen and kicked off her heels, then walked to the picture window and stared out onto the lawn, where just a few weeks ago their baby daughter's wedding reception had taken place. A lump welled up in her throat as she thought back to when she herself was the happy bride. A part of her still loved Bradford but she wasn't so sure he loved her anymore. Sometimes she thought he never had. Or if he ever did, he had a crazy way of showing it.

And she was clueless as to how to fix things. When it came to Bradford and his women, she was lost. When he was under a lot of pressure at work, she tried being patient. When he came home and didn't want to talk, she tried to be understanding. She had tried the sexy negligees, the gourmet meals. She'd threatened to leave and even once stayed with her aunt for a month.

Nothing worked. Like an idiot, she went along with all this for years, using vodka to soothe the pain when it became unbearable. So what if she didn't have her husband one hundred percent? She was still Mrs. Bradford Bentley. Half of him was better than all of most other men. It had been easier to believe that kind of crap when she was full of booze.

But she had been sober for two years now, and lately, with the clarity of sobriety and the wisdom of age, all the "things" Bradford's money could buy were starting to mean less and less to her. She had reached a point where she thought she could give it all up to be in a loving, trusting relationship with a man.

She had even gone so far as to get a divorce lawyer's name and number from an old friend down in Smithfield a week ago. She didn't dare ask Marilyn or anyone else in Silver Lake, or even in Prince George's. They all had connections with Bradford, and she didn't want him knowing that she was asking around until she was sure she was ready to make her move. The day after Rebecca's wedding, he had made it clear that he would fight her if she left him. She didn't want another heated argument like that.

Should she call the lawyer now? She was sick of all the Sabrinas. She sighed. She could definitely use a drink, but she was determined never to go back to those dark days of drowning all her sorrows in the bottle. Alcohol had turned her into a person she despised — whiny, helpless, pitiful. Bradford thought she was all those things anyway. When she was drinking, she thought them about herself.

She would decide about the lawyer a bit later. Right now she was going to head upstairs for a nap. She picked up the mail that Phyllis had left on the black granite countertop and flipped through it. Most of it was junk, and she tossed it aside for the trash until she came across a real estate brochure called *Extraordinary Properties* from Long and Foster. It was a booklet of luxury homes in the Washington metro area that they got once in a while, but what interested her most were the short bios and photos of realtors at the back of the book. One or two of the agents were sometimes black, and Marilyn had been featured once.

She tucked the brochure under her arm, picked up her bag and walked up the back stairs that led directly to the master bedroom. She hoped Bradford was down in the media room watching a movie or in the exercise room working out. She didn't feel like seeing him now. She just wanted to crawl into bed and read a bit before falling off to sleep.

She was in luck, she realized as she dropped her bag and the brochure on the love seat in the sitting room. Her husband was nowhere in sight. She closed the drapes, then turned down the bedcovers. In the dressing room, she removed her suit and slipped into a knee-length nightgown. The she climbed into bed and flipped through the pages of the Long and Foster brochure.

Maybe a job was just what she needed. It would give her some clout of her own. She would be somebody besides Mrs. Bradford Bentley. She was going to call Marilyn and ask her about real estate classes at Long and Foster as soon as she finished her nap. She yawned, put on her eye mask and pulled the covers up.

As soon as her head touched the pillow, she jumped back up. She had felt something odd under the pillowcase. She moved her hand around inside until her fingers touched something soft and wispy, like nylon. She yanked it out, snatched the mask off her eyes and held it up. A black G-string stared back at her. She had never owned such a thing in her entire life.

Dammit. She gritted her teeth to stop the scream from exiting her throat. The fabric felt like a hot flame on her fingers. She threw it on the floor and kicked off the bedcovers. She couldn't take this anymore. She was going to kick that bastard out now and then call the lawyer.

She grabbed the G-string, held it out between two fingers and ran out of the room and down the stairs without bothering with the silk slippers sitting neatly at the edge of her bed. She skipped down the stairs, taking them two at a time.

When her bare feet reached the carpeted basement, she was breathless. But she didn't stop. She ran straight into the media room. He wasn't there, so she spun around and ran down the hallway to the exercise room. Bradford was lying flat on his back on a bench, lifting a 150-pound weight. She ran up beside him and threw the scanty G-string in his face. It caught on his nose and dangled down his cheek.

"You bastard!" she shouted. "I am so damned sick of this."

"What the hell!" He shook the G-string off his face, then carefully dropped the weight into the rack. He sat up on the bench and glared at her. "Jesus, Barbara!" he exclaimed. "You scared the crap out of me! Do you know how dangerous that is? You trying to kill me or something?"

Oh, he was good, she thought. Trying to turn the tables on her. Well, he should be good at this. He'd had plenty of practice. "What is that?" she yelled, pointing to the offending object. "I demand to know. And I want the truth."

He reached on the floor for the G-string and held it up. He narrowed his eyes. "Where did this come from?"

"You tell me," she snapped. "I found it inside my pillowcase just now."

"You found this inside your pillowcase?" He looked as surprised as she'd been when she'd found it.

"Yes. And it wasn't there this morning. Who does it belong to? Sabrina? Or have you already moved on to someone else?"

"Barbara, really. I've never even seen this before. Are you sure it isn't yours?"

Barbara stomped her foot. He knew good and darn well it wasn't hers. "I won't have this going on in my house, Bradford, or any of your nonsense anymore. I'm sick of it."

He held his palms out, faceup. "If I try to explain what I think may have happened, you won't believe me."

"You're right, I won't, because you always lie. Whoever left this for me to find is sick."

He stood up. "I agree. I'm really sorry about all this."

"And . . . and as far as I'm concerned you can pack . . ." She paused and stared at him suspiciously. Come again? He was agreeing with her? And apologizing? He must be up to another one of his tricks. "Don't bother apologizing. And don't bother lying. I don't want to hear it. Just —"

"I admit it, she was here."

Barbara stopped cold. "Who was here? Sabrina?"

Bradford let out a deep breath of air and nodded his head. He looked eager to talk about it. "She showed up at the golf course this morning and caused a big scene in front of my buddies, so I left and came home. A few minutes after I got here, she rang the bell."

"So you took her to our bedroom and had sex with her?" Barbara sneered. "That solves everything, doesn't it, Bradford?"

"I didn't take her into the bedroom, and I didn't have sex with her. Hell, I didn't even know she was up there. I know it looks like I did, if you found this." He held up the G-string, his face appropriately twisted with disgust.

She narrowed her eyes with doubt. "I don't believe you, Bradford."

"I'm telling the truth. Honest to God, I swear it. I let her in, and we talked in the living room for a few minutes. Or argued, rather. Then, after about ten minutes, she said she needed to use the bathroom. I guess she snuck upstairs and slipped this inside your pillowcase. She was planning to do this all along."

"How does she even know which side of the bed I sleep on?" Barbara snapped.

He let out a deep breath. "Oh . . . well."

"You've had her here before, haven't you?"

He nodded reluctantly.

"In our bedroom?"

He nodded again.

Barbara swallowed hard. This was new. As disgusting as it was, he was admitting it. "How many times?"

"Only once — about three months ago."

"Where was I?"

"On that overnight shopping trip to London, when you took the Concorde with Rebecca and Robin."

"Oh, Bradford. How could you?" She nearly sobbed. "It's not enough to screw her, you had to do it in our bed?"

He shook his head slowly. "I'm sorry about this whole thing with her. It was stupid. But at least I'm trying to be honest with you now."

Barbara was beginning to think that maybe she was better off not knowing.

"And I've got another problem," he said.

She frowned. What more could there be?

"It's turning into a *Fatal Attraction* kind of thing, and I'm worried."

Barbara's frown deepened. "What do you mean, 'fatal attraction'?"

"She's been harassing me almost daily. She calls the office five, six times a day. She shows up at the golf course."

"This is ridiculous, Bradford!" Barbara exclaimed in alarm. "I don't want her coming anywhere near me or our daughters."

"She would never do anything like that," he said firmly. "She's wild but not crazy."

Barbara wasn't so sure. She thought about Sabrina coming at her with a butcher knife just before Rebecca's wedding. "You need to call the police and get a restraining order."

"What will I say to them? That a woman has been following me around? Don't worry. I'll handle it. I'm thinking of getting away for a week or two to give it a chance to cool off."

Barbara tried to calm down. "Do you think that will help?"

"That's what I'm hoping. Listen, why don't you come with me?"

"Excuse me?"

"Our thirtieth anniversary is coming up," he said. "I was thinking that we could spend a few days at the condo in Wintergreen or drive to the Greenbrier resort. We always talk about going there. Or at least we used to talk about it."

Barbara couldn't believe her ears. He wanted them to go away together? They'd grown so far apart, she wouldn't even know how to act alone with him for any length of time. "You aren't serious, are you?"

"Why wouldn't I be? I know it's been a while since we've done anything like that. You even hinted around about divorce a few weeks back. But that's not what I want. A trip would probably do us a world of good."

Barbara clutched her hands uneasily. His behavior was confusing her. A few moments ago, she had been about to do a lot more than hint — she was going to throw him out. She chuckled hesitantly. "I don't know, Bradford. Things have been so bad between us for so long. Sometimes I think maybe we should just . . ." Did she dare say it? He was being so honest with her for a change. Did she really want to give up on their marriage?

"Maybe what?" he asked impatiently.

Barbara looked down at her fingers.

"We've built quite a life together, Barbara. We really should try to work things out. I'm willing to try if you are."

She was silent for a moment. What if they were beyond trying? No, no. She couldn't think like that. This was her marriage they were talking about. She had been Mrs. Bradford Bentley for thirty years now. "All right," she said softly. "I'm willing to give it a try."

"I'm thinking of getting involved in David Manley's campaign for P. G. county executive."

Jolene lowered the mystery novel she was reading to the bedcovers and turned to face her husband, standing on the other side of their king-size bed and removing his robe and slippers. He had just come up from watching TV in the family room.

"Huh?"

"I said, I may get involved with David Manley. I went by his campaign office last week. The election is coming up in November and they need volunteers."

She flipped her weave off her shoulders and picked her novel back up. "Right, Patrick."

"I'm serious."

She eyed him from above the book as he sat down on the edge of the bed. "What about your job?"

He shrugged. "This would be part-time, evenings and weekends."

She placed the novel facedown on the bed. "Where is this coming from, Patrick?

You've never said one word about getting involved in politics before this very moment. I didn't even know you were interested in politics. This is coming clear out of the blue."

"Well, all you ever want to talk about these days is the house we're building. But I've been thinking about this for a while now. I've got a lot of ideas for Silver Lake and the surrounding area. I may even run for office myself one day."

Jolene rolled her eyes to the ceiling. Patience, patience, she told herself.

"Make fun if you want," he said. "But I'm serious about this. I'm really concerned about the kids around here, especially the young boys and the public school system. You drive a few miles up the road and they're hanging out on the street in their baggy jeans and black caps starting trouble."

"I admit it's a problem. But we live in a gated community, and Juliette is in private school." She shrugged.

"But those young boys are still our neighbors. They're more than that. They're our future."

"Patrick, that's all very honorable, but what can you do about it?"

"Some community projects might help, like a sports center, after-school programs."

Jolene scoffed. "Patrick, please. What half of them need is prison. Look, I don't mean to make fun, but c'mon. You know nothing about politics. Spend that extra time you're planning to work on Manley's campaign at Digitech if you need something to do. We could use the money."

"Everyone has to start somewhere, and I'm tired of sitting behind a desk all day. I interact more with the computer than with people. I need a change."

Jolene waved her hand. "Fine. It's a free country."

"Are you with me? I offered to plan and organize a fund-raiser in Silver Lake. They liked my ideas, and you'd be good at that."

Jolene shook her head firmly and held her hand out. "Uh-uh. Go ahead if you want, but don't ask me to get involved. I've got enough on my plate as it is with work and the new house. And I want to have a big housewarming party soon after we move in. We can invite —"

"Jolene, that's not what I want to talk about now," he said impatiently. "I could really use your help on the fund-raiser. It's a chance for us to do something together and get involved with the community."

"We *are* doing something together. We're building a house."

"No. *You're* building a house."

"See?" she said. "If that's your attitude about the house when you know it's important to me, why should I give a damn about this politics thing? My father was a judge until he retired, and you know I hate anything to do with politics."

"Your father was appointed."

"It was still very political."

He sighed. "Can I at least get your word that you won't interfere with my effort?"

"I said it was fine. As long as you don't ask me to help and don't use our money."

"What money?" he asked sarcastically. "You're spending it all on the damn house."

She rolled her eyes and picked up her novel. She stared at the pages, but she was only pretending to read. How could she focus on fiction after he had just dropped this bombshell?

He lay down beside her and propped his head up with his hand, facing her. "What's that you're reading?"

"A novel, as if you care," she said curtly.

He chuckled. "You know, you still look sexy to me when you get upset."

She felt his hand move to her thigh under the covers. What the hell was getting into him? He knew they only had sex the first weekend of the month. And she certainly wasn't in the mood now, not after his surprise announcement about getting involved in politics. She quickly shoved his hand away. "Not now, Patrick. I'm reading. Or trying to."

He threw the covers off and stood up. He grabbed his robe and stormed out the door, probably to go back down to the family room and watch TV. Thank God. She was still savoring her lunch hour of passion the day before with Terrence. The last thing she was in the mood for now was Patrick.

She slammed the novel shut. Politics? Running for office? This was so unlike Patrick. Years ago, after he finally got his college degree in computer programming from the University of D.C., he had toyed around with the idea of starting his own computer firm. That spark of ingenuity had lasted for about a month. These days he went to work, then came home and parked his butt in front of the TV until he went to bed.

Politicians were leaders, and leaders were motivators. Patrick couldn't even motivate his own lazy butt. So where the hell did he get some notion that he could run for public office? She blinked as a bizarre thought hit her.

Could another woman be behind this? Jolene shook her head. Nah. Affairs took lots of planning and scheming and running about. Patrick didn't have it in him.

She'd give his idea a few weeks to play out. Let him tinker around at the edges of this crazy scheme and see how time-consuming it was. Then she would push him to ask for a promotion at work. They needed more money for the new house. This was no time for him to be thinking and acting like a damn fool.

She chuckled and opened the novel. Running for political office. Patrick? Puh-leeze.

Chapter 15

"How could you do this to me, Mom?" Ashley asked scornfully. "I'm furious with you."

Candice barely had a chance to get out of her Ford Taurus before Ashley pounced on her. "What on earth are you talking about, Ashley?"

"I'm talking about you snooping behind my back," Ashley snapped. "That's what I'm talking about. You called Jolene Brown and asked her about Kenyatta. You're spying on me."

Candice shut the car door. She needed a second to think this through because she was guilty as hell. But how on earth had Ashley found out about it? As far as she knew, Jolene had no relationship with Kenyatta or his mother.

"I'm not spying on you," Candice corrected her calmly. "I simply asked Jolene a few questions about him."

"Oh my God. I am so not hearing this. What did you ask her? And why didn't you come to *me* if you had questions about him?"

Candice walked up the path leading to the

house, and Ashley followed close on her heels. Candice told herself to stay calm. Otherwise this would turn into a shouting match. The truth was that she felt a little guilty about what she'd done, especially since nothing much had come of it.

"*Jolene, I hate to even bother you about this, but, well . . . it's been on my mind.*"

"*I'm sure it has, Candice. But I really don't know much about Kenyatta, or Pearl for that matter, or anyone else who lives in those town houses. You might try calling Barbara Bentley, since Pearl does her hair.*"

"*Well, that's the problem. You see, if Ashley ever found out I was doing this, she'd be furious. And Barbara might say something to Pearl. So . . .*"

"*Hmm. I see what you mean, Candice. Well, I do know another woman who goes to Pearl's salon. I'll call her and get back to you.*"

"*Would you, Jolene? I can't thank you enough. And for what it's worth, this has nothing to do with Kenyatta being, you know . . . with him being black. It's more about his age. He's older than Ashley. And the hair. He seems so . . . so radical. Now, for all I know he could be a fine young man. But I . . . I just want to be sure, you know. I'd do the same thing if he was white and older with purple hair or something. You know I —*"

"I understand, Candice. No problem."

Candice opened the front door and stepped into the foyer. It had been almost a month since she had placed that call to Jolene, but so far she had heard nothing back from her neighbor. Candice didn't know whether it was because Jolene couldn't dig up anything about the Jacksons or whether she had decided that she didn't want to spy on Kenyatta for her white neighbor.

Candice placed her shopping bag on a side table in the foyer, then turned to face Ashley. "I asked Jolene what she knew about him and his mother," she said calmly. "That's all."

Ashley folded her arms across her waist-line defiantly. "That's not what I heard."

"Well, what did you hear?"

"That you asked Jolene to find some dirt on them."

"That's not true." Candice knew that she wasn't exactly innocent, but it was going too far to say that she had asked for dirt. No way. She had simply asked for more information. Now if dirt had come up . . . well.

Obviously, Jolene had talked to someone. But who? And what did she say? Thanks, neighbor.

"Well, you must have said *something* to

Jolene," Ashley said suspiciously.

"Who told you this, anyway?"

"Don't even go there, Mom," Ashley said indignantly. "How could you do this to me?"

"I told you, it wasn't like that. I just asked Jolene a few questions, and she offered to ask around. I never asked anybody to dig up dirt. That's not even like me, Ashley. You know me better than that."

"I thought I did. But ever since I've been dating Kenyatta, you've been acting so weird."

"*I* haven't been acting weird," Candice retorted. "It's *you* who's acting weird. You never dated a black man before. I'm trying to be patient about this, Ashley, but —"

"What's so different about dating a black man and having black friends? Huh? You never had a problem with us having black friends. Why is this so different?"

"Don't act stupid with me, Ashley. You know what's different about it."

"You know what, Mom? I would never have figured you for this shitty behavior before. But you're more like Granddad than I thought, and he's the biggest bigot around."

It was all Candice could do to keep from slapping her daughter at that moment.

"Don't you dare talk like that around me. I'm still your mother. And don't say that about your grandfather."

"Well, it's true. He uses 'nigger' all the time."

"He's from the old school."

Ashley waved her arm defiantly. "You always have excuses. Why can't you just stay out of my business? Stop calling around asking questions, period. It's embarrassing. And this family isn't exactly perfect. What about *our* background?"

Candice frowned. "What about it?"

"Oh, please," Ashley replied indignantly. "Our ancestors were slave owners. When I did that history project in the tenth grade and learned about that, I was so embarrassed."

Candice sighed. "You can't compare that with this, Ashley. Everyone in the South owned slaves back then unless they were poor. It's nothing to be ashamed of. Your ancestors were many things besides slave owners, things you can be proud of."

"Yeah, right," Ashley said sarcastically.

"It's true. Your great-great-great-grandfather owned a lot of land near Richmond, Virginia. And his son George started a business in Massachusetts after he moved up there."

"Big deal," Ashley retorted. She grabbed a lock of hair and twisted it around her finger. "And you know what? I always thought it was weird that we only have one picture of George and none of his first wife."

"Oh, Ashley," Candice said with annoyance. "Now *you're* making a big deal out of nothing. They didn't have instant cameras back then. It wasn't so easy to take a picture. You had to hire a photographer and —"

"But there are plenty of his second wife and children on our side of the family. If George's dad was this big-shot landowner, they could have afforded to take more pictures."

"Maybe George's first wife died before they had pictures taken or maybe he left them behind when he moved to Massachusetts. I don't know."

Ashley shook her head doubtfully. "There's something fishy about old George. There are no stories about his childhood in Virginia, like where he went to school, or about his first wife. It's like he suddenly materialized in Massachusetts with a new wife."

"Ashley, if you want to know more about your ancestors you can always do the research. I've been meaning to do that myself.

But what has all this about dead ancestors got to do with anything we're talking about now?"

"I'm just saying that our family background isn't perfect," Ashley said. "Remember that before you start spying on other families."

Chapter 16

They pulled up under the portico to a line of Benzes and Jaguars, and the doorman opened Barbara's side of their Benz sedan. As Bradford directed the porter with their Louis Vuitton luggage, Barbara climbed out and looked across the vast estate, now blazing with fall colors. She breathed deeply, taking in the crisp, clean mountain air.

Finally, she was here — at the Greenbrier in White Sulphur Springs, West Virginia. The elegant resort hotel was a world away from the dirt-poor Virginia where she grew up.

They checked into their suite, dressed for dinner and then had a wonderful multicourse meal at one of the restaurants for which the Greenbrier was noted. Bradford was charming and attentive — pulling her chair out as they sat, asking how her meal was and listening closely to everything she said. It felt like one of their early dates. God, he was such a handsome man, she thought as he signaled the waiter and ordered cognac for himself and coffee for her, especially under the glow of this romantic candlelight.

"I'm glad you decided to come with me," he said after a toast. "We should do this more often. Just you and me, alone together."

"We used to get away a lot. But . . ." She stopped and shook her head sadly.

"I know." He opened his suit jacket, then reached across the table for her hand. "I haven't been the best husband to you. I know that. But I'm going to change," he said earnestly.

"I've heard this all before, Bradford."

He nodded understandingly. "But I mean it this time." He paused and chuckled. "I've said that before, too, I guess. But I really understand the error of my ways now." He shook his head. "I'm not a total cad, you know."

She looked down at the table.

"What I'm trying to say, Barbara, is that I really want us to try and make things better. I don't want us to just drift like we've been doing or you toying with the idea of leaving, which I assume you have . . ." He paused, waiting for her reaction.

She took her hand out of his grasp. She wasn't going to deny it. Let him squirm a bit. "I'm tired of the way things are, Bradford."

"That makes two of us. You and the girls

mean a lot to me. I understand that now, and I really hope you'll try to work things out with me." He paused and reached into the inside pocket of his jacket. "Maybe this will help you to at least begin to forgive me."

He held out a Tiffany box with a white bow, and she smiled. Those little blue boxes always lifted her spirits. Maybe not as much now as they did when she and Bradford were first married, but it was still a thrill to have one placed in her hand.

She opened it and gasped at what lay inside — a beautiful sapphire and diamond ring.

"You've outdone yourself," she said. Over the years each one of his gifts of jewelry seemed to top the last. First it was pearls, then emeralds, then diamonds. Now it was a combination. She removed the jewel and placed it on her right ring finger. It fit perfectly. She held it out subtly and admired it against the light. The waitress came by and cooed appreciatively.

"It's beautiful, Bradford."

He smiled broadly, looking quite pleased with himself. In a way, what he was saying made sense. She had given this man thirty years of her life. He wasn't as caring and honest as she would have liked, but they had come so far together. And she still enjoyed the respect and recognition that came with being Mrs. Bradford Bentley.

Maybe Sabrina's outrageous behavior had knocked some sense into him. He certainly seemed shook up by it. Or perhaps her hints of divorce made him realize how much he stood to lose.

She smiled at him, and he smiled back. Even after all these years and a few extra pounds, he could still send a chill up her spine. She supposed that was another reason why it was so hard to let him go.

Still, if she stayed, there were going to have to be some changes. "I'm glad to hear that you really want to try and work things out now. And I have to admit that my unhappiness isn't entirely your fault. I need to get out there and develop my own interests. So . . ." She paused and squared her shoulders. "I'm going to get a real estate license."

"Excuse me?"

"A real estate license. I'm going to get one."

"What for?"

"To sell houses. What else?"

"C'mon, Barbara. You haven't worked in years. And what do you know about selling houses?"

"I sold furniture before we got married and I was damn good at it."

"Furniture is a long way from real estate."

"I helped you build our house."

He chuckled sarcastically. "Do you even know what an I-joist is?"

She let out a deep breath. "I can learn. With the girls both grown now, I need to do something meaningful, something besides committee meetings and charity events."

Bradford looked up in exasperation. "What about working in Bloomingdale's as a part-time sales clerk if you're determined to work? Or Saks. You love to shop, and isn't that your favorite store?"

She ignored his sarcastic comments.

"Fine, Bradford," she said with tight lips. "I can see you haven't changed one bit." She shifted her gaze away from him and sipped her coffee.

He sighed. "OK. You're determined to try this?"

She tapped her foot.

"If you're serious, I can ask a business associate of mine who's a real estate lawyer to —"

"No," she interrupted firmly. "I'll do it on my own."

"I was only trying to be of help."

"You can help by supporting me emotionally."

He smiled in resignation. "I'll do my best.

Real estate, huh? Tell me more what you're thinking."

After dinner they strolled around the hotel and grounds. They talked, window-shopped the many boutiques and held hands as they walked back to their suite. She slipped into a new floor-length silk night-gown and dabbed a touch of Creed perfume between her breasts. It had been so long since they'd made love that it felt like she was on her second honeymoon.

Chapter 17

The park bench was still damp from the previous night's rain and so was her blanket. Lee moaned and pulled the cover up over her head. Her body was sore from spending so many long cold nights on hard benches. Her stomach hurt from skipping too many meals. And her heart ached from missing her mama.

She heard a noise and peeked out from under the blanket. The sun was just coming over the horizon, and she could see a man in a black cap standing near her feet and going through her purse. Lee knew from the funky odor hanging in the air and his tattered clothes that he was a homeless drunk.

Her teeth were chattering, she was hungry as hell. She didn't need this punk coming up in here starting shit. She had half a mind to pop him. The gun was right there under the towel she used as a makeshift pillow. Everything else she had in this world was in that bag. It wasn't much, but it was *hers*. She threw the covers off, jumped up and lunged at him.

"Get the hell away from there, you lameass punk," she yelled as she pounded him with her fists, "before I put my foot up your ass."

The man was obviously caught off guard by her attack. He probably thought she was fast asleep. He stumbled back and threw his hands up to defend himself, and that was when Lee realized that he wasn't black, as she had thought. He was white, but dirty as hell.

She hissed, "Get the fuck out of my stuff."

She pushed him as hard as she could. But he had steadied himself by now. He sneered, pushed her back onto the bench and landed on top of her. Lee didn't know if he was just clumsy drunk or had other things in mind. But he stunk something awful, and for the first time in weeks, she thought of Uncle Clive and his foul hands. She thought of all the nasty things he had done to her.

She went mad.

She screamed and cussed so loud her throat ached. She attacked the homeless man with every limb on her body — arms, legs, hands. She bit his cheek and spit in his face. "Get off me, you bastard," she cried.

The man jumped up, holding his face. "Crazy bitch," he screamed, his face turning into an ugly scowl.

She reached under the towel and jumped up, holding the gun at arm's length and huffing and puffing to catch her breath. "Get the fuck out of here before I empty this sucker on your punk ass."

He vanished.

Her shoulders shook with fright as she lowered the gun. A lone tear fell down her cheek and she quickly brushed it away. She wanted to go home so badly. She had no business out here all alone.

But then she thought of Uncle Clive's lifeless body lying in a pool of blood on the living room floor, and she sat down and lowered her head to her lap.

This was all Mama's fault. Why didn't Mama stop him?

Lee heard a key in the lock and nearly fell out of her seat at the kitchen table. Mama never got home from work before dark, and her baby brother went to an after-school program up the block until Lee picked him up at six.

She slammed her history book shut and leaped up. It had to be Uncle Clive. She hated that man. He was so skinny, he looked like he was on dope. And he was so pale he could pass for white if it weren't for that nappy head of his. But worst of all, he sat around the house with his legs wide open and his hands resting on his crotch.

He appeared in the doorway of the kitchen dangling his keys in his hand. "You done ate yet, Lee?"

"No. I ain't hungry." She grabbed her shoulder bag off the back of the chair and held it close to her body. She had to get out of there.

He dropped the keys into his pocket and left his hand in there. "Now where you off to? It ain't but four o'clock."

Her eyes followed his hand. She could see it moving around inside the pocket and she knew what he was doing. He never did that when Mama was home. She backed away.

"I'm going out," she spat.

His eyes narrowed. "What about your homework?"

Who was he to ask? He wasn't her daddy. Her daddy was handsome. And rich. Nothing like him. "I'm done. I'm rolling over to the playground now, till it's time to pick up Vernon."

"You better sit your black ass back down there. You know your mama don't want you hanging around out there with that trash on the playground, Lee. You best stay put here with me till she gets in."

Better the trash out there than the garbage in here, she thought. She hated the way he was fondling himself. And she hated the way he always called her black like it was something

182

evil. She was getting out of there, and the sooner the better.

But he was standing right in the doorway with his hand in his pocket, and somehow she had to get by him without letting him touch her. She focused on his work boots.

"I ain't gonna be out long," she said, trying to keep from spitting the words out.

He smacked his lips. "Me and you could go out and get us some Chinese at that takeout place up the street. Then we can come back and eat it here and watch some —"

She flew past him and nearly knocked him down. She ran through the living room and tripped over the tattered ends of the carpet, but she caught herself and kept on running.

"What the fuck is wrong with you, you little nigger? I'll whip that black ass till . . ."

She didn't hear the rest. She was slamming the front door shut and running down the stairs. She didn't like hanging out in the streets around these parts at all. But she despised being up there with that nasty man.

And now he was dead. And good riddance. And to Mama, too, since she didn't stop him from doing all those nasty things to her. Mama was smart about a lot of things but dumb as hell when it came to men.

She wiped the tears away with a corner of the damp blanket, then stood and put the gun in her bag. She had long since dumped the car, when it ran out of gas. It was just as well. It would be too easy for them to find her with it.

Right now she had to get something to eat. She was starving. She almost got caught the last time she lifted bread and bologna at Safeway, so this time maybe she would try to find a Giant supermarket somewhere.

She sighed as she tucked the blanket under one arm and wearily threw the shoulder bag over the other. The days of sleeping in the car and eating at McDonald's seemed like a luxury compared with this. She didn't know what she was going to do when it got too cold to sleep outside. But she had to think of something. Winter was just around the corner.

Chapter 18

Terrence threw the sheets back and jumped up out of bed. A feeling of desperation washed over Jolene as she lay beneath the covers and watched his nude body walk across the hotel room and shut the bathroom door. Something was wrong, very wrong. She could see it. She could hear it. She could feel it.

And it was her fault. Over the past couple of months, she had talked constantly of him leaving his wife. She had whined and nagged, but she couldn't stop herself. She wanted him all to herself so badly. She thought he was the answer to her dreams. Had she pushed him too far?

"I thought you loved me, Terrence."

Long pause. "I do, baby. Don't I tell you that?"

"Then why do you stay with your wife? Why do you insist on staying with her if you love me."

Deep breath. "I told you. My boys."

"They will still be your boys. It's your wife you'd be leaving. Not them."

Gritted teeth. Silence. Still, she pushed.

"I don't understand what's stopping you,

Terrence. We've been —"

"For God's sake, Jolene. Will you get off my back?"

Lately the vibes between them were all wrong. They weren't acting like lovers. They were acting like, well, a couple. A couple at the end of their relationship. He was different. *They* were different. Take this room for starters. It was a fucking Holiday Inn on the outskirts of D.C.

A few months ago, Terrence would have booked them a room at the Hyatt, and they would have slipped in separately and discreetly to snatch a few precious moments together on a Sunday afternoon. This cheap, obscure hotel out in the middle of nowhere was definitely a step down. When she called him to ask where they would meet after church and he said the Holiday Inn, she thought she was talking to the wrong man. This sounded like something that cheap-ass husband of hers would have cooked up. Not Terrence.

She and Terrence had once spent a very romantic night together at the Inn at Little Washington, about an hour's drive outside the city. They had a fabulous, leisurely dinner at the restaurant, one of the best in the country, and spent a memorable night in one of the suites. It was beautifully decorated with antiques, and the bed was in a loft overlooking the sitting room. That was the most romantic time ever for Jolene. Everything was so elegant, and she had the man of her dreams at her side.

And now it had come to this. The Holiday Inn.

Terrence came out of the bathroom fully dressed and sat in a chair across the room to put on his shoes without so much as looking in her direction. Her heart sank. There was a time when he could barely keep his hands off her whenever they were alone together. Instead of sitting as far away as he could get, he would have sat on the edge of the bed to be near her.

She sat up against the headboard and pulled the sheet over her bare breasts, nearly up to her chin. It felt like she was in the room with a stranger.

"Did I do something wrong, Terrence?" she asked softly.

"No. You're just being you, Jolene."

"What's that supposed to mean?"

"It's nothing."

"Don't tell me nothing. You seem so . . . so distant lately. It's got to be something."

He shrugged. "I've got some things on my mind."

"Us?"

"No. Work, mainly. Clients."

She nodded grimly. "Figures."

He looked up from his shoes. "What does that mean?"

"There was a time when you would have told me you were thinking of us. Of *me*."

He looked back down at his shoes. "Look, everything is not about you, Jolene. Running an architectural firm takes a lot of work. I do have other things to think about besides us."

His voice was cold and aloof. Bitter even. She was losing him. She knew it. Tears welled up in her eyes. Damn. This was not like her. She didn't get emotional about men, not since high school. Not since Jonathan Parker. If Terrence didn't want her, so be it. She took a deep breath as if she could suck in her feelings.

"You're not crying, are you?" he asked with annoyance.

She stood up, taking the bedsheet with her. A few weeks ago, she would have gotten up and paraded around the room naked, knowing he loved to see her that way. Now she wasn't sure how he would feel about it. She went into the bathroom and slammed the door. She splashed cold water on her face, then picked up a towel and buried her head in it.

She couldn't believe this was happening. She had let herself get too wrapped up in Terrence and she should have known better. After all, he was married, and even if Laura was a lame bitch, she was a Spelman graduate. And he was an architect, a prominent businessman. Why would he want somebody like her?

"Have you told the boy yet, Jolene?"

"He doesn't want to marry me, Daddy."

"No other decent boy will want to marry you either, now, Jolene."

"Why not, Daddy?"

Look at you. Pregnant and so black. Missed the brown-bag rule by a mile.

Shame on you, child, for shaming the family like this.

Jolene looked up and stared at her reflection in the bathroom mirror. Stupid bitch. Ugly fool. She felt like slapping herself. When would she learn?

There was a knock at the door. She jumped.

"Jolene? How long are you going to be in there? I have to go to the office now."

She didn't want him to see her face. Not like this. Cheeks puffy, eyes rimmed with black mascara. Ugly.

She grabbed a face cloth. "Give me a minute. I'll be right out."

"I really should go, Jolene. I have to pre-pare for a big client tomorrow. I'll call you later this week."

Is she younger? And prettier? Are you screwing her, too? Jolene yanked the door open, black-rimmed eyes and all. He was standing at the foot of the bed buttoning his overcoat. "Damn you, bastard. Don't bother. OK?"

He jumped back. "What?"

"I said, don't bother to call me. You can't even wait a fucking couple of minutes for me anymore."

"What's gotten into you? All I said was, I'll call you next week."

"And all I said was, Don't bother."

"Meaning?"

"Figure it out for yourself, asshole." She slammed the door shut.

He knocked again immediately. "Jolene. Open up."

She stared at the door. Should she open it? Did he really care about her the way she did about him? Did she still stand a chance to win him?

No, no and no. "Good-bye, Terrence. It was nice knowing you."

"C'mon, Jolene. Open the door."

"I mean it," she said. "I'm tired of being your mistress. Call me when you're ready to leave your wife."

Silence. A cold, hard silence. Still she waited and hoped to hear his voice. She prayed. She held her breath.

She opened the door. The room was empty.

Pearl sat Barbara down in her salon chair. "So you had a nice trip?" she asked, removing the rollers from her client's hair, one by one. "Was it romantic?"

Barbara smiled. The trip to the Greenbrier was everything Barbara had hoped for, and it had probably saved her marriage. "It was very romantic. And Bradford gave me the most beautiful sapphire and diamond ring for our thirtieth wedding anniversary."

"Oh!" Pearl exclaimed. "Where is it, girl?"

Barbara chuckled. "I'm saving it for special occasions."

"So, you've been married thirty years? Mmm-umph. I didn't know it had been that long. What's your secret?"

Looking the other way, Barbara wanted to say, but she never talked about Bradford's indiscretions, not to anyone. She shrugged. "Patience, I guess. So, how about you? Got a man in your life?" She had become an expert at quickly changing the topic of conversation whenever her marriage came up.

"Humph! I work so hard I don't have time to meet them."

"Any single men at your church? That could be a good way to meet someone."

"Oh, girl. I've been single for so long, I've gotten used to it. How's Rebecca? No grandbabies coming yet?"

"I wish, but not that I know of. Not yet."

"It's still early in the marriage."

"For them, yes, although never too early for the hopeful grandparents. How about Kenyatta? Is he still seeing that young woman he was with at the wedding?" Barbara frowned. "Oh shoot. I'm having a senior moment. I can't remember her name. I swear, sometimes it feels like my brain is turning into mush."

"Tell me about it, girl," Pearl said with a chuckle. "After I turned forty-five . . ." She paused and shook her head. "Whoo. I have to write everything down or I'll forget it as soon as I turn around. The other day I forgot I had already done the beds. Went back up twenty minutes later to make them. Now is that dumb or what?"

Barbara smiled in recognition. "I keep a notepad on my nightstand."

"And I have that." Pearl pointed to a stuffed Day-Timer sitting on the shelf in front of the mirror amid combs, brushes and hair picks, bottles of hair oil and cans of hair spray. "It goes everywhere with me. Even to bed."

Barbara laughed. She had always felt comfortable around Pearl. Their lifestyles were different, but they had similar roots since both of their fathers had deserted the family and left their mothers to raise their daughters alone. Pearl was a welcome relief from her society friends, like Marilyn and Jolene, who all grew up in two-parent middle-class black families.

"But really, how is Kenyatta?" Barbara asked.

"Oh, he's doing just fine. And yes, he's still seeing Ashley. Thanks for warning me that her mother is calling around checking up on us."

"I didn't mean it like that. Jolene Brown called and said Candice called her and asked about Kenyatta. That's all I know. I thought it was nice of Jolene to call me, though."

Pearl nodded. "Do you know Candice?"

"Not that well. She works for Bradford, and I've seen her at some of the annual Digitech Christmas parties and the summer picnics. I've seen Ashley and her sister once or twice. They all seem nice enough."

"Humph. I'm sure they are, but that girl is not right for my son. I mean, I know they say love is color blind and all that," Pearl continued as she combed Barbara's curls out, "but society isn't. I try to explain that to him, but he won't listen. He's been asking for weeks to have her over for dinner so we can all get to know each other."

"That's not as serious as it was in our day. I can't count the number of guys Rebecca and Robin brought home to meet us."

"Yes, but for dinner?"

"Hmm. Maybe not for dinner," Barbara conceded. "What did you tell him?"

"At first I said, No way. I ain't cooking for one of his white girlfriends."

"No, you didn't!" Barbara said incredulously.

"Heck, yeah. Why not? We've always had an open relationship. We both say what we think. I encouraged that. So he throws it up in my face that I'm always complaining that he never introduces me to his girlfriends. Humph. So I had to give in and . . . well."

Barbara smiled. "You finally said yes, didn't you?"

Pearl grunted. "She's coming next week."

"It's probably nothing to worry about,"

Barbara said. "They're both so young. And it will give you a chance to check her out."

"I pray you're right, Barbara. This Ashley is not what I imagined for Kenyatta. Not by a long shot."

"For what it's worth, I've always liked Candice. Some of Bradford's white employees never seem comfortable with us in social situations, but Candice does. Have you talked to her about how she feels about all of this?"

"No, I haven't. And after she went around snooping on me, I don't intend to," Pearl said indignantly. "She didn't need to go and do that."

"Maybe not, but try not to take it out on Ashley when she comes to dinner. They're young and in love."

"Humph." Pearl smacked her lips defiantly. As far as she was concerned it was impossible to be too tough when it came to her son.

Candice lifted a gray cardboard box from the top shelf of her closet and placed it on the bed. She had no idea how old the box was. It was torn and obviously a mere fragment of its original self. But it had been in the family for as long as she could remember — first in her grandmother's home, then in her mother's. Now it was in her care.

She removed the top gently and looked inside. The box contained the only information she had about her distant past, about a time long ago before her mother and grandmother were born.

There wasn't much to go on — a few letters written to her great-grandfather George and several black-and-white photos of his second wife and their children.

There was only one photo of George, and it was faded and tattered and had the look of a picture that had been handled many times over the years. You could barely make out George's face, but he was dressed like a farmer and posing with his horse.

She turned the photo over in her hand. She knew so little about him, except that he was born just before the Civil War to Andrew and Sara Blair. He had a sister named Rose, and the family lived on a plantation outside Richmond, Virginia.

Candice also knew that George had first married when he was very young, but that that wife died a couple of years later and he moved to Massachusetts, where he met and married Candice's great-grandmother. It seemed that George remained close to his sister Rose even after he moved to Massachusetts, for they kept in touch by mail for several years.

Candice picked up a small white envelope. It was one of the letters from Rose to George and it was postmarked Richmond, Virginia, 1906. The handwriting had faded over the years, but it always surprised Candice to realize that it was so old.

She removed the letter and glanced at Rose's neat penmanship. As in most of her letters, Rose talked about how much she missed George and couldn't wait until he would visit Richmond again. She never asked after George's new family in Massachusetts, even though by this time George and his second wife had several children.

This was the strangeness that Ashley often spoke of. In her more defiant moments, Ashley would suggest that perhaps George was a bigamist, leading a double life in Richmond and Massachusetts. To Ashley that would explain why Rose seemed to be unaware of his family in Massachusetts. Caitlin thought that maybe George was a crook.

Candice thought her daughters had vivid imaginations. Too vivid. Only a few letters from Rose had survived, hardly enough to make such wild judgments about someone's life.

Ashley was right about one thing, though.

The family background was vague. Candice realized that she knew next to nothing about her heritage beyond her grandmother. But that was her own fault, since she hadn't bothered to dig into the past.

Well, it was time to change that and put a stop to all this nonsense about bigamy and crooks. If Ashley and Caitlin knew more about their heritage, they would have more pride in it and not be so suspicious about the gaps.

But where should she start? It seemed like a daunting task. Her grandmother had died two years ago at age ninety-five and taken much of the family history with her. Candice's mother and father had moved to a retirement community in Florida a year ago, but Candice didn't think her mom would know much more than she did. She really regretted not listening more closely when her grandmother talked about their ancestors.

Well, no point crying over spilled milk, as her grandmother used to say. Her mom seemed as good a place to start as any. It certainly wouldn't hurt to try her. Candice placed the photo of her great-grandfather down on the bed and picked up the telephone.

"Mom?"

"Hi, Candice," Mom said cheerfully. "How are you? And how are Jim and the girls?"

"I'm fine. We're all fine. How's Dad?"

"He's well. A little arthritis now and then, but that's about it."

Candice nodded into the phone. "Is he using the heating pad I sent?"

"Yes, it helps some."

"Good. Mom, I wanted to ask you some questions about our ancestors."

"Well, there's not much I can tell you that I haven't already. What do you want to know?"

"What do you remember about George's mom and dad?" Candice asked.

"Oh, you mean Andrew and Sara? All I know about them is that they owned some land down there near Richmond, Virginia."

"Do you know what happened to it?" Candice asked.

"My mother used to say that they sold a lot of their land after the Civil War, but I don't know who they sold it to. I never knew Grandpa George, you know. He and his folks all died before I was born."

"I know. Did Grandma Helen ever say much about Rose DuPree, George's sister?"

"She's the one who kept in touch with Grandpa George after he moved to Massachusetts. Mama used to say that George would sometimes go to Virginia to visit a sister named Rose. He would take the train down to Richmond every now and then and stay a few weeks."

"Did he ever take his family down to Richmond with him?" Candice asked.

"I don't think so. Mama used to say that he would go alone once or twice a year until he died."

Candice frowned into the phone. "Does that seem strange to you?"

"No. Not really. It was different back then," Mom explained. "It was a lot harder to get around. And Grandpa George died fairly young. Maybe he died before he had a chance to take his family down to Richmond."

That was exactly the point Candice always stressed to Ashley. You couldn't hop on a plane back then, or even a bus. "That's what I always assumed. Do you know if there are any other photos of George or his first wife besides that one of George standing with his horse?"

"That's the only one I know of. Mama used to say that he didn't like getting his picture taken."

"Oh? I wonder why," Candice said.

Mom laughed lightly. "Beats me."

Candice studied the photo in her hands. "He looks Italian or something, with that dark hair and the thick mustache."

"Italian? Goodness, no. They were Scottish," Mom said firmly. "I don't know of anyone ever saying we have any Italian ancestry."

"His complexion looks a little swarthy in the picture."

"Oh, honey," Mom said. "I wouldn't read too much into that. I think that may be the old photo process that they used back then."

"That could be it," Candice said. Obviously, her mom wasn't going to be of much help. If she wanted to learn more about George and the others, she was going to have to look elsewhere.

Chapter 19

Jolene pulled her Mercedes-Benz C240 onto the driveway in front of the big Tudor house on Sixteenth Street in Northwest D.C. She always had mixed feelings about visiting her folks, especially when her sister was up from Atlanta with her husband and two children. They were all so damn perfect — Paul Cooper, the top-flight chemical engineer husband; Jackie, the housewife who worked part-time for Atlanta's mayor for self-fulfillment, not because she needed the money; and Paul Jr. and Pamela, the twelve-year-old twins, both geniuses and angels wrapped in tidy little packages.

"Looks like they got a new car," Juliette said with admiration as she shut the passenger-side door to the C240.

"So it does," Jolene said, trying to keep the jealousy out of her voice as they walked past a brand-new black Mercedes S500 with Georgia license plates. The big thing made her own puny C-class Benz look like a damn Toyota Tercel. One of these days, she thought, eyeing the big car with envy. The right house, the right car, the right husband. That's all she asked for.

Terrence immediately came to mind and her heart sank. They hadn't spoken to each other since that dreadful Sunday afternoon at the Holiday Inn last month. She had called him twice and left messages. He hadn't called back. It was just as well, she finally reasoned. He would never leave his wife and children. She was better off getting over him and moving on.

"That's a *bad* car," Juliette said as she rang the front doorbell.

"Mm-hmm. I wouldn't have gotten it in black, but it is nice."

"Mama, get real, I'd take that car in *any* color."

Jolene chuckled and put her arm around Juliette. At the last minute Patrick had said he would be late for Thanksgiving dinner with the family and that he would meet them at her mother's house. It had something to do with David Manley's campaign for the P. G. County executive seat. But Jolene couldn't be bothered with the details. She despised politics and was still hoping that Patrick would soon come to his senses.

Jolene's mother answered the door wearing a white lace apron over a tailored cranberry-colored coat dress. It was the perfect outfit for Thanksgiving Day.

"Here they are," Mama said cheerfully.

She kissed Jolene and Juliette both on the cheek as they stepped into the foyer. Mama was hanging up their coats when Jackie came out of the kitchen looking immaculate in a smart navy suit and heels, with her naturally long hair swept up in a neat French twist.

Jolene smoothed the skirt to her own red silk cocktail dress after they all embraced. She had spent hours trying to pick the perfect outfit and fussing with her hair weave, and still it felt all wrong. It was too dressy. She should have worn one of her simple, chic St. John knits instead of this stupid thing. Oh hell. She could never do anything right when it came to this family.

"Where's Patrick?" Mama asked.

"He's coming later," Jolene replied. "He had a conference call."

"On Thanksgiving Day?" Jackie asked, her eyebrows raised in surprise. "He sounds awfully busy."

"Daddy's into politics now," Juliette said with pride. That was OK, Jolene thought. Even if she didn't like the idea, it was the kind of thing Jackie would approve of.

Jackie raised an eyebrow. "Oh? That's interesting. What's he doing?"

"He's working on David Manley's campaign for county executive," Jolene said casually. "I don't know much more than that. You'll have to ask him to fill you in when he gets here. I'm focusing on the house we're building in Maryland."

Jackie's eyes lit up. "Mama had just mentioned that when you rang the doorbell. Where is it? In Montgomery County?"

"No. It's in P. G.," Mama said before Jolene could open her mouth.

"Oh. So you're going to stay over there in P. G. County?" Jackie murmured.

Jolene twisted her lips. The way Jackie said it, you would have thought someone had farted. Some people thought all of Prince George's County was the dumps simply because a lot of blacks lived there. Many whites avoided it like the plague, but worse than that to her mind, some uppity blacks did, too. Like her folks. They didn't understand that the county was full of contrasts — from the upscale communities like Silver Lake to the depressed areas inside the beltway. Jolene wanted others to realize that she didn't live in the hood, but more than that she didn't want her daughter to be ashamed of where they lived.

"In the community where we're building," Jolene said haughtily, "some of the homes go for a million or more. It's very nice there."

Jackie and her mother exchanged glances full of doubt.

"Mama, you've seen them," Jolene said. "Some of the houses are very nice, especially on the northern side of Silver Lake, aren't they?"

Mama twisted her lips. "There are some beautiful homes in Silver Lake, but it's still P. G. County. It changes the minute you drive out of the gate."

Jolene sighed hopelessly.

"Well, you'll have to tell me all about it," Jackie said. "We're thinking of building outside Atlanta. How many square feet will it be?"

"Um, about seven thousand." A small exaggeration of about a thousand, but absolutely necessary around these folks as far as Jolene was concerned.

"Oh," Jackie said excitedly. "That's about the size we're living in now. How many bathrooms?"

A hundred fifty, bitch. That's what Jolene was tempted to say. Instead she smiled sweetly and lied again. "Six."

Mama shooed them out of the foyer as if she sensed that a bit too much tension was building in the air. "Go on in and see your father, Jolene. He's waiting in the living room."

Mama led them into the room where Daddy and Paul sat in stuffed armchairs sipping red wine and smoking fat cigars. They both stood when the ladies entered, and there were more hugs and kisses all around. Jolene sat on the couch near her father, and Juliette left to play games with her twin cousins in the recreation room as Mama and Jackie went back into the kitchen.

"So, how's your portfolio these days?" Paul asked Jolene.

Portfolio? Did he mean as in stocks and bonds? Puh-leeze. Nearly every dime that belonged to the Brown name, and then some, was going into the house they were building. She had managed to hold on to a few thousand in a mutual fund, and she was thinking seriously of pouring that into the house, too.

She turned and stared at Paul, with his receding hairline, rimless glasses and smug smile. He was so light-complexioned he practically blended into the tan chair he sat in. One good thing about Patrick, at least he wasn't a nerd. "It's fine," Jolene said.

"You own stocks, Jolene?" Daddy asked, clearly surprised.

"A couple of mutual funds."

"That's great," Paul said, pushing his

eyeglasses back up on his nose. "I was just explaining to your father that a friend and I lost a small bundle last year on an IPO."

"Really?" Jolene muttered, trying to sound knowledgeable. She had no fucking idea what an IPO was. And didn't care.

"You talking five figures or six?" Daddy asked as if he had this kind of conversation daily.

Paul let out a big sigh. "Low six, unfortunately."

Daddy whistled.

Damn, Jolene thought. She and Patrick should have six figures to lose.

Daddy shook his head. "Those new things are too risky for me. I'll stick with IBM and P&G."

Paul chuckled. "That's appropriate for you, since you're both retired. You don't really want to stick your neck out there with IPOs at this point in your life."

"I wouldn't have done it before I retired," Daddy said, laughing.

Jolene cleared her throat. All of this was way over her head. And frankly, it was also depressing to listen to folks talk about losing big sums of money with less concern than she would have if she lost her wallet.

"The roof finally went up on the house last week," she said as soon as there was a lull in all the money talk.

"You don't say?" Daddy said, blowing a puff of smoke to the ceiling. "Will you still be able to move in before Christmas?"

Jolene twisted her lips. "No, they're backed up."

"That always happens when you build a custom house," Paul said. "Where are you building?"

"Silver Lake," Jolene said.

"Is that a new development over in Potomac?" Paul asked.

Jolene almost gasped. Potomac was one of the most exclusive areas in the state of Maryland — and also one of the whitest. The only blacks living over there were, well, like Paul and Jackie — very well off and very snooty.

"No."

"They're over there in P. G. County," Daddy explained.

"Oh," Paul said. "I've heard of it. It's the wealthiest majority-black county in the country, isn't it?"

Jolene smiled. "Yes, it is. And Silver Lake is very —"

Daddy scoffed. "That's what they say. But don't let that fool you. P. G. County has its problems — crime and the school system." Daddy shook his head woefully.

"Really?" Paul said.

"I don't get over there much myself," Daddy said. "So tell me, Paul, what would you recommend for this market other than IPOs? Stocks? Bonds?"

Paul cleared his throat, and Jolene stood quickly, before he could launch into another one of his lectures. If her father would rather talk to Paul about stocks and bonds than to his daughter about their new house, she didn't want to be in the room. The way her father brushed her off was plain cold in her opinion, although nothing new.

"Excuse me. I think I'll go and help Mama and Jackie." She made her way to the kitchen door.

"Your guess is as good as mine," Mama was saying. "I don't know why they stay over there."

"Obviously, they like it," Jackie said.

"But there's so much crime over there," Mama said with concern. "I worry about them all the time, especially Juliette."

"What about the schools?" Jackie asked. "How are they?"

Mama scoffed. "They're sending her to a private school, thank goodness. The public schools in P. G. County leave much to be desired."

"And she's doing just fine," Jolene said

210

coolly as she stepped into the kitchen. "Most of the crime in Prince George's County is inside the beltway in places like Seat Pleasant and Landover, not out where we live. People fail to realize that, and it gives the whole county a bad rap."

Mama and sister both fell silent, with guilty looks on their faces.

"C'mon," Jolene said, a smile toying around her lips. "You don't have to clam up on account of me. I know you both hate Prince George's."

"We just think you'd be so much better off here in Northwest D.C. or in Montgomery County."

"We wanted land and you get more for your money out there. And frankly, we like living in a suburban community with a lot of other middle-class black people."

"You have a daughter to think about," Mama said softly.

"Yes, there are better places to raise children," Jackie added.

"And the shopping over there is horrible from what I've heard," Mama said.

Jolene realized that she felt almost as much out of place here in the kitchen as she did in the living room as Mama and Jackie went on and on about the horrors of Prince George's County and the virtues of living just about anywhere else on earth. She got tired of defending the county and gave up.

Then Jackie got into the thousands of dollars they were spending on private schools for Paul and Pamela, on Paul and Pamela's activities in Jack and Jill, the snooty social group for black children, and on their plans to remodel their old McMansion or build a new one. Yakety-yak.

Jolene was ready to bolt within about five minutes of listening to all this bull. Nothing made her feel so cheap as a visit to her childhood home.

It didn't get any better when Patrick arrived. Unlike Paul, Mister Perfect, Patrick had all the wrong credentials. He didn't belong to the right male social groups like the Boule. He hadn't attended Morehouse or Howard or Harvard, and his father wasn't a doctor or a judge. Patrick went to the University of D.C., and his daddy was a high school dropout. Patrick was the ultimate outsider.

Years ago, she consoled herself whenever she thought of these dismal facts by reminding herself that Patrick's heart was bigger than Paul's. He had saved her when she was young and dumb and pregnant, and she would always be thankful to him for that.

Her folks were always polite to Patrick, but they would never accept him as they had Paul. She and her husband could suddenly strike it filthy rich, and still Patrick would never be one of them. New money didn't get you into the black elite. Take Bradford and Barbara Bentley. Even with all that dough and a multimillion-dollar home, they wouldn't be accepted by her snooty family.

But money like the Bentleys' could make you feel a hell of a lot better about not being accepted. With that kind of money, you could thumb your nose at the snooty old-guard blacks with style.

The minute they got back home tonight she was going to invite the Bentleys over for dinner. Instead of getting involved in politics, Patrick should be busting his ass trying to get Bradford to give him a raise. He should be working overtime instead of going to political meetings. He should be sucking up to the Bentleys any way he could. Politics? Please. Money was the key, honey.

Candice stepped out of the doors of the train and onto the platform at the Archives–Navy Memorial metro stop in Washington, D.C. She hated coming downtown. There was too much traffic and too many people, and parking was a nightmare. But this trip to the National Archives had suddenly become urgent. Her daughters had no respect for their heritage, and she had to change that.

She went through security, signed in and was issued a visitor's badge with a chain to wear around her neck. She took the elevator up to the fourth floor, signed in again and was handed a long sheet of paper with guidelines and her seat number at the top.

She entered a dimly lit room with high ceilings, an industrial-grade blue carpet and row after row of microfilm readers, most with folks sitting at them, their eyes glued to the screens. It was her understanding that she could look up her ancestors in the census reports here and learn the names of other family members who lived in their households. It seemed amazing when she thought about it. The building might be old and dingy but the records went back hundreds of years and contained valuable information about her ancestors.

She found her assigned table and hung her jacket on the back of the chair.

Candice squinted through her glasses at the microfilm. The scribbling on the 1860 census report was so faint she thought she would go blind trying to read it. But it looked like she had finally found George's father. The name of the head of the household was right — Andrew Blair — and his age — thirty-six — seemed about right, too.

Oddly, there was no mention of Andrew's wife, Sara. Three young girls were listed in the household along with a woman named Caroline. Who were these people? And where was George's mother, Sara?

George was supposedly born around 1862, so Candice wasn't expecting to find him in the 1860 census. But she had assumed that his mother would be listed. She decided to go back further, to the census for 1850.

As her eyes scanned this new piece of microfilm, she grew more baffled by the minute. In 1850, still no one named Sara was living in the Blair household, but the woman named Caroline was there.

Could Caroline have been the first wife of Andrew? Maybe Caroline died, and then Andrew met Sara and started a second family sometime after 1860. Candice had never heard of Andrew having another wife and children before Sara. But it was possible. And it was the only thing that made sense. If that was the case, then Sara might be listed in the 1870 census.

She moved up to the later census and found Andrew again, but still no Sara, or Rose or George, who had been born by this time. Candice removed her reading glasses and sat back in her chair. This was getting weirder by the minute.

She put her glasses back on. There was no way she was going to figure all this out here and now. She decided to put Andrew aside for the moment and focus on George and his first wife in Richmond, Virginia.

Candice spent more than two hours searching back and forth through the censuses for Virginia. But she found no George Blair who seemed a match for her great-grandfather.

She leaned back in her chair and took a deep breath. This was so disappointing, but her eyes couldn't take any more of this today. She had hoped this trip would answer some long-standing questions. Instead it seemed only to raise new ones. If anything, her past was even more murky now than before.

"Learn anything interesting at the National Archives?" Ashley asked from the doorway of her mother's bedroom.

"Oh, so you're back?" Candice peered over her glasses and placed the genealogy

216

book she was reading facedown on her bed. "How was the movie?"

"Great. Kenyatta's downstairs talking to Jim. I came up 'cause I wanted to hear what happened at the archives. What did you find out?"

Candice shrugged. "Not as much as I hoped, that's for sure. It turned up more questions than answers."

"Really?"

Candice nodded and held up the genealogy book. "I found this at the local library on my way back. I was just reading up on some other places to search."

Ashley came in and sat on the edge of the bed. "Sounds like you're totally into this ancestry stuff now."

Candice smiled. "I admit I'm hooked."

"So. C'mon. I'm curious. What kind of questions did you turn up?"

"What kind of questions did I *not* turn up would be a shorter answer," she replied. "Well, let's see. I may have found Andrew, your great-great-great-grandfather, in the census."

Ashley's green eyes lit up. "Really? You found him? That's amazing."

Candice smiled thinly. "Don't get too excited. I hit a brick wall on his wife, Sara. She may have married Andrew and died between censuses. I don't know. People died young then."

Ashley frowned. "What about George? Did you find out anything about him?"

Candice sighed in frustration. "I'm drawing a complete blank with him, and his sister, Rose, too. I did find a woman who may have been Andrew's first wife."

Ashley's frowned deepened. "You mean Andrew was married twice? I never knew that."

"Neither did I, but if this is the right family, it looks that way. We'll see. I still have a lot of work to do."

"What does Grandma have to say about all this?"

"Not much. I called Mom when I got back, but she wasn't much help."

"This sounds so weird, don't you think?" Ashley asked.

"Well, it was a long time ago. It's going to take a while to straighten it all out. It's possible that the census taker made a mistake. From what I've been reading, they went around from house to house back then and wrote down the names and ages of the people they found there. That doesn't sound very reliable. Maybe they overlooked Sara somehow."

Ashley squinted doubtfully. "And George

and his sister, too? That doesn't sound right, Mom. Maybe it's something else."

"Such as?"

"I don't know. Maybe something got twisted over the years when the stories were being handed down, like some of the names and ages."

"Mom seems pretty certain about the few details we have."

"Uh-huh." Ashley twisted a lock of her hair between her fingers. "I always wondered about something. Where's that cardboard box of old photos?"

Candice frowned. "It's right under the bed." What on earth was Ashley cooking up now? Candice wondered as her daughter kneeled and reached for the box. Ashley sat back on the bed and placed the box between them, then picked out the photo of George and studied it as she twisted her hair. Candice wanted to tell her to stop all the twisting. It was getting on her nerves. "What is it, Ashley?"

"Well, George looks olive-complexioned and —"

"It's an old photo," Candice corrected. "And this was the South. Maybe he had a tan."

"Or maybe he was ethnic or Jewish. That would explain so many things."

"That wouldn't explain why I couldn't find them in the census."

"But it would explain the photo and maybe why Sara and George were so mysterious. They may have been outcasts or —"

"Ashley, I think you're getting carried away. No one in our family has ever said anything like that."

Ashley held up her hands in defense. "Fine, Mom. It was only a thought." She stood. "Should I tell Kenyatta that you'll be down to say hello?"

Candice blinked and tried to keep the look of frustration off her face. Ashley had hinted around at something like this before but had never been so blunt about it. No doubt it had to do with her seeing Kenyatta. "Give me a minute to get dressed."

Ashley trotted back down the stairs as Candice stood and slipped back into her skirt. Ashley was probably downstairs this minute telling Kenyatta that one of her ancestors was ethnic. Candice never thought she would find herself wishing Ashley was dating one of those white guys from high school with orange hair and nose rings.

Her quest to find her ancestors seemed more urgent than ever.

Chapter 20

Jolene parted the living room drapes and peeked out. Still no headlights, no big Benz or Jaguar convertible, no Barbara and Bradford arriving for dinner. She dropped the drapes and looked at her watch. Well, no wonder. It was only 7:10 and they weren't due to arrive until 7:00. Of course, they had to be fashionably late.

She took a deep breath and straightened the sleeves to her black-and-silver St. John pantsuit. She flipped her long hair weave over her shoulders. She was going to have to calm down or she would be a nervous wreck by the time they arrived.

The cognac! Did Patrick pick up some Napoléon cognac? Patrick had said that cognac was Bradford's favorite after-dinner drink, so they absolutely had to have the best here for him. She dashed across the living room to the bottom of the stairs.

"Patrick!" she yelled. "Patrick."

He appeared at the top of the stairs, fastening his cuff links. "What is it?"

"Did you get the cognac?" she asked anxiously. "I don't remember seeing it in the kitchen."

"It's in the pantry up on the top shelf. I bought it yesterday."

She started toward the kitchen, then abruptly turned back. "Why aren't you dressed? It's after seven."

"I'll only be another minute."

"Well, hurry, would you?" Jolene said impatiently. "They're due any minute. You can't keep your boss and his wife waiting."

Patrick rolled his eyes to the ceiling and walked back to their bedroom as Jolene dashed into the kitchen and past the Cornish hens she had roasted so carefully. She had cooked everything in advance so she could relax and enjoy her guests. She hated it when the hostess was so busy she couldn't even entertain properly. That was so tacky, so amateurish.

Of course, she had wanted to hire a cook for the evening, but Patrick was dead set against it. He even threatened not to show up if she did. He claimed they couldn't afford it with the house they were building. Mister Cheapo.

She opened the pantry door and grabbed the bottle of cognac. Damn. It was the wrong brand. She had distinctly told Patrick to get Napoléon. It was top of the line. Of course, Patrick bought a cheaper brand. That man could never do anything right.

But it was too late to do anything about it now.

She placed the cognac with the other liquor on the drink cart in the dining room, then stood back and ran her eyes over the setting. She had checked and double-checked everything, but the Bentleys were coming to dinner so it wouldn't hurt to check it all again. She wanted to make a good impression.

She had to admit the table looked fabulous, good enough for a magazine spread. And it should. She had copied it from a photo in one of B. Smith's books, using brightly colored place mats instead of a tablecloth to highlight the dining room table. And she didn't have to worry about Juliette since she was at a sleepover until tomorrow afternoon. Everything was perfect. Now where were her guests? And what was keeping her husband?

She checked her watch again. Damn. This was starting to tip the scales from fashionably late to downright rude. Why was everybody running behind but her? She marched across the dining room floor toward the stairs. Patrick had to come down this minute. After all, this was for his benefit. This was his boss they had invited over for dinner. He was the one who needed a raise. The least he could do . . .

The doorbell rang, and Jolene stopped in her tracks. It was about time. She took a deep breath and made a point of strolling slowly and calmly to the door. Patrick came down the stairs just as she turned the knob and swung the door open.

They all smiled and greeted each other with cheek kisses. Barbara had brought a cake for dessert and she gave it to Jolene. Patrick took Barbara's mink coat and Bradford's cashmere to the hall closet while Jolene placed the cake on a sideboard. Then she led them into the living room.

"You both look fantastic," Jolene said as Bradford sat on the couch and Barbara settled into an armchair across from him. It was true. Barbara was wearing a lovely bottle-green suit that set off her complexion nicely. The suit was far too plain for Jolene's taste, but Barbara looked happier and more relaxed than ever. And Bradford was still his old sexy self.

Patrick came into the room and fixed drinks for everyone as Jolene sat down on the couch next to Bradford. He was regaling them with tales of his latest conquests at Digitech, something about a big multi-million-dollar contract they had just landed to update computer network security.

Jolene crossed her legs and turned them to face Bradford. She smiled a lot and laughed at his jokes. She was flirting, no doubt about it. But she couldn't help it. Bradford had a kind of animal magnetism that some men were blessed with. Besides, she'd do anything to help Patrick get that promotion he so fully deserved. She'd probably screw Bradford if it would help. Hell, she'd screw him anyway.

But judging from the looks of the women in his life, Bradford wouldn't be interested in someone brown-complexioned like her. Barbara was light, and Jolene had heard that Sabrina and many of his mistresses followed suit. Some black men thought they needed women like that once they reached the top. What a pity. Bradford didn't know what he was missing. Hadn't he heard that old saying: "The blacker the berry, the sweeter the juice"?

Barbara took a sip of her spring water and watched Jolene closely. She was going to have to keep her eyes on this woman. No doubt about that. Jolene had been flirting shamelessly with Bradford from the minute they walked through the front door. The way she was crossing her legs and flipping that fake weave in front of Bradford was almost sinful. Not to mention all the cleavage she had on display.

She glanced at Patrick. He didn't seem to notice or maybe he didn't care. But Barbara did and she hadn't missed a thing. Her marriage had been better than ever for the past few months. Bradford was home at a decent hour most evenings, and no one was calling the house and hanging up whenever she answered the phone. Barbara wasn't about to let any other woman spoil the picture now without putting up a good fight.

Pearl had decided to go all out for Ashley's visit. Nobody would ever be able to say she didn't know how to treat guests in her home. She had the catfish frying, the macaroni and cheese baking and the sweet potato casserole topped with marshmallows, too. The string beans were simmering, and homemade rolls were ready to pop into the oven. Last night she baked a rum cake and poured a hot rum and butter sauce all over it. The cake was always a big hit. She loved to cook and any old excuse would do, even a dinner invitation to Kenyatta's white girlfriend.

Besides, cooking had a way of soothing her soul and her soul was mighty irritated these days. A big meal like this gave her an excuse to be in the kitchen fussing with food rather than out there trying to make small talk with Kenyatta and his girlfriend. Twice already Ashley had stuck her little white head in the door asking if she could help, and twice Pearl shooed her out of her kitchen. She had agreed to break bread with the child but not to let her help in the kitchen and get all up into Pearl's domain. That was going too far.

One thing was a relief. Ashley wasn't one of those lily-white, blond-haired women. She had green eyes, but her hair was brown and she had a lot of color in her cheeks.

Pearl removed the macaroni and sweet potatoes from the oven and set the dishes on top of a towel on the countertop to cool for a minute. She adjusted the oven temperature and slid the rolls in.

She was sprinkling thyme on the string beans when the door to the kitchen opened. This time it was Ashley *and* Kenyatta.

"How much longer, Ma? We're starving."

"And it smells delicious," Ashley said.

"Five minutes," Pearl said. "And until then I want you both out of my kitchen. Go on." She shooed them out, then removed a small Corning Ware dish from the cabinet. It felt so odd having that white girl over for dinner, she thought as she scooped the string beans from the pot to the dish, especially since the girl was her son's new love. Pearl would put up with her just this once to show Kenyatta that his mama wasn't a complete monster. And hopefully, he would quit nagging her about having Ashley over.

Once they were all seated around the dining room table, Pearl tried her best to be pleasant while they made idle chat. When Ashley reached over and touched Kenyatta's arm, Pearl pretended not to notice, even though she was tempted to smack the girl's hand away. When Kenyatta went for seconds and Ashley immediately asked for another serving of sweet potatoes, Pearl smiled and passed her the bowl, even though she was beginning to wonder if the girl had a mind of her own. Although Ashley could definitely afford to eat everything on the table and more, with her skinny self. Girl couldn't weigh much more than a hundred pounds.

"Here, have some French vanilla ice cream with your cake," Pearl said after she placed a slice of rum cake on Ashley's plate.

Ashley covered the cake with her hands. "Oh no. No ice cream for me. Thanks."

"You can't eat the cake like that. Got to have some ice cream. Lord knows you can afford it."

Ashley smiled sheepishly and put her

hands in her lap while Pearl dished out the ice cream.

"I can't remember when I've eaten so much," Ashley said. "But it's delicious." She picked up her fork and dug in.

"Judging from the looks of you, you don't eat much at home," Pearl admonished. "You're not much bigger than a beanpole."

"I like her this way," Kenyatta said. "She could be a model."

Humph. What's to like? Pearl wondered. Nothing there but skin and bones.

"Oh!" Ashley exclaimed with her mouth full. "This cake is to die for."

Pearl smiled, probably for the first time that evening. Ashley was obviously trying to butter her up with the compliments, but she had seen others react to her rum cake the same way. "Thank you," Pearl said. "Glad you like it."

"Everything has been delicious," Ashley said sweetly. "Can I get the recipe for the cake?"

The smile fell off Pearl's face. Heck, no. "Sorry, but that's a family secret. I don't give it to anybody." Least of all some white girl. Although she would gladly give it away to Kenyatta's *black* wife someday.

"Don't feel bad," Kenyatta said. "She won't even tell me."

"That's only 'cause I know you would give it away to anybody who asked," Pearl said. "And you don't cook, anyway."

Kenyatta chuckled.

"Do you like to cook?" Pearl asked Ashley.

"I'm not really into cooking and all that stuff. Mom does most of it. But sometimes I'll throw a steak in the oven, nothing fancy, especially lately, since Mom has been going to the archives after work a lot."

Not into cooking and all that stuff? It was all Pearl could do to keep from frowning. Lordy, it was obvious that this girl was not wife material.

"Ashley's mom is researching their family's roots," Kenyatta announced with pride.

"Oh," Pearl said cautiously. "Isn't that something."

"Tell her what you told me," Kenyatta urged Ashley.

"Well . . . maybe I shouldn't," Ashley said, glancing doubtfully from Pearl back to Kenyatta.

Pearl sensed that Ashley seemed reluctant to say whatever it was in front of her. That was fine. She'd rather be upstairs watching cable TV anyway.

"Go ahead," Kenyatta said.

"Don't push her if she doesn't want to," Pearl said.

"But it's so interesting, Ma. She thinks some of her ancestors were ethnic or Jewish."

Pearl blinked. "Oh really?"

"I don't know for sure," Ashley said shyly. "But my great-great-grandfather had a lot of gaps in his life."

Pearl stared at Ashley. "I see what you mean." But she really didn't see. What she saw was a white girl who was trying to snare her son and would say anything to get him. Good Lord.

Why was it that everybody seemed to want to be anything but white these days? Especially the young ones. They tried to lock their hair. They wanted to dance and sing like us. Humph! All they really wanted was to take the good stuff and pretend the bad stuff didn't exist. Let them walk into a department store and be followed around by security or rejected for a loan they knew they were qualified for. They would change their minds about being black or ethnic real fast.

"You have to see his photo, Ma," Kenyatta said. "He looks kind of dark. Interesting, huh?"

"Yes," Pearl admitted. "What does your

mother say about all this, Ashley?"

Ashley shrugged. "She has a thousand other excuses for the dark photo and everything else, of course."

Pearl smiled wryly. "I bet she does. I'm sure it will take a lot more than a photo to convince your mother of that."

"Mom says we're Scottish," Ashley said, rolling her eyes skyward. "And she'll never let that idea go in a million years."

"You could be some of both," Kenyatta said.

"Tell me something, Ashley," Pearl said. "You seem hopeful about it. Why?"

"I think it's way cool. We're all so mixed up in this country anyway, you know? In the end, people are just people. That's why I admire Kenyatta. He's so open-minded about things."

Pearl was beginning to see why her son had fallen for this girl. She was open-minded herself and cute as a button. She would make some nice white man a good wife, as long as he could do his own cooking. But she wasn't right for Kenyatta. Not in this world.

Now how did this happen? Barbara wondered as she fussed with the hemline of her skirt. She was sitting here with Patrick discussing P. G. County politics, and somehow Bradford had wandered off with Jolene after dessert. Presumably Bradford was taking a look at a problem Jolene was having with her laptop computer, something that Patrick, a programmer, couldn't fix. Yeah, right. Knowing Jolene, her *top* had probably found its way to her *lap* by now.

Barbara cupped her hands on the dining room table. She had to stop these naughty thoughts. If she and Bradford were going to make it, she would have to learn to trust him.

"We're planning an event to raise funds for David Manley next month," Patrick said.

"I didn't know you were involved in politics."

Patrick smiled. "It's new for me. Do you have any interest in politics?"

"Me?" Barbara tapped the tabletop lightly. She could sure use a cigarette about now. "No, not really. But you should talk to Bradford. He's got a lot of connections."

"I mentioned the fund-raiser to him. I was hoping you both could be there."

Barbara nodded absentmindedly. Everyone wanted her someplace. She and Bradford. They got dozens of invitations a month. Didn't these people understand she couldn't be everywhere? And where on earth were Bradford and Jolene?

"Can I get you more water?" Patrick asked anxiously, as if he sensed something was bothering her. "Or something else?"

"No thanks, I'm fine." It was a pity that water was all she could drink. She put her hands in her lap. No booze, no cigarettes. Husband missing. What was a girl to do? Make small talk, that's what. That would take her mind off Bradford and Jolene. Besides, she was being rude to her host, one of her husband's employees. "Um, your house is lovely. Will you put it on the market when you move into the new one?"

"Oh yeah. Without a doubt. We can't afford to keep both of them."

Barbara nodded and smiled. She was tempted to get up and go find Bradford. But that would never do.

"Let's go sit in the living room," Patrick suggested. "It's more comfortable there."

Barbara jumped up. "Good idea." She thought she would go mad if she had to sit still another minute.

Just as they entered the living room, Jolene and Bradford returned from their little journey to who knows where.

"Any luck fixing her top? Er, laptop computer?" Barbara asked. It was a struggle to keep a smirk off her lips. She thought her comment was clever, even if no one else noticed.

"Not really," Bradford said. "It's probably time for a new one."

"That's what I told her," Patrick said. "Thanks for taking a look at it, anyway, Bradford."

"No problem. Anytime."

Bradford sat on the couch, and Barbara and Jolene collided as they both moved to sit next to him.

"Are you sure you wouldn't be more comfortable in the armchair?" Jolene asked, smiling sweetly as she relinquished the seat to Barbara.

"Not at all, I'm fine here," Barbara replied as she settled into the couch.

Jolene slumped into the chair.

"So, how's the new house coming?" Bradford asked.

Jolene and Patrick looked at each other.

"Slowly but surely," Patrick said.

"Too slowly for me," Jolene added. "We're looking to move in by late spring."

"It was supposed to have been finished by now," Patrick said. "But someone keeps changing her mind about this and that."

Bradford chuckled. "Oh no. That will do it. We went through something similar when we built our house."

"So many decisions have to be made," Barbara said. "Paint, tile, wallpaper."

"That's the fun part to me," Jolene said. "We're going to have a party and invite the neighbors soon after we move in."

Patrick scoffed. "If we have any money left over."

Bradford and Barbara exchanged looks.

Jolene chuckled nervously. Patrick was starting to embarrass her. He sounded so ridiculously cheap, constantly harping on money. She wanted to tell him to shut up. "That rum cake you brought was delicious," Jolene said to change the subject.

Patrick leaned back and rubbed his stomach. "Oh man. You're quite a cook, Barbara."

"I wish," Barbara said, laughing. "My hairdresser made the cake."

"You mean Pearl Jackson?" Jolene asked with obvious surprise.

Barbara nodded. "She's having her son's girlfriend over for dinner today, so she baked an extra one for us."

"That was nice of her," Patrick said. "Where do I sign up?"

Barbara laughed.

"I'm serious," Patrick said. "We need someone for refreshments at the fund-raiser

I'm planning, and I prefer to give our money to someone black."

"Well, you know, her salon is in Bowie, Maryland, not far from Digitech," Barbara said. "And Pearl loves to cook. In fact, she used to do some catering on the side, mainly desserts, for extra money when she was sending Kenyatta to college. But I don't think she's done much of that since she opened her own salon. I'll ask her, though."

"Will you?" Patrick asked. "I'd appreciate that. Tell her I said that cake is the bomb. In the meantime, I need to work some of this one off." He stood up. "Can I interest you in a game of pool, Bradford?"

Jolene laughed. "A lot of exercise that is, guys, standing around the pool table shooting balls. You'll be drenched in sweat. Should drop, oh, maybe an ounce or two."

Barbara smiled.

"Well, it sounds good to me," Bradford said, chuckling as he stood to join Patrick.

"So, you said that Kenyatta is taking Ashley to dinner at Pearl's house," Jolene said after Bradford and Patrick left for the recreation room. "I thought Pearl was against that relationship."

Barbara shrugged. "I know that Pearl was reluctant to have her over. But what can you do? She doesn't want to alienate her son."

"Did you mention to Pearl that Candice called me and asked about Kenyatta?"

Barbara nodded. "Thanks for telling me about that, especially since you and Candice are next-door neighbors and you don't really know Pearl." And it was well known that Jolene was no fan of the families who lived in the town houses.

"I felt trapped when Candice called me," Jolene said. "She's a good neighbor, and I sympathize with her. But it wouldn't have felt right to talk about him to Candice." Ratting on a sister, any sister, to her white neighbor was a no-no. "How does Pearl feel about this whole *Jungle Fever* romance thing?"

"The same way Candice feels. She would prefer that he stick to his own race."

"I just hope Juliette picks the nice, clean-cut type. I don't give a damn what color he is as long as he's planning to be a doctor or lawyer or maybe a dentist."

"As long as he has money, you mean? Or will have it."

"Well, of course."

Barbara shook her head emphatically. "Money is not the key to a good relationship, Jolene. Trust is much more important. You can be pretty miserable without it, I don't care how much money you have. Take my word for it." As soon as Barbara said all of that, she regretted it. It sounded too personal, and spilling her personal troubles had never been her style, especially to someone like Jolene.

Jolene smiled awkwardly. She had expected Barbara to agree that money was important. After all, Barbara had married Mister Moneybags himself. But maybe she shouldn't be surprised. Everyone knew Bradford had a roving eye. He had probably slept with half the women in Silver Lake. Was this little outburst evidence of serious trouble in paradise?

This had started out as a meeting to butter the Bentleys up, in hopes of getting a promotion for Patrick. But now Jolene found herself wondering about the strength of the Bentley marriage. Was it all a sham? Was Bradford perhaps available to the right woman? To *her?* Jolene wanted to draw out more clues, but she had to be careful not to irk the boss's wife.

"Would you like something a little stronger to drink?" Jolene asked sweetly. She knew that Barbara once had a drinking problem, and it was wicked to even ask. But liquor did wonders to loosen the tongue.

"No, thank you. I don't drink alcohol." As if she didn't know, Barbara thought, folding her arms tightly across her waist. The little vixen was up to something.

"Oh, *that's right,*" Jolene said, flipping her weaving innocently. "Can I get you some more water or something else then?"

"No. I'm fine."

Jolene cleared her throat. "Well, I must say that I'm surprised by what you just said, Barbara. I've always thought of Bradford as quite the catch, and, well, it's no secret that he's loaded. And the two of you look so happy. You are happy, aren't you?" Jolene smiled sweetly and waited impatiently.

Barbara hesitated. How brazen. How rude. She had already told Jolene more than she should have, and here the little sneak was hunting for more. Her relationship with her husband was nobody's business but her own. "What I meant is that it's not his money that makes Bradford such a catch, as you put it." That was a little curt, but this hussy was asking for it.

"Uh-huh," Jolene said, her voice full of doubt.

"He's a wonderful father," Barbara said. "And he's very resourceful. I always know he'll look out for us."

Jolene was utterly disappointed. Resourceful? A good father? Puh-leeze. What the hell happened to all that stuff about needing trust and honesty? Maybe if she said some negative things about her relationship with Patrick, Barbara would feel more at ease spilling the bad beans about her marriage to Bradford.

Jolene nodded. "I know what you mean. Bradford is the take-charge type. Patrick is the exact opposite. I probably shouldn't say this, but I have to push to get him going on anything. It's so tiring."

This conversation is what's tiring, Barbara thought. She didn't like it one bit. It made her uneasy talking about personal things with her husband's employees and their spouses, especially *this* spouse. She needed to change the subject immediately. "Patrick seems to be really into this political thing," Barbara said. "That takes a lot of initiative."

"Please," Jolene said with a wave of her hand. "I give it a few more weeks to play out. He'll grow tired of it and be right back to sitting on the couch watching cable TV most evenings in no time. I'm sure that's not the case with Bradford."

Barbara chuckled. "That definitely is not Bradford. Sometimes I wish he would be more like that. Bradford is always on the go, always reaching."

"I admire that. I wish I could say the same

about Patrick. But there is one advantage to someone like Patrick, though. I don't have to worry about him running around on me. He doesn't have it in him to have an affair."

Barbara clammed up. She thought she had shifted the conversation to Patrick and politics. How on earth did they get to this talk about affairs all of a sudden? If this woman thought she was going to get her to talk about such a delicate subject, she was dreaming. Barbara never talked about that to anyone.

Damn, Jolene thought. Judging from the way Barbara had suddenly stiffened, their conversation had hit a brick wall. Jolene was disappointed not to get much more out of Barbara about her relationship with Bradford, but she didn't dare push the boss's wife any further. She had probably already gone too far.

"Um, may I offer you something more to drink, Barbara? Water, tea?"

Chapter 21

"Hey, Big Daddy. Wanna have some fun? I can be nasty or sweet, however you want."

Lee leaned over in her red booty shorts and stuck her head into the passenger window of the tan Toyota. She opened her white fake fur jacket so the occupant could get a good glimpse of her pert sixteen-year-old breasts. She didn't have all that much to display, so she figured she had to flaunt what was there. She had been doing this a couple of months now and had learned a few tricks of the trade.

He was a balding white man in a cheap suit, probably just getting off from some two-bit government job. He took a quick glimpse at her, then glanced furtively into his rearview mirror. "Uh, how much?"

"Fifty bucks," Lee said, smacking on her gum. "It'll be the best fuckin' fifty you ever spent, sweetie."

"Where?"

"I got me a cozy place around the corner I can take you."

"Nah. It's probably a dump. What about in here?"

Lee shrugged. "Fine with me, sweetie.

Whatever floats your —"

A police siren blared in the distance and the bald white man nearly jumped out the window. Lee backed away quickly. She knew from the scared look in the man's eyes that he was about to take off, and if she was still hanging in the window he would drag her with him.

She was right. It was as if the Toyota suddenly turned into a Lear jet the way it flew down the street. Lee stomped the pavement with her black patent leather knee-high boots and wrapped her jacket tightly around her breasts. It was so damn cold she could see her breath hanging in the air. She would give anything right now to be inside some man's nice warm car instead of standing on this godforsaken curb freezing her buns off in the middle of December.

She was more than ready to turn in for the night but she needed to turn a couple more tricks for Tony or she'd be sleeping out here, too. And that would be far worse than turning even a hundred tricks in this weather.

But first she would take a short break. She glanced around to make sure Tony's car was nowhere in sight. If he caught her slacking on his time, he could be a bigger problem than any kind of weather. That sucker was an expert at beating his girls and leaving no bruises.

She stood near a building and lit a cigarette as a cold blast of air whipped around the corner. It had gotten so she could turn these tricks without even thinking about it. The first week was the worst. Every time she was with a man, she would relive the first time Uncle Clive put his foul hands on her. She shivered and pulled her jacket tighter. Even thinking about it now sent a chill up her spine that was far worse than anything from the frigid night air.

Lee stepped out of the shower and grabbed her towel off the rack. She had to dry off and get to the bedroom fast. She was running late for school, since she had a bad cold and had a hard time getting out of bed that morning. But what she was really worried about was Uncle Clive coming back to the house. He was in and out all day between drug deals, and she hated being there alone with him. But with Mama working two jobs, waiting tables all day and cleaning office buildings at night, it was getting harder and harder to avoid being alone with Uncle Clive.

She wrapped the towel around her slender body and blotted the water from the ends of her hair. They were extensions, and she needed to have them redone, but Mama didn't have the money just yet, said to give her two weeks. Lee hoped the braids didn't all fall out in the meantime.

She studied her chocolate-colored face in the mirror above the bathroom bowl and noticed a tiny pimple on her chin. She peered closely. She was seeing more of these ugly things on her face lately. Mama said it was normal at her age, something about hormones changing. Well, she would sure be glad when her hormones settled down.

She heard the front door open and shut and remembered that she was still not dressed yet. Damn. Please, let that be Mama coming home early from work to check on her cold after dropping Vernon off at school. Please, please, please.

Lee took a deep breath, cracked the door open and stuck her head out. She heard the refrigerator door shut, but she didn't dare call out. She opened the bathroom door all the way and stepped into the hallway, planning to run to the bedroom as fast as her legs could carry her.

But before she could take even one step, Uncle Clive appeared in the hallway and planted himself right in front of the bedroom doorway. He took a swig of beer, then looked her up and down from head to toe as he wiped his mouth with the back of his hand. He stuck one hand in his pocket and smiled, showing a mouthful of rotten teeth.

He didn't say a word. He didn't need to. She knew what was on his mind. But it would be a cold day at the equator before she let him put one stinking hand on her. She might be a girl, but he was a scrawny old man. She would bite, kick, hit and everything else if he dared to mess with her.

His hand was moving inside his pocket, and she looked down at the floor and pretended not to notice. She didn't want him to see the panic on her face, the fear. Should she run back to the bathroom or try to make it past him to the bedroom? It didn't really matter. None of the doors in this cheap-ass apartment had locks on them worth a dime. How could she have let him catch her half naked like this?

She bit her bottom lip. Then, without knowing why, she turned and fled back toward the bathroom. He was on her heels like a hungry shark, and her heart leaped. She let out a low moan and tried to shut the bathroom door behind her, but he burst through and sent her hip smashing against the white basin. She screamed as he grabbed her.

Next thing she knew, she was sprawled across the bathroom floor on her back with her legs lying out in the hallway and he was on top of her, his pale face and nappy head within inches of her own. The smell of beer on his breath was *so strong it seemed she could taste it. He clamped a hand over her mouth as she tried to wiggle free, but she could barely move under his weight. He was so much stronger than he looked.*

She bit his hand, and he yelped. She opened her mouth to scream but he covered it again with his foul-smelling palm. He grabbed the neck of the beer bottle and held it within inches of her face.

"Shut the fuck up, bitch, or I'll smash this right into that ugly black face of yours."

She kicked but that seemed only to arouse him more. He tossed the bottle onto the floor and ripped the towel from her body. He fondled her breasts, then reached down toward his pants. She knew what was coming or thought she did. No one had ever touched her this way, and she was scared out of her mind. Would it hurt real bad? Would she bleed?

She closed her eyes and tried to block everything out. There was nothing else she could do. She couldn't even lift a hand to wipe away the tears falling down her cheeks.

A car pulled up to the curb. A window rolled down. Lee stomped out her cigarette, spit the wad of chewing gum in her mouth out on the sidewalk and stuck a fresh stick in. She opened her fake fur jacket, walked up to the open window and leaned in.

Chapter 22

Candice walked off the Metro escalator and pulled up the collar of her wool jacket. The street was full of slippery mush from the recent snow, and she had to step gingerly in her boots as she crossed the intersection to keep the mess from splashing over her ankle-length skirt.

She was definitely not looking forward to spending another afternoon at the National Archives. It seemed like she'd been coming here forever, but if that's what it took, so be it.

She had finally found George and his second wife in the census for Massachusetts. But George's mother and sister from Virginia were still a mystery, one Candice was determined to solve one way or another.

After closely rereading the letters from George's sister, Rose DuPree, Candice realized that she and her family had settled in Charlottesville, Virginia, after the Civil War. So Candice planned to look up the DuPrees in the censuses taken after the war. That might provide the names of Rose's children and hopefully lead down to

someone alive today whom she could contact to learn more about George's mother,
Sara.

She went through the metal detector,
signed in and draped her jacket on the back
of a chair as she had countless times before.
Then she retrieved a microfilm and scanned
it eagerly until she found the section she was
looking for. And there it was: DuPree,
Peter. He was the right age to be Rose's husband, and there was a woman in the household named Rose.

Four children were also listed, two girls
and two boys, Candice noted with delight.
She was finally having some luck. She
quickly removed a pad of lined paper and a
pen from her shoulder bag and began jot-
ting down all the names and ages. As soon
as she finished with this roll of film, she
would scan the next census to see if Rose
and Peter had more children in later years.

She finished writing everything down and
was about to rewind the microfilm when her
eyes caught a column that she hadn't paid
much attention to recently. It was always
filled with the letter W, which stood for
white, next to the names of her relatives.
She had also noticed the letter B in that
column, which stood for black, but never
next to the names of her relatives.

But now she noticed the letter M in that column next to the names in the DuPree family. What did that stand for?

She turned the knob on the microfilm reader and scrolled quickly up toward the first row. What she saw hit her heart with a thud.

The mystery M stood for mulatto.

Candice blinked. Her right eyelid began to twitch, and that hadn't happened since her divorce.

How odd this was. Everything else about this family of DuPrees seemed to match. But according to the census taker, this Rose and her family were mulatto, which meant they were mixed — part black and part white.

She removed her glasses and rubbed her eyes. Could the census takers have made a mistake with the color designation? It looked like they had missed Sara and George entirely in the earlier years, and now it looked like they had marked George's sister Rose as mulatto. Either those census takers were a bunch of nincompoops or . . . or . . .

Candice's heart picked up a beat, slowly at first and then faster until it was pounding in her ears. Or her family had made a mistake about their heritage — a big one — and

Rose and George and all the rest of them really were part black. *Her* George. *Her* family.

She stood up so fast her chair fell over backward. Oh God. This was like watching a horror movie and her ancestors were the cast. Her family couldn't possibly have been so wrong about something like this all these years. That was absurd. She looked at her hand. It was white. *She* was white. *They* were white. A little piece of film more than a hundred years old couldn't change that.

She picked up her chair and sat back down. She pressed the button and stared at the reel as it rewound. Her eyelid was jumping furiously now. Her throat felt hot and scratchy. She could see all those names scrolling by in front of her with big black M's next to them. Hundreds and hundreds of M's scrolling by as if to mock her. Mulatto, mulatto, mulatto. Black, black, black.

How could this be?

Chapter 23

Jolene stepped onto the elevator and pressed the button for the fourth floor. This little ploy of hers absolutely had to work, since she had gone through so much trouble to plan it. Ever since Bradford and Barbara had come over for dinner, Jolene had known that she had to get Bradford alone to find out if he was available. And she would move heaven and hell to do it. A woman simply did not miss out on a chance to get close to a man like Bradford Bentley. Not this woman, anyway.

At first she had been tempted to pick up the phone and call to ask him out to lunch, but that was a bit brazen, even for her. They were both married, and she didn't want to look like a fool if Bradford wasn't interested in her.

Then she got lucky. Patrick told her on Friday that he would be in Baltimore all day that following Monday to visit one of Digitech's clients, and in no time Jolene had hatched her little plan and put it in motion. She had her hair weave redone on Saturday at Kim's, a chichi salon in D.C. She'd had to bribe Kim to bump another woman and take her at the last minute with the promise of a fifty-dollar tip, but it was worth every penny. Then she got a manicure and pedicure. On Sunday she drove to Saks on Wisconsin Avenue near D.C. and bought a new St. John suit, fitting tight as you please.

That morning she had called in sick at the office, then slept a little late to get some extra beauty rest. She woke up around ten for a long hot bubble bath. There was nothing like a leisurely soak in the tub to get her feeling sexy. Not that she needed help in that department. She was a natural. But she wanted to be at the very top of her game for this day. She then did her makeup and slipped into her new suit and a pair of three-inch heels. She took the time to make sure everything was flawless.

Now she was at the Digitech offices, and judging from the lustful glances she was getting from the men she passed on her way up, she was looking like a billion bucks. She would casually stroll in and pretend to have a lunch date with Patrick. When the receptionist told her he was out for the day, she would feign surprise, then ask to see Bradford.

It was a perfect plan — almost. The only flaw was that she had no way of knowing if Bradford would be in. But there was nothing she could do to ensure that. She had to take her chances.

She stepped out of the elevator and into the fourth-floor hallway. Digitech was on her right, behind double glass doors. A black man in a navy suit who appeared to be in his early thirties exited the office and held the door open as he looked her over with obvious approval. She smiled and threw in a little extra hip wiggle for him as she walked through the door. It always pleased her to see that she could still turn a man's head, especially a younger one.

The receptionist was seated behind a big wooden desk in the outer lobby of the suite. She looked up and smiled. Jolene had never been crazy about Brenda. She looked like a lot of the women in Bradford's life — tall, thin and fair in complexion. She was one of those African-American women who looked almost white, with long wavy hair and light green eyes. Jolene wondered if Bradford had ever had an affair with her.

"Good afternoon, Brenda."

"Good afternoon, Mrs. Brown. How are you?"

"Never better," Jolene said. "I'll go on back. Patrick is expecting me."

Brenda raised her eyebrows. "Is he? Then he must have forgotten. Patrick is going to be out of the office all day today."

Jolene did her best to look surprised. "But that can't be right. We're meeting for lunch."

"Do you want me to buzz him to see if he's there? I'm almost sure he's out."

"Would you, please?"

While Brenda dialed, Jolene removed her compact and checked her hair and makeup. Brenda hung up and shrugged. "He's not there. Sorry."

"You're kidding?" Jolene asked innocently.

"I'm afraid not," Brenda replied. "He came in early this morning but then he left to go to Baltimore around ten and said he wouldn't be back here until tomorrow morning."

"Oh darn," Jolene said. She flipped her weave over her shoulders. "He must have forgotten our lunch date. Men. I tell you. Well, you know what? Since I'm here, I may as well stop in and say hello to Bradford. Is he in?"

"You mean Mr. Bentley?" The receptionist seemed perplexed.

"Yes," Jolene answered coolly. "Him."

"Um, I can check." Brenda picked up the phone and spoke for a minute, then hung up. "His secretary said for you to go on back. It's through these doors, all the way to the end."

Jolene smiled triumphantly. So far so good, she thought as she walked down the hallway. And then there it was. She could see big double doors with his name in elegant bold letters. "Bradford Bentley III, President." Ooh. Her heart fluttered in anticipation.

She paused and hiked her skirt up a bit, ignoring the puzzled look on his secretary's face. Then she knocked and entered when she heard his voice. He was buttoning the jacket to a very expensive-looking gray pinstripe suit. He came from around his desk, took both of her hands and kissed her on the cheek.

"Now what did I do to deserve this delightful visit?" he asked as he led her to a small plush couch sitting against the wall. They sat down next to each other.

She smiled sweetly. "Well, I came down here to have lunch with Patrick. But I think he forgot all about me. I just learned that he's in Baltimore today. So I thought I would stop in and say hello."

"Well, shame on him. But I couldn't be happier. Patrick's loss is my gain. You look fabulous, Jolene."

"Thank you, Bradford." He was obviously flirting with her. She crossed her legs, and her short skirt rose up high over her thighs. His eyes caught every move and every inch of leg.

"Give me a minute," he said, standing. "I want to get my secretary to hold all my calls. It's not every day that a beautiful woman comes to the office to visit me."

Jolene put on her biggest, sexiest smile as Bradford walked to the desk and reached for his phone. She could hardly believe how well this was turning out. He was flirting with every move he made — the way he smiled at her, touched her, spoke to her.

This was starting to feel like that first visit to Terrence's office and the way they had flirted shamelessly with each other. In some ways, Bradford reminded her of Terrence. They were both very successful, very good-looking and, unfortunately, very married. Although there was one big difference that immediately came to Jolene's mind. Bradford was a heck of a lot richer than Terrence.

In fact, next to Bradford, Terrence looked like a damn pauper. And Bradford didn't seem to be nearly as devoted to his wife as that sap Terrence turned out to be. Poor Barbara. It looked like her marriage was a total sham. Well, it certainly wasn't *her* fault if Barbara didn't know how to keep her man happy, now was it? Jolene smiled as Bradford put down the phone and sat next to her. He moved in closer than before.

"Now, where were we?" He touched her knee gently with his finger as his gaze traveled from her thighs up to her breasts. Fortunately, she had left the top button to her suit jacket open and was not wearing a blouse, so his eyes had plenty to feast on. To her total astonishment, he shifted his fingers from her knee to the crevice between her breasts. It was a light feather touch and very tantalizing.

She caught her breath. Whoa. Down, boy. Bradford was ready to pounce on her right then and there. It was tempting, but this was a bit fast, even for her. She had learned a lot with Terrence, and she wasn't going to be so easy this time. If she let him, Bradford would bang her and then drop her before she knew what had happened. She was going to play this one a lot more carefully. Let him chase her a bit. Then he would appreciate her more when he finally caught her.

She had to gain control of the situation without offending him. She smiled and turned her knees away gently. "I was just saying that I came down to meet my husband for lunch but he's not here."

He backed away. "Yes. Well, like you

said, I believe he's out for the rest of the day."

"And how have you been, Bradford?"

"I'm just fine. And you?"

"Mmm . . . a little disappointed that I won't be having lunch with Patrick after coming all the way down here, of course." Hint, hint.

"Oh well. I'm here," Bradford said, and spread his arms.

She smiled coyly. "So you are."

"Where would you like to go?"

"You mean for lunch? Us?"

"Yes, if you're up for that," he added. "And you don't mind my company."

"Not at all. I'd like that very much."

"Then why don't we ride into town to B. Smith's? Or Georgia Brown? How does that sound?"

"Wonderful," she said with delight. "I can't think of a better way to spend my time. Er, if, um, if Patrick's not here."

"Good."

He held the doors open for her and stood a lot closer than he needed to in the elevator. Not only was he a very sexy man, he was also a gentleman.

She sank into the passenger seat of his silver Jaguar convertible and it felt like she was wrapped in fur.

"You look like you were made for that seat," Bradford said.

Her thought exactly. She laughed. "I could definitely get used to this in a hurry."

He stopped at a traffic light, and she turned toward him, making sure he had a good view of the cleavage he had touched moments ago. "When are you going to give Patrick a promotion so I can ride in style like this?"

Bradford threw his head back and laughed. "Are you sure he didn't put you up to this?"

Jolene chuckled. "Patrick? Hardly. He doesn't really care much about things like this." She rubbed her fingers over the smooth leather of the car seat. "But I do."

He nodded with understanding. "Neither does Barbara. She thinks it's too flashy. You surprise me, Jolene. You're not what I might have expected. I mean, I always found you attractive but I thought your personality would be different than it is."

"Oh really? How, Bradford?"

"Somehow I had pictured you as more conservative, I think. More straitlaced."

She smiled. "And what do you think now?"

"You're a go-getter, a woman who knows what she wants and goes after it."

"Hmm. That's a compliment in my book."

"I meant it as a compliment. That can be very alluring in a woman."

"Thank you, Bradford. You know, you're exactly what I expected."

"Oh? And what did you expect?"

"Smooth, sharp, sexy as hell."

He nodded as if he had known it all along, and Jolene smiled. What a man. He was so much like her. Cool and confident. And she loved the vibes jumping back and forth between them. She could feel the heat bouncing off the walls and ceiling.

Bradford was obviously well known at the restaurant. The maître d' sat them at a quiet table in a corner, and they continued to flirt shamelessly. By the time the waiter brought dessert, they were playing footsie under the table. She had removed her right heel and ran her stockinged toes up and down his calf.

This was moving a little faster than she had planned, but so what. She wasn't complaining. She found this man so much more irresistible than she'd ever imagined.

"What are you doing to me, Bradford?" she said softly. "I feel so naughty around you."

"I'll take that as a compliment," he said.

"Because you are the most captivating woman I've come across in a long time."

"You know what they say, don't you, Bradford?" she asked coyly.

"I'm sure you'll tell me."

"The blacker the berry, the sweeter the juice."

He threw his head back and laughed, a deep throaty laugh. "Well, now, I sure hope I'll get a chance to test that."

"You inspire me, Bradford. I've always admired you tremendously. You remind me of my father in a way. He's a retired judge, you know — very confident and commanding."

"So, your father was a judge? I'm impressed. What is he doing now?"

Jolene smiled. "He and my mother live off of upper Sixteenth Street. They do a lot of traveling. In fact, they're in the Caribbean now."

"Hmm," he said, arching his eyebrows with obvious approval. "The gold coast. Nice area."

Jolene smiled. Her casual comments about her parents seemed to have the desired effect. She wanted him to know that she was of far different stock than Bradford's previous mistresses, at least that nut Sabrina. Not even Barbara, with her country beginnings, came close to having her illustrious pedigree, filled with judges, doctors and lawyers.

The waitress brought the check, but they were so fixed on each other that they barely glanced in her direction. Although Jolene pretended not to notice, she couldn't help but see the big smile that the twenty-something little blond waitress bestowed on Bradford whenever she approached the table. It seemed every woman on the planet was drawn to this man. And could she blame them? With his good looks and thousand-dollar suits, he oozed power, authority, money.

Well, get out of the way, bitches. He was hers now. "What do you have planned for the afternoon?" She prayed he would want to see her. If not now, sometime soon.

Bradford pulled out his platinum American Express card and placed it on the table. Then he looked back at her. "You, I hope."

She thought her heart would jump out onto the table. For the first time in her life, her mouth went dry.

"I'll be honest with you, Jolene," he continued. "Right now I'm thinking of a suite at the Ritz and you lying nude between the sheets. I'd love to spend a leisurely afternoon playing hooky and getting to know each other. But if it doesn't suit you, I understand."

Jolene quickly found her voice. She hoped it didn't sound hoarse. "What are we waiting for?" The hell with taking things more slowly this time around and letting him chase her. She had come to seduce him, hadn't she? Although now she wasn't so sure who had seduced whom.

The waitress returned the credit card, and Jolene excused herself to go powder her nose. But it was really her heart that needed tending. She was off to a hotel room with Bradford Bentley. It didn't get much better than this.

And it had been so damn easy. To think she was worried that he might reject her. Silly girl. She smiled at her reflection in the ladies' room mirror. She wanted to believe that it was this pretty brown face and perfect body that made everything go so smoothly. But she knew better. Bradford was a player, plain and simple. He was probably just waiting for the right woman to come along to replace Sabrina. Or maybe the right couple of women. For all she knew, he was already seeing someone else.

But she would do her absolute best to clear the field. Move over, bitches. Jolene is here. That meant Barbara, too. Even a man like Bradford would settle down for the right woman, and obviously that was not Barbara. If she played her cards right, maybe it could be her. Mrs. Jolene Bentley. Ooh. That sounded positively perfect.

She was going to dig up every bit of information about him that she could find — his likes and dislikes, his quirks and habits. And then she would become the woman of his dreams. Did he like women who cooked? She would take a damn gourmet cooking class. Did he like them athletic? Hell, she would take up golf or tennis or learn to jump out of planes. Whatever it took.

But first things first. Right now she was going to have to summon everything she had learned over the years to be the best lover he had ever slept with. If there was one thing she knew about men like Bradford, it was that they liked sex, and lots of it. Good sex was the bait that lured the big fish like Bradford out of the sea. Then you could go in for the kill — the ring, marriage, the whole bit. The key was to get him to feel that he could get his every need satisfied with her and her only.

She touched up her makeup, quickly checked her suit and opened the door.

Candice brushed by the reception desk

and barely looked in Brenda's direction. It was already after lunchtime and she was just getting into work. She wasn't getting much sleep at all lately. She would wake at two or three in the morning and stare at the dark ceiling, then finally doze off around four or five. It had been that way ever since that frightening discovery at the archives last week.

Her emotions were all over the place, jumping around like a yo-yo. One minute she'd brush the findings off, quite certain that there was a huge mistake, that the census taker or someone at the archives had screwed up. All she had to do was look in the mirror to see that.

The next minute she'd find herself wondering if something so bizarre could possibly be true. She was starting to notice things she never had before, to see things differently. The other day it had dawned on her that Brenda had the hair and features of a white woman and that if her complexion were a shade lighter, she would look white. And she had noticed that a lot of blacks on the street looked like Brenda.

She sat at her desk and twirled around in her chair to face the window. But it wasn't the view that she saw. It was microfilm and a column of M's and B's, one after the other.

Black, black, black.

How did that happen? How did we all get so mixed up?

What was most distressing was that she didn't have a single person to talk to about all of this. Not even her husband, and especially not her daughters. It was too private, too personal and too damn scary. She had no idea how Jim would react. She could only imagine.

"Honey, I have some news."

"What is it, dear?"

"I might be black."

"Huh?"

"Black, African-American, Negro."

"Well, I'm out of here."

Would he leave her? Would he want to touch her and hold her anymore?

And her folks. What would her dad do if someone told him that his wife's grandfather was born a slave? He didn't even want to live on the same street with black people.

Oh God. She had to stop this and get some work done. She put on her glasses and swung around to face the computer. She opened her graphics software and called up a web site she was designing. Some of the links needed work, and Bradford was expecting to see it tomorrow. She tried to focus, but five minutes later, visions of that damn microfilm clouded her thoughts. *Black, black, black.*

Dammit. What was the matter with her? It was silly to let a little piece of microfilm get to her like this. No more ancestor research. It was too confusing and too aggravating. Look at the mess she had uncovered.

She laughed out loud. Of course, that was it. She would give it a rest and come back to it when her head was clearer. That made sense.

It made sense, but she couldn't do it. She had to get to the bottom of this *now*. She snatched her shoulder bag off the desk and headed out the door.

Jolene put her hand on the bathroom doorknob. She was wearing her birthday suit and nothing else. And Bradford Bentley — rich, powerful, gorgeous — was waiting for her. *Her.* Jolene Cooke Brown. Eat your heart out, sis. And all you snobby upper-Sixteenth Street denizens. For all the airs they put on, they were paupers compared with this man. And she had him now.

Good-bye Terrence and the Holiday Inn. Hello Bradford and the Ritz.

She opened the door and smiled at the man sitting up in the king-size bed. She struck a pose in the doorway and held it. Let

269

him soak in all her luscious assets — the big boobs and butt, the slim waistline. Lord knew she worked hard enough to keep it all in tiptop shape. And Patrick never even noticed. She took her sweet time strolling across the carpet.

He threw the sheets back and she got a preview of *his* assets. Bradford was indeed a man of means.

Within her next few breaths, they were all over each other. It was like an athletic event, a competition to see who could most satisfy the other, with lots of thrusting, panting and loud moaning. They rolled around on the bed and fell on the floor with a thump and barely missed a beat.

They finished on the love seat in the sitting room and then collapsed, completely exhausted. Jolene flopped back on the couch, and he slid down to the floor and lay flat on his back.

For a minute neither of them said a word and Jolene focused on catching her breath and savoring the moment. She had just experienced the wildest sex of her life with Bradford Bentley!

She had never felt so happy. Not with Jonathan or Terrence and certainly not with Patrick. Could this be love?

She sat up and looked down at him. His

eyes were closed, and a tiny smile played around his cute lips. If the Lord made a perfect creature, it was Bradford Bentley. Love? The very thought scared her silly, because if she couldn't have him, it would tear her apart.

Was it possible that he felt the same way about her? He had just yelled her name, hadn't he? He had called her "baby," "sweetheart" and "juicy," hadn't he? She smiled at the last one. No one had ever called her juicy before.

"That was sensational," he said as he opened his eyes and smiled at her. He sat up on the floor and rested his back against the base of the love seat.

See? He thought she was sensational. That was certainly encouraging. It wasn't exactly "I love you" or even "I think I'm in love with you," but it would do for now. She smiled and slid down on the floor next to him.

"Bradford, that was better than sensational. It was the best sex I've ever had. You take my breath away."

He took her hand and kissed her palm. "You're quite a woman, Jolene."

She rested her head on his shoulder. She had to be careful. She wanted to tell him that she was falling for him, but she knew better than to go that far just yet. It would scare him away if he didn't feel the same. She had to be patient.

They sat in silence for a few minutes. She could stay here all afternoon, just like this. Maybe they could go at it again. Did she dare suggest it?

He tapped her on the arm. "Baby, I need to get back to the office."

So much for hanging around all afternoon, she thought as she lifted her head from his shoulder. She was disappointed but she didn't dare let on. "I understand."

They both stood up and he took her in his arms and kissed her. She moaned and clung to him tightly, hoping to hold him there just a while longer.

He took her by the arms and pushed her away gently. "Whoa," he said softly. "You'll get me going again if we keep this up."

"That's the general idea," she said. "I don't want you to go, Bradford. Can't we stay a little longer?" OK, so she was losing her cool. She couldn't help herself.

He glanced at his Rolex watch. She knew it was around four o'clock, and they had been together since noon. "Do you realize that we've been together for almost four hours?" he asked.

"Mmm." She wrapped her arms around

him. She kissed his neck, his face, his lips. "Is that all?"

He didn't push her away this time. Instead he lifted her in his arms and carried her back to bed.

Chapter 24

"But Bradford, we always drive down to Smithfield after the holidays to visit my aunt for her birthday," Barbara said as she put her coffee cup down on the kitchen table. "You know how important she is to me. She raised me. And I don't want to disappoint her, especially after what happened September eleventh."

They had visited her aunt in the winter every year since they were first married more than thirty years ago, no matter how they were getting along. Why was he backing out at the last minute?

"It can't be helped," Bradford said, looking up from the Sunday business section of the *New York Times*. He shrugged. "I've got some important contract negotiations coming up over the next few weeks. Go on without me."

"But it takes three or four hours to get down there by car. You know I don't like to do that much driving alone, and I'm not ready to fly again yet."

He shrugged. "Get Robin to drive with you."

"I can't go," Robin said. "I start a new

semester next week."

"See?" Barbara said. "And it won't be the same without you there, Bradford. Aunt Gladys will be looking for you."

Bradford chuckled. "I doubt she'll miss me. You know we just tolerate each other. And barely. She thinks I'm a ruthless cad."

Barbara smiled wryly.

"Oh, so you think that, too, huh? Thanks, dear."

"I didn't say a word."

Robin chuckled. "She doesn't really think you're that bad, Daddy. But she's from the old school, and, well, you're a businessman doing what you have to do to survive these days."

"Please explain that to your mother. Sometimes I don't think she understands that."

"That's not the point, Bradford. We only visit Aunt Gladys and Uncle Marvin once a year. Now you're backing out of that."

He sighed. "We could wait and go in the spring."

"Bradford, please. I don't want to disappoint her, especially this year."

"Mama has a point, Dad."

Bradford flicked an imaginary speck of dirt from his pajama leg while he thought. "I'll tell you what. If everything goes well, I might be able to get away for a couple of days and join you down there later. But I can't promise anything."

Barbara sighed with disappointment. A lot of things still made her suspicious, especially whenever Bradford changed his plans at the last minute. Old habits died hard when your husband once acted like he thought he was king of the players.

But she and Bradford had been getting along much better recently, and there had been no signs of Sabrina or any other woman lately. Thank goodness. She felt more relaxed and contented than she had in years. Perhaps she shouldn't nag him about this if she wanted to keep the peace.

She lit a cigarette. "If that's the best you can do, Bradford, I'll have to live with that."

Robin stood and placed her coffee cup in the sink. "Well, I'm off. I have to go over to George Washington to pick up my textbooks for classes, then I'm going to stop by a friend's house."

"Will you be home for dinner?" Barbara asked.

"Probably not," Robin said, blowing kisses from the doorway as she ran off.

Bradford folded the paper and stood up. "I'm going to get dressed and go out to hit a few balls."

"In January?" Barbara asked with surprise.

"Yep. It's warm for this time of year, almost fifty degrees out there."

She took a drag off her cigarette. "Mm-hmm. Speaking of classes, I signed up for a real estate course with Marilyn's firm. It starts next week."

"Well, good for you," Bradford said as he headed for the door.

"Wait. Is that all you have to say?"

"What do you want, Barbara? Cartwheels?"

"Very funny."

He came back and kissed her on the forehead. "Good luck with your class. Let me know if I can do anything to help."

"Will you be home for dinner?"

"Probably. I'll call if not."

She watched as he tightened the belt to his robe and walked off, then smashed her cigarette out. She was trying with every fiber in her body to trust him again, but it was hard as hell. Take this playing golf in the middle of January. Who the hell played golf in January? Talk about ridiculous. And suspicious.

She lit another Benson & Hedges. She was so glad she had signed up for that real estate course. It would leave her less time to sit around alone feeling sorry for herself and smoking these awful cigarettes.

Pearl couldn't believe her eyes. Was that Jolene Brown's husband walking through the door of her salon? What on earth did he want here? Pearl appreciated Jolene sending her a warning through Barbara that Candice Jones was snooping around behind her back. But she still didn't like Jolene much, not after she formed that group to try and stop the town houses from being built. They had even gone so far as to plant their behinds on the construction site to block the workers at one point. And then they killed her idea for a community sports complex. The woman seemed to think that thugs were trying to take over her precious Silver Lake.

"Hello," Pearl said, looking up from the head of her client's hair. Her hands were full of suds, so she could only nod and smile at Patrick in greeting. She had one client under the faucet, two under the dryer and a fourth sitting on the couch waiting her turn. She couldn't afford to stop even for a minute if she didn't have to. Kenyatta was always telling her that she needed to get better at managing her time, and he was probably right. But the problem was that she didn't have the time to figure out how to manage her time. "What can I do for you?"

"Hi," he said. "I'm Patrick Brown. Jolene Brown's husband. We live in Silver Lake."

He was dressed casually in brown corduroy slacks and a leather bomber jacket and he looked like he felt out of place, as most men do in hair salons. Pearl couldn't help but smile. "I know who you are. How are you? And Jolene?"

"We're both fine. How are you?"

"Busy," Pearl said with a chuckle. "But I'm still here."

He smiled. "So you are. I believe you know Barbara Bentley."

Pearl nodded. "She's a client of mine."

"Yes. Well, Barbara and Bradford Bentley came to our house for dinner a few weeks ago and they brought a cake for dessert. Barbara said you made it."

"Oh yes. A rum cake, right?"

"That was it. Best cake I ever tasted."

Pearl smiled. "Thanks, but if you're looking for the recipe, sorry. I don't give that out."

He chuckled. "Can't say I blame you. But no. What I was wondering . . . well, Barbara also said you've done some catering in the past."

"Yes, but I don't do that anymore. Ever

since my salon took off, I don't have time for much else. I might bake one for a friend or a client now and then, but —"

"Well, if you'll consider me the friend of a client . . ." He smiled, and Pearl noticed that he was rather handsome in an understated sort of way.

"I'm helping to plan a political reception next month, and we're willing to pay whatever you ask," he said.

She started to shake her head.

"It's for a good cause," he added before she could speak. "David Manley. He's running for county executive."

She nodded and looked at him more closely. She was so busy with the shop these days that she had no time for politics. She never voted except in presidential election years. But she had helped her ex-husband when he campaigned in Detroit so she knew a thing or two about what it involved — lots of parties, fund-raisers and town meetings. Somehow she had a real hard time seeing Jolene involved in all of that. But Patrick had a nice smile and the kind of solid good looks that crept up on you slowly. He was probably good with people.

Still, this was not a good time. "Look, I appreciate that you like my cakes and all and I wish you the best of luck. But I really don't have the time to do any catering now. I'm real sorry."

He nodded. "If you can't, you can't."

He looked so disappointed that Pearl felt sorry for him. "I'm sure you'll find someone else."

He forced a smile. "Yeah, yeah. I understand. Well, I don't really understand but I'll have to live with that." He reached into his jacket pocket for his business card and held it out. "In case you change your mind, you can reach me there."

She nodded toward the shelf in front of her, and he put the card down, then he turned to leave.

"You know, my ex-husband ran for office in Detroit," she said. "I helped him campaign." Pearl didn't know why that came out. She hadn't talked about those days in years. But there was something about this man. He seemed trustworthy and genuinely upset by her decision. She wanted to cheer him up a bit.

He turned around to face her. "You don't say? What office was that?"

"City council. Way, way back."

"So, you were holding out on me, then," he teased. "You're an old pro at this. Did he win?"

She shook her head. "Nope. And he

281

didn't deserve to if you ask me."

"Oops," he said.

She shrugged. "That's just my opinion, but it was an interesting time."

He chuckled. "I'll bet. Did you enjoy campaigning?"

"Mmm. I guess you could say I did. I love getting out and meeting people."

He nodded eagerly. "So do I. It's a welcome change from my job as a programmer."

She smiled. "Somehow I don't see you sitting behind a computer all day long. You look more like a people person."

"Thanks. I'll take that as a compliment."

"And you should."

"Well, you have my card. If you change your mind about the cakes, please give me a call."

She nodded. "Good luck."

He waved good-bye and stepped out the door.

"He sure was cute," Vicky said breathlessly as Pearl lifted her head from the sink and wrapped it in a towel.

"You think so?"

"Yeah, right, Pearl," Vicky said. "Like you didn't notice."

"He's married, you know."

"Shoot, girl." Vicky waved her arm.

"That don't mean he can't be cute."

Pearl chuckled as she toweled off Vicky's hair. She thought Patrick was very attractive. But she had turned that dial off a long time ago, ever since her march out of Detroit.

She sat Vicky under a hair dryer, then wiped her hands and picked up the business card Patrick had left on the shelf. She was surprised to see that he worked at Digitech, Bradford Bentley's company. She had no idea. Maybe she ought to reconsider, since he worked for the husband of her favorite client.

Nah, she thought. She had too much on her plate already. Patrick would find someone else to make desserts for his political reception. Of course, they wouldn't be as good as her cakes.

She walked into the adjoining room and called her next client.

Candice stared at the phone. Should she do it? Should she make the call? She shifted her gaze to the slip of blue-lined paper on the nightstand in front of her.

JOSEPH DUPREE
804-555-4255
RICHMOND, VA.

On her last visit to the archives, she had searched the census reports and discovered that Rose and Peter had two children between 1900 and 1910. So she had dialed the operator to get the phone number of the youngest son but now she was too scared to make the call.

She frowned at the slip of paper. If this was the right Joseph DuPree and he was still living, he would be more than ninety years old. Chances were slim that she would reach him. And even if she did, he might not be well enough to talk at that age.

But none of it mattered, anyway, since she couldn't get up the nerve to call him.

"What are you doing?"

She jumped at the sound of Jim's voice behind her in the bedroom doorway but managed to slip the piece of paper into the little drawer in the nightstand before he entered the room.

She turned to face him. "Oh, nothing."

He stood in front of her with his hands in the pockets of his khakis. "What's been eating you lately, hon?"

She hesitated. How much had he seen? "Nothing."

"Don't tell me it's nothing, Candice," he said with annoyance. "You've been edgy for several days now."

She wanted to tell him everything so badly. But she wasn't ready to do that yet. She wasn't ready to tell anyone.

"Is it about Ashley and Kenyatta?" he asked.

She nearly laughed out loud. If only it were that simple. Ashley and Kenyatta were going full steam, sure enough. But right now her daughter dating a black man was no longer at the top of her list of concerns. *What if I told you that your wife is black, Jim? How's that for something to be worried about?*

"No, it's not that," she said. "I'm just tired."

He sat next to her on the bed. "I don't buy that," he said firmly. "It's more than that. You're different somehow. You go to work, then you come home at night and read or watch TV. On weekends you mope around the house all day in your robe and slippers. Or you're off to the National Archives. Sometimes I see you sitting and staring at nothing. What's bothering you?"

Everything, she wanted to shout. Her whole world was spinning upside down, and sometimes it felt like she could barely catch her breath. One night she got up and ran into the bathroom so Jim wouldn't hear her sobs.

"I said it was nothing," she said shortly.

"Will you please just get off my back?"

His face dropped with sadness and he stood up. "OK. Fine. If that's how you want to be."

Boy, she had handled that well. Now she had her husband upset with her. "I'm sorry, Jim," she said softly.

He shrugged in defeat and turned back toward the door.

She stood up. "Jim."

He turned back to face her.

She didn't want him to be upset with her. "Um. I . . . I am going through some things now that . . . that I can't discuss. Not yet, anyway. I need more time to think about what to do. It's . . . it's complicated."

He frowned. "Maybe I can help you decide what to do if you just tell me what the problem is."

She paused. He was her husband. If there was something to all this, he had the right to know.

Or did he? Did anyone have to know besides her?

"This is something I need to deal with on my own for now," she said gently. "Try to understand. Please."

He looked at her strangely, then nodded. "I'll be here when you're ready to talk."

He turned and left the room, and she let

out a big sigh of relief. Oh hell. Had her behavior changed that much?

She sat down, opened the drawer and
stared at the slip of paper. Look at what this
was doing to her and her family. She
snatched the sheet of paper and ripped it to
shreds. Then she jumped up and threw it in
the wastebasket.

Good-bye. Good riddance. She was going
to forget all this ancestry crap and get back
to her life as a happily married woman with
two beautiful daughters — her life as a *white*
woman.

Chapter 25

As usual, they were starting their day with a big fight about the new house. The closer they got to completion, the more they bickered. Jolene was so damn tired of it. Now that she was seeing Bradford Bentley, these arguments were getting harder to take.

"Damn it, Jolene. You think money grows on trees? We can't afford a Viking stove. What the hell is wrong with GE? We've already maxed out every credit card we have. We're neck deep in loans, and we have a daughter to send to college."

Jolene flipped her weave. Patrick was shouting so loud she could see the veins in his neck. She thought for a minute that he was going to cut himself with the razor blade he was shaving with. She fastened her black lace bra and slipped her arms into the straps. Then she sat on the bed to put on her panty hose. "Do you have to shout and cuss, dammit?" she snapped. "I'm sitting right here. And Juliette hasn't left for school yet."

"She needs to hear how silly her mother can be when it comes to finances. Because I swear, this shit is getting out of hand. We owe Visa, MasterCard, American Express and Diners Club thousands of dollars."

"Oh, chill, Patrick. You're such a damn tightwad. I don't want just any old stove in my kitchen. It's —"

"For crissakes, Jolene. You don't even like to cook. And look at this mess." He threw his razor into the sink and raced from the master bath into the bedroom. He grabbed a pile of bills from the top of his chest of drawers.

"Do you see these?" he said, lowering his voice only a little. He threw them on the bed beside Jolene. "And in case you've forgotten, we're paying two mortgages until we put this house on the market."

Jolene sighed and rolled her eyes to the ceiling.

"At this rate, we're going to have combined mortgages of one and a half million at some point. Jeez. One and a half million."

She stood and faced him. "Well, have you asked Bradford for a raise yet? Or can you get up the nerve?" She sneered.

"Even with a raise, we can't afford to spend this way. Unless he doubles my salary, which he won't. Why do you always have to be so over the top? We'll never be like your snooty folks. You need to accept that."

She clenched her fists. "You don't have to

be so damn nasty about it. We can't even talk without you putting me down."

"Oh, like you're being Miss Congeniality. You could win a prize in the nastiness contest for the way you talk to me." He stomped back into the bathroom and picked up his razor blade. She followed him and stood in the doorway, eyes ablaze.

"If you weren't so goddamn cheap, I —"

"Mama?"

Jolene froze. She turned toward the bedroom doorway to see Juliette standing there dressed for school except for bare feet. She was holding up one navy blue kneesock.

"What in the world are you two fighting about now?" Juliette asked, placing her hands on her hips.

"We're not fighting," Jolene said. "We're just talking."

Juliette narrowed her eyes doubtfully. "Yeah, right."

"What do you want?" Jolene asked. "And why aren't you ready for school?"

"I can't find my other wool navy sock."

"You have more than one pair of navy socks, honey," Jolene said.

"All the rest of them are dirty."

"Ha," Patrick snickered as he rinsed his razor blade. "You can thank your mother's wonderful housekeeping skills for that."

Jolene turned a cold eye toward her husband. How dare he talk to her that way in front of Juliette. She wanted to hurl every profanity in the book at him, but she would never stoop so low in front of their daughter. "That was so uncalled for," she whispered between clenched teeth.

She led Juliette from their room to help her find a matching pair of socks for school. When she returned to the bedroom, Patrick was sitting on the bed putting on his shoes, and her moment of wanting to curse him out had passed. She had nothing more to say to him.

They finished dressing in total silence, and Patrick left for work just as she started to put on her makeup. That was fine with her. She was meeting Bradford for lunch that afternoon at the Ritz in Tyson's Corner, Virginia, just outside of D.C. And nothing Mister Cheapo said or did could spoil her excitement about that.

She and Bradford had been meeting at hotels for lunch for almost a month now. Barbara was going down to Virginia this week to visit her aunt, and Bradford was looking into getting them a cozy cabin in the Blue Ridge Mountains for the weekend. For the first time, Jolene was going to get to spend some real time with Bradford, something besides a lunchtime rendezvous. She didn't know what she would tell Patrick and she didn't care either. If Bradford got a place for them to stay over the weekend, nothing would keep her away.

She smiled as she thought about Bradford. He was quite the romantic. The couple of times she and that asshole Terrence went away together, she did all the planning and paid most of the expenses. Not with Bradford. He arranged every detail and picked up the bill. He was a real man.

He did say they had to be discreet. That's why they usually met outside of the city and a good distance away from Silver Lake. Fine. Whatever. Although if it were up to her, they would shout about their affair from the rooftops of Silver Lake. Let the whole damn world know. And the sooner the better. But if he wanted to be discreet, fine. The day to let it out would come.

In the meantime, she could still fantasize, couldn't she? Mrs. Jolene Bentley. She giggled. How fantastic did that sound? She had visions of herself lounging around the pool and supervising the help. She would leave her job, of course, and devote herself to Bradford. Juliette would go to the best private schools, and they would take long, luxurious vacations. She would be the envy of every woman in Silver Lake — black, white and every color in between, just as Barbara was now.

Did she feel any guilt about Barbara? Any pity? She had thought about that for all of five minutes. Hell, no. The woman had her chance and she blew it. Bradford Bentley slept in Barbara's bed every night, and if she couldn't hold on to him, that was nobody's fault but her own.

Pearl sat her client under the hair dryer and told the receptionist that she was going to duck into her office for a quick lunch break. Then she went into a room at the back of the salon and shut the door. The small office was cluttered with boxes of hair supplies and a desk piled high with paper. There was barely enough room to turn around in, but she loved it back here. It was the only place in the shop where she could take a few minutes to herself and recharge her batteries.

But more than that, she was surrounded by the fruit of her labor, or maybe the seeds — boxes of shampoo and conditioner, computer printouts and spreadsheets filled with numbers and data about her business, an extra salon chair. It reminded her of how far she had come as a businesswoman.

She sat at the desk, opened a brown paper bag and removed two pieces of broiled chicken, a salad tossed with olive oil and balsamic vinegar, and a bottle of spring water. This was week three of her low-carb diet. It was all the rage now, and since she had tried every other diet known to woman-kind she figured she might as well give this one a chance.

She took a bite of chicken, then picked up a business card and held it in her hand. She had decided to call Patrick Brown after all and agree to make the cakes for his political reception. He worked for Barbara Bentley's husband and one didn't take unnecessary chances with a client like Barbara. Clients switched hair salons almost as often as they did hairstyles. Barbara had remained a loyal and generous customer for many years, and Pearl didn't want to give her any reasons to switch.

Besides, she liked Patrick and had a feeling he would be pleasant to work with. He had taken the time to send her a small African violet plant with a note asking her to reconsider. The plant fit perfectly in the pic-ture window of her salon, and she suspected he'd put a bit of thought into it.

And she could always use some extra money.

She took a sip of water and dialed the number. She didn't know why she felt so jittery. It wasn't like she was calling to ask him out on a date. He was only a man and this was a business call.

A receptionist answered and she asked for Patrick.

"Hello?" came a male voice.

"Patrick Brown, please."

"This is Patrick Brown."

"Hi. It's Pearl Jackson. I got the plant. That was very thoughtful of you."

"I'm glad you liked it and I'm also glad you called. Does this mean you've reconsidered?"

"Yes, actually. You're a friend of Barbara Bentley's, and she's one of my best clients. And you need it for a good cause, so I'm open to doing it if we can agree on the terms."

"That sounds fair enough," he said, obviously pleased. "I have a contract that I use for this kind of thing. Do you have a fax?"

"No, I'm afraid not," she said with a little embarrassment. "I'm hopelessly out of date. Been meaning to get one for the longest time."

"Don't worry about that," he said sympathetically. "I can mail it to you, but I'd rather bring it over myself to get things moving. The reception is in about two weeks, so I'm in a big hurry."

"Two weeks?" she said with surprise. "You're right. That will be a bit of a rush."

"Will that be enough time for you?" He sounded worried.

"Yes, yes," she assured him. "I should be able to manage."

"So how about meeting for lunch? Is there a restaurant nearby that you like?"

"To tell you the truth, I usually grab a bite at my desk here. I hardly ever have the time to get out for lunch. Maybe once a week, if that."

"Well, which day will that be this week?" he asked.

Pearl chuckled. "You're persistent."

"When there's something I want, yes."

"I see," Pearl said. "OK. Hold on while I get my appointment book." Pearl stepped out to the receptionist's desk and grabbed her schedule. "This week is so full," she mumbled as she flipped the pages. "How about Friday?"

"That works for me. At noon?"

"I have a client coming on her lunch hour. But I can do it at one. Make it one-thirty. Do you like Italian?"

"It's my favorite."

"Good," she said. "There's a small place

nearby that makes great pasta."

"I'll see you then." Pearl hung up and a let out a deep breath of air. Only then did she realize how nervous she was the whole time she was talking to Patrick. What was the matter with her? He was married, and to Jolene Brown at that. And this was business. She kept repeating that to herself as she tidied up after lunch and called her next client.

Bradford rolled off of Jolene. "Oh, baby. That was fantastic," he said between deep gulps of air.

Jolene laughed in agreement. "The best."

As soon as her breathing slowed a bit, she propped up the pillows, leaned back and closed her eyes. This being a world-class hotel, there were six luscious pillows to snuggle into.

This was the happiest time of her life. No question about it. Bradford Bentley rocked her world. He could be as wild as a tiger one minute and gentle as a kitten the next. And the man had so much class.

She was madly in love. Plain and simple. Hell, if she had her way they'd both dump their spouses and head to Vegas for a quick marriage right this very minute.

But he hadn't told her how he felt about

her yet. And a man like Bradford could not be rushed. He had to take the lead, or at least think he was taking the lead. He had to tell her how he felt first. So she would have to be patient and play a perfect game if she wanted the big prize.

Bradford sat up and kissed her palm. She loved it when he did that. It sent tingles all up and down her spine.

"I'm glad we finally found each other," he whispered in her ear.

"So am I," she said softly. She loved the way he said sweet things like that. If only he would say the magic three words.

"I mean it. I had my eye on you for a while, but seeing as you were with Patrick, I didn't think I should interfere. So —"

"I had my eye on you, too, but you have Barbara."

"Well, if I had known we would click like this, I would have made a move a lot sooner."

Jolene snuggled closer to him. She loved the way he smelled. "Better late than never, I always say."

"Right you are. Wait there just a minute." He picked up his suit jacket from the back of a chair and fumbled around inside until he came up with a long rectangular navy box from Bailey Banks & Biddle.

She gasped before he even handed it to her and sat up excitedly. "For me?"

He got back in bed and leaned up on one elbow. "Go ahead. Open it."

She giggled as she lifted the jewelry case out and flipped the top. It was a white gold and sapphire bracelet. She placed her hand on her bare breast. "Oh, Bradford. It's beautiful."

"You like it?"

"I love it." She spread kisses all over his face. Then she lifted the bracelet and draped it around her wrist. She held it up to the light. Without a doubt, it had to be the most expensive piece of jewelry she'd ever worn. She would have preferred an "I love you" from him, but if this was the way he expressed his feelings, she could live with it. "It's gorgeous, Bradford. Fabulous."

"I'm glad you like it."

She rested her head on his shoulder. She loved the way he smelled even more now. "Bradford, there's something I've been wanting to say to you but —"

"What is it?" he asked as he draped an arm around her.

Should she? The feeling was so strong it felt like it would burst out of her chest if she didn't release it.

"I'm falling in love with you."

He sat up so abruptly her head fell off his shoulder.

Uh-oh. She'd made a big fool of herself. Fuck. "I didn't mean to scare you. Sorry." She moved away from him and stared straight ahead.

"You're not scaring me. I'm just surprised. I'm . . . I'm flattered, actually. Um, I think I'm falling for you, too."

"Really?" Jolene almost gulped. She couldn't believe her ears. He had said the magic words. Almost.

They slipped back down under the covers, and when they came up an hour later, Jolene thought she would die with happiness. She couldn't wait until Barbara went away, and they would finally get to spend some real time together.

"Where will we be going for the weekend?" she asked from the bathroom as they both dressed to get back to the office.

"Going?" Bradford asked from the bedroom.

Jolene stopped in the middle of putting on her lipstick and walked back into the bedroom. Had he forgotten already? "I thought you were going to get us a cabin in the mountains since Barbara's going down to Virginia to visit her aunt and uncle."

"Oh yeah, right," Bradford said. He

cleared his throat and bent over to tie his shoe.

Jolene's arms dropped to her side. "Well?" she asked nervously. "Is Barbara still leaving town or what?"

"Yeah, she's still going."

"Then what?" Jolene asked anxiously. "Don't tell me you decided to go with her."

He stood up and reached for his jacket. "No, no. I'm staying here."

Jolene sighed with relief, but it was short-lived. Had he changed his mind about spending the time with her? No, that didn't make sense. He had just told her he loved her, and she had a beautiful new bracelet on her arm to show for it. "Well, are we still going to get away together? I was looking forward to it."

"So was I, but I can't. Not this weekend. I thought I told you that I have to stick around here for some business meetings."

Jolene frowned. "On the weekend?"

"Afraid so. It can't be helped."

Dammit. What rotten luck. "Too bad," she said, struggling to keep her voice calm. "It would have been the first time we could spend more than a couple of hours to-gether."

"I know, baby. But this came up at the last minute. Anyway, we can still spend some time together Saturday night. We just can't go out of town. That will have to wait for another weekend."

"Can we go out for dinner or something? Someplace romantic. We've never been anywhere together except to hotels."

Bradford cleared his throat as he straightened his necktie. "You know I'd love nothing more than to take you out someplace nice for dinner. But we have to be real careful about that, baby, especially around here. Someone who knows Barbara or Patrick could see us."

Frankly, she wouldn't give a damn. Being with Bradford was worth the risk. But obviously he was going to need more time to come around. It was a pity, because she was so ready for this, for him. She didn't want to have to wait much longer. "I thought you said you loved me."

He stopped straightening his tie. "What?"

"If you really loved me, you wouldn't be so worried about who might see us."

"We have other people to think about, Jolene. I don't want to hurt anybody."

"You mean, like your wife? I didn't want to say this, but I have a hard time understanding why you're still with her." Jolene was beginning to feel as if she was singing a song on a broken record. She had gone through the same bull with Terrence. "I know you both grew up in the country, but you've grown so far beyond that, Bradford. And Barbara is, well, she's still such a country girl."

"Barbara's a good woman," he said patiently, going back to his necktie. "She's never done anything to hurt me."

"Well, neither have I," Jolene said pointedly. "You need someone more like yourself, and I could help you in your career. My family has a lot of connections. My father is a judge, two of my uncles are lawyers, and —"

"It's not about that. Barbara doesn't have those kinds of connections, no. But I can trust her, and I know she'll never leave me."

"You mean no matter how many times you cheat on her?" Jolene said sarcastically.

A look of irritation crossed his face. "And I know she'll never cheat on *me*. Barbara would never do that to her husband."

"What the hell is *that* supposed to mean?"

He sighed. "Look, I really enjoy our time together, Jolene. I always look forward to it. But let's face it. We're too damn much alike. Anything more than this would never work between us."

"I could change for the right person. Couldn't you?"

He shook his head in exasperation. "I also have Robin and Rebecca to think of. Leaving their mother would devastate them. You should understand that. You have a daughter."

He had ignored her question. Instead he was hiding behind his daughters. Excuses, excuses. She was so damn tired of the excuses. With Terrence it was his boys. Now it was Bradford's girls, even though they were grown women. What about *her* feelings? If he loved her the way she did him, he would be willing to risk others being hurt to be with her. She was willing to risk that with Patrick and even Juliette. They would all get over it soon enough. But apparently Bradford wasn't ready to take that step. And it would be suicide to push him.

"I understand about your daughters. I just want us to spend more time together. Is that so wrong?"

He put his hands on her arms. "Not at all," he said gently. "Come over to the house Saturday evening and stay the night. What will you tell Patrick?"

She shrugged. "I'll think of something. For a whole night with you, wild dogs wouldn't be able to keep me away."

He laughed and hugged her, then checked his watch. "We should get going. I've got a big meeting and —"

"I know. I know." At least she was going to be with him overnight. It looked like she was going to have to settle for that for now.

"Hello, may I speak to Grace Johnson, please?"

"Speaking."

Candice couldn't believe her luck. She had finally gotten around to calling Rose DuPree's son Joseph. A daughter named Thelma answered the phone and said that Joseph had died several months ago, but she suggested that Candice call his sister Grace, who was living in Northwest Washington, D.C. Thelma had said that Grace was in her nineties and her hearing was going bad but otherwise she was in good health.

"My name is Candice Jones. I got your number from Thelma Henry."

"My niece?"

"Yes."

"Oh, how is she? I haven't seen her in a while."

"I haven't met her, but I spoke to her on the phone and she sounded fine. Actually, I'm calling because I'm doing some research and —"

"You're doing what?"

Candice remembered that Thelma said

Grace's hearing was going bad, and she raised her voice. "I'm doing research on my family, and I'm looking for information about a man named George Blair."

"Oh? That was my uncle."

"Yes, yes. That's what Thelma said. I'm trying to find out if your uncle and my great-grandfather George were the same man." Candice also wanted to know a lot more about this family. Were they white or black? But that wasn't going to be so easy to determine over the phone. Like Thelma, Grace's voice was clear and proper, and the only accent she could detect was a Southern one.

"Where are you from?" Grace asked.

"I live in Maryland. But my ancestors lived in Virginia and Massachusetts."

"Mm-hmm. Then do you mind if I ask *you* something?"

Candice frowned. "No. Not at all."

"Was your George married to a woman named Marianne?"

Candice was so startled to hear this woman mention her great-grandmother's name that she nearly dropped the phone "Yes. Yes, he was," she said softly.

"Oh my," Grace said, her voice growing with excitement. "And her daughter Helen was your grandmother?"

Candice jumped up beside her bed. This

was too damn much — hearing a stranger mention her ancestors' names. "How . . . how did you know about Grandma Helen?"

"Because I knew that Uncle George and his wife had a daughter named Helen, although I never met any of them. My mother exchanged letters with George and used to talk about him all the time. She mentioned him the day she died."

Candice sat back down. "Really?"

"Oh yes. What else do you want to know, dear?"

"Um, anything you can tell me."

"Excuse me? Can you speak up?"

Candice knew she wasn't speaking loud enough for Grace. But she could barely find her voice. "Yes," she said louder. "Listen, from what Thelma told me, I'm not that far from you. Would it be all right if I came by?"

"Of course, dear. It's so hard for me to hear on the phone, anyway. Come over, and I'll tell you everything I know. We always wondered what happened to that side of the family."

As she took down the address, Candice wondered exactly what Grace's last comment meant. There was something about the way she had said "*that* side of the family."

Chapter 26

The Lincoln Town Car came to a screeching halt, and Lee felt herself being shoved out violently. She hit the pavement on her hands and knees with a thud, and the car took off.

She jumped up. "Come back here, you punk-ass thief," she yelled. "I want my damn money. I'll go get my man on you, and he'll put his foot up yo' ass, motha fucka. For real."

It dawned on her that she was ranting at thin air. She shut up and stomped the pavement. She paced up and down. "Shit. Fucking thieves. Coming up in here with that crap." She was sick and tired of it. Her gun was right there in her shoulder bag, and she was going to take out the next sucker who did this to her.

She remembered the first time she thought about blowing someone away. She had been fed up with his crap, too.

"If you ever say one fucking word about this to your mama or anybody else, I'll put a foot up yo' brother's black ass till it's blue. And then I'll throw all of you niggas out on the street. You, Vernon, your fat-ass mama, all y'all. You got that, bitch?"

Uncle Clive stood above her and slowly zipped up his pants as she lay crumpled in a heap on the bathroom floor, her face buried in her hands. She sniffed.

He kicked her in the gut. "Answer me, bitch, unless you want your baby brother sleeping on the pavement. Do we understand each other?"

Lee nodded.

"Good. And quit that sniffling. I ain't hurt you. This woulda happened to you sooner or later anyhow. Shit. Damn ugly thing like you ought to be glad somebody would even look at your black ass."

She never told her mama. She was too scared of what Uncle Clive would do. But she did tell her best friend at school, a boy everybody called Mookie and who was a year older than she. Mookie got mad and threatened to "break that punk's fucking face." When she said that would only make Clive mad and then he would come after her, Mookie vowed to "blow his scrawny ass away." She begged him not to, so he offered to get her a gun to protect herself. Said he could hook her up for twenty bucks. She told him he was crazy. She didn't know nothing about no guns and didn't want to.

Then Uncle Clive did it again one Saturday afternoon a week later when Mama was waiting tables and Vernon was back in the bedroom playing with one of his toy action figures.

Uncle Clive came home unexpectedly just after she and Vernon had finished lunch and snuck up on her in the kitchen while she washed the dishes. He grabbed her hair extensions and pulled her back into the bathroom, with her fighting him all the way. She couldn't scream because she didn't want to scare Vernon, and Uncle Clive knew it.

She vowed never to be at home alone with Uncle Clive again. After school, she would pick up Vernon and hang out with Mookie or her girlfriends until ten or eleven, getting in just before Mama came home around midnight. She made Vernon promise not to tell.

One morning Mookie convinced her not to go to school at all. He hot-wired a car at Landover Mall, and they went joyriding until it was time to pick up Vernon at school. Then they went to Roy Rogers for dinner and rode around and smoked joints while Vernon did his homework in the backseat. Mookie dropped them off at the house at about the usual hour.

She did this for several days until Mama came home early one Friday and caught her. Mama was waiting in the living room in her work clothes when Lee walked in the door holding Vernon by the hand. Mama reached out and snatched Vernon away from her.

"Where you been all this time, girl? I been calling all over the place looking for y'all."

"What you trippin' for, Ma? I picked Vernon up after I left school just like I always do, and we went out to eat."

Mama shook a finger in Lee's face. "Don't you lie to me. The school called and said you ain't been there all week."

Oops. Lee shrugged. "Ain't no big deal. I was just out rolling with Mookie."

"Didn't I tell you I didn't want you hanging around that trash? He looks like a fool, with that stupid black stocking cap on his head all the time and his pants hanging down to his knees. And where did he get a car? He ain't but sixteen."

Lee folded her arms defiantly. "It belongs to his daddy."

Mama narrowed her eyes. "Girl, you better not be lying to me. I don't know what's gotten into you lately — cutting school and staying out half the night. And your grades bad enough to make me want to cry."

Lee scoffed.

"Well, I'll tell you one thing, Miss Smarty-Pants. This better not happen again. If the school ever calls me or I find out you not coming home after school, girl, you gonna be real sorry. And I'm gonna call here and check on you every day."

Lee's arms dropped. She clenched her fists. "But I don't like it here. I —"

"Shut up. Did I ask what you liked? You come straight home from school and do your homework."

"But Mama, you don't —"

"I said shut up. I'm your mama. You do what I say."

Lee folded her arms.

That night, while Uncle Clive showered and Mama lounged on the couch watching TV, Lee tiptoed into the bedroom and found Clive's wallet sitting on a table. It was thick with bills, probably drug money, and she didn't think he would miss one twenty. The following Monday, she took Mookie up on his offer to get her a gun.

She would come home from school every day just as her mama wanted, then go straight to the drawer holding her two prize possessions — the photo of her daddy and the revolver. She would sit at the kitchen table, hide the gun behind one of her textbooks and dare Uncle Clive to come home and mess with her.

Lee looked down at her knees. They were scraped and bleeding from the fall onto the pavement. She damn sure couldn't turn any more tricks all bloody like this. She had to go to her place and get cleaned up. Tony was going to be mad at her if he found out, but what else could she do?

It was a one-room affair that she shared with two other girls who worked for Tony.

There was a sink in one corner and a much used bed in another. In the middle of the room stood a wobbly table and two chairs. She had stacked some cardboard boxes on one wall to keep her things in. They shared a shower and toilet down the hall with four other apartment units.

She removed her fake fur jacket and washed and dried the cuts on her knees. Then she picked up a brush lying on the edge of the sink and raised it to her head to spruce up her hair extensions. But she saw her reflection in the mirror, and her arm dropped to her side. The way she had aged over the past several months wasn't funny. She was sixteen now but looked closer to thirty.

Shit. How had this happened? The last time she could remember being happy was more than a year ago, before they moved in with Uncle Clive. Now she was a damn whore living in a fucking hole in the wall that was even worse than Uncle Clive's place.

This was all Mama's fault. Mama was smart about a lot of things, but she was dumb as a dog about dudes. Lee threw her brush at the boxes stacked against a wall. She kicked one, then another. They fell and her clothes spilled out — skimpy tops and booty shorts — stuff she wouldn't have dared wear before. It was disgusting, all of it.

She stomped over the clothes and kicked them until she came across the snapshot of her daddy and mama. She stopped and stooped down to pick it up, then stared into her daddy's smiling face, probably for the thousandth time. She turned it over, hoping to find some new clue about him, but the only thing it said was "Smokey, Silver Lake, Maryland."

At night, whenever she had trouble sleeping, she would think about her daddy smiling in the photo. She wanted to find him so bad. But she had no idea where this Silver Lake was, and even if she could find it her daddy might not be living there anymore. Or he might not want to see her.

She set the photo down and put her jacket back on.

Chapter 27

Patrick strode through the door of Pearl's salon on Friday at exactly one-thirty. He unbuttoned his all-weather coat and stood off to the side with his hands in the pockets of his slacks, and Pearl smiled. He looked odd in a room full of women getting their hair done. Cute, but odd.

She was rinsing the conditioner out of a client's hair and nodded toward him to let him know she'd seen him. She put a plastic cap over the woman's head and sat her under a dryer. Then she removed her salon smock and grabbed her black leather jacket off the rack and slipped into it, all the while giving instructions to her assistant on how to finish up. She told the receptionist she would be back in about an hour, and they stepped outside into one of the Washington, D.C., metro area's mild winter afternoons. Patrick pointed at his car and walked ahead to open the passenger-side door for her.

"It's a nice day, and the restaurant is only about four blocks from here," Pearl said. "Are you up for a short walk?" She could use the exercise, she thought. She had dropped eight pounds since starting her diet and was real proud of herself.

"Sounds good to me," he said. "I love to walk."

"It must be nearly sixty degrees out here," she said as she unbuttoned her jacket.

He removed his coat and flung it across his shoulder. "I'm not complaining. I'm more than ready for summer. It's my favorite time of year."

"Mine too," she said.

"I started to get into a little golf last summer. It will be good to get back out there again to practice my swing." He made a little motion with his arms. "Do you play?"

She shook her head. "I always wanted to learn but I never have the time. First it was my son eating up all my time, now it's the salon. I'm lucky if I can get a garden going in the summer."

She wondered what he thought of big women like herself. Some men liked them. Others wouldn't touch them. Not that she should even care what he thought. This was a business lunch, and he was a married man. She was having to remind herself of that a lot more than she should.

"That must be tough," he said.

"What? Running a salon?"

"That too, but I meant raising your son alone."

She chuckled. "Oh Lord. There were days when I wanted to pull out every hair on my head, I kid you not." There were still days like that, she thought wryly as Ashley came to mind. "But with patience and a little help from the Lord, I managed."

"Did his dad help much?"

"Humph. Not one bit. But I think I did pretty good by myself. Kenyatta graduated from college and he's got a good job." Never mind that he was in love with a white woman. Hopefully, that would pass.

"You should be proud of yourself."

Pearl shrugged. "You do what you have to when it comes to your children. How many do you have? I know you have at least one daughter."

"Just the one. Her name is Juliette."

"Right. I've seen her around the neighborhood. How old is she?"

"Fourteen going on twenty."

Pearl laughed. "She's a beautiful girl. So poised."

He smiled with obvious pride. "Thanks. She's the light of my life. Just hate to see them grow up."

"Tell me about it. Enjoy her while you can. Here it is," she said as they approached an Italian restaurant on a corner.

"Let's eat and talk cake." He held the

door open for her.

The restaurant was small, with only a half dozen tables. The owner knew Pearl and greeted her warmly. She asked for a quiet table, and he sat them in a corner. They talked about business, P. G. County politics and their families, and before she knew it an hour had whizzed by.

Patrick was a pleasant surprise. He was nothing like she would have expected, given that he was married to Jolene Brown. She had been around Jolene only a few times and that was more than enough, since the woman always acted like she didn't think Pearl was good enough for her. But Patrick was so easygoing and down to earth. She felt comfortable with him immediately.

Why was it that men always went for women like Jolene and only wanted to be friends with women like herself? They loved the ones who dressed like whores and flaunted every physical asset they had and acted like bitches half the time. Pearl didn't understand it.

They stood up and shook hands over the cake deal, then he walked her back to the salon. He took her hand at the door and smiled warmly. He had a kind smile, with perfectly shaped lips and a thin, neat mustache. That million-dollar smile would do him a world of good in politics. And those mischievous eyes would do him a world of good with women. Whoa. What was she doing analyzing his mouth and eyes?

"I enjoyed that," he said.

She smiled and lowered her gaze. For some strange reason, he made her feel shy. And at her age, not many folks could do that.

She realized he was still holding her hand. She wanted to pull away but she didn't. She cleared her throat. "Well, I better get going." Yes indeed. She needed to get out of there. It was starting to feel hot, and she was sure her hand must be getting clammy. But he held on.

"This is going to sound strange, Pearl," he said slowly, "and I don't want you to take it the wrong way, but . . ."

He paused, and she glanced down the block. What on earth was he about to say to her? She cleared her throat. She was tempted to yank her hand away and run into the safety of her salon.

"I really enjoy talking to you. For some reason I don't feel I have to put on an act around you, and I find that refreshing."

"Well, thank you. I, um, I like talking to you, too." No harm in saying that, right? He probably just wanted to be her friend.

That's all most men wanted from her anyway.

He was still holding her hand. Why was he holding her hand?

"Can I call you sometime?" he asked.

What did *that* mean? They had a business deal. She was gonna bake half a dozen cakes for him. Of course he could call her. No harm in that.

"Yes," she said softly.

"Yes?" He leaned down to make sure he'd heard right. "You mean . . . I mean, I'd like to see you again. Socially." He smiled.

Socially? As in a date? He couldn't possibly mean that. But he did and she knew darn good and well he did. Lord. She was so out of practice with this stuff. He meant call, take her out and get to know her. Of course she could never agree to that. Of course she had to say no to that. Of course . . .

"That's fine. I'd like that, too." What the heck was she saying? Did her brain just fall out of her head and roll down the sidewalk?

He squeezed her hand, then let it go, finally. He held the door open for her. "I'll call you over the weekend, maybe on Sunday after church," he said. "Just to talk."

She smiled her consent, and he turned

and walked to his car. She stood in the picture window near the plant he'd bought for her and watched until he pulled away from the curb. So he was a churchgoing brother. She liked that. Yes, she really liked that.

"Pearl. Pearl."

She realized that the receptionist was calling her name and holding up her phone messages. *Get a hold of yourself, girl.* She patted her short hairdo in place, took the pink slips and called her next client. She sat the woman in her salon chair, and they chatted, or rather the client did. Fortunately, it was Dawn, who could pretty much carry on a conversation all by herself. Pearl just smiled and nodded as she put on her smock and Dawn talked about her job, her kids and everything else in between.

She was rusty, that was it. It had been so long since an attractive man had paid her any attention that she didn't even know how to act. That was the only way to explain her behavior. What she had just done was plain stupid, not at all like her.

Humph. She would straighten this mess out as soon as he called. If he called. He probably wouldn't even contact her, except about the cakes. Look at her. Fat, boring. She would be shocked if he asked her out.

She shook out a towel and draped it

around the client's shoulders. She took a deep breath. She had to put all these thoughts about Patrick aside. Right now she had a job to do.

"So how have you been, Dawn?"

Dawn stopped in mid-sentence and stared at Pearl. "Girl, have you heard a word I just said?"

Jolene was beginning to realize that getting a man to leave his wife was tough as hell. She had been with Terrence for months and couldn't pull it off. It was starting to look like a repeat with Bradford.

She wiped her sweaty forehead with the towel draped around her shoulders, then increased the incline on the treadmill. Bradford claimed he didn't love his wife, but he was still married. So go figure. Why did he insist on sticking with Barbara? Especially now that he knew *she* was available.

Bradford had said that he didn't think the marriage would survive another affair if Barbara found out about it. Unfortunately, the wife was usually the last to know about these things. She had always wondered why Terrence's wife never became suspicious, even when he was with her two or three evenings a week.

Maybe she should give Barbara a little

nudge, open her eyes up to what was really going on behind her back. If Barbara knew that Bradford was up to his old tricks, maybe she would leave him. But how in the world could she accomplish that without implicating herself?

Chapter 28

Candice climbed out of her Ford Taurus and popped her umbrella open. It had been raining all day and she had to step carefully as she walked up the wet path to the house on Kansas Avenue. It was a tidy little brick affair in the middle of a block of row houses. The lawn was trimmed neatly, and the porch was covered in grass carpeting that had recently been swept clean.

She walked up the short flight of stairs to the porch and shook out the umbrella, then raised her hand to the doorbell and paused. Her nerves were all over the place. She took a deep breath and pressed the button.

She heard a thump, a door shutting or something, and then soft footsteps on a wood floor. The front door opened and an elderly woman peeked out from behind the screen door. She was black with a medium complexion and pure white hair pinned back in a bun. Her skin was wrinkled but had a soft dewy texture. She had warm brown eyes and a youthful smile.

Candice had prepared for this moment, thinking out all the possibilities. The minute she reached the neighborhood, she thought the family living in it was probably black. But just because a distant cousin was black didn't mean that her great-grandfather George was black. This woman could have been adopted. Rose could have been white and married a black man. Anything could have happened. It was not yet time to panic.

Candice smiled. "Mrs. Johnson?"

"Yes. And you must be Candice Jones?"

Candice nodded.

Grace Johnson unlatched and opened the screen door. "Come on in," she said. "And get out of the rain. Such nasty weather we're having. May I take your coat?"

"Yes, the weather has been awful." If Grace was at all surprised that Candice was white, she didn't show it. Candice wasn't sure what that meant. This was all so confusing.

Grace hung her coat up on a rack near the door and led Candice into a small living room. It was filled with wood furniture that had been well kept over the years. A Persian carpet covered most of the floor. Handmade doilies graced the arms of the couch and a stuffed armchair. And an old console television sat up against a wall.

"Can I get you something?" Grace asked. "Some water or a soda?"

"No thanks. I'm fine." Immediately she regretted not asking for something. Her throat was like gravel, but she wanted to get on with this.

She sat on the couch and Grace sat in the armchair across from her. "My daughter had to go out. I'm sorry about that because I wanted you to meet her."

Candice smiled. "I'm sorry I missed her."

"Another time maybe. So. You wanted to hear about Uncle George, right?"

Just hearing that name coming from this woman's lips sent a shudder up Candice's spine. She nodded. "Yes."

Grace clasped her hands together in her lap, and Candice noticed that she was holding a white lace handkerchief.

"Well, let's see. As you know, George and my mother were brother and sister. After his first wife died — she died pretty young and I never knew her name — George moved up north, where he met his second wife, a woman named Marianne. I believe you said they were your great-grandparents when we spoke on the phone?"

Candice nodded. Strangely enough, she felt so calm. It was like she was having an out-of-body experience. Here she was sitting across from a ninety-something-year-old black woman and they had some of the same ancestors. She was a sweet, charming woman, but a black woman nevertheless.

"Do you know anything about George's parents?" Candice asked.

Grace nodded and dabbed her cheeks with the handkerchief. "His father's name was Andrew Blair. He owned a plantation outside Richmond and he also had a city mansion in Richmond."

Candice sat up eagerly. If Andrew owned that much land, it confirmed that he was white. "And he was married twice, right?"

Grace shook her head and fiddled with the edges of her handkerchief. "As far as I know, he had only one wife. He never re-married after she died."

Candice frowned. "But based on my research at the National Archives, a woman named Caroline showed up as his first wife, and Sara was his second wife. She . . ." Candice paused. A strange look had come over Grace's face.

"Sara wasn't his wife, dear," Grace said softly as she twirled the handkerchief around her fingers. "She was a slave."

It felt like the couch had collapsed underneath her. Candice chuckled nervously. "Whatever makes you say that?"

"Well, my mother told me, of course. You see . . ." Grace looked down at the handkerchief and opened it flat on her lap. Candice wished she'd leave the damn thing alone and go on with what she was about to say.

"Andrew Blair had two families, really. His white family and his black family. He and his slave Sara had two children together, my mother, Rose, and George." Grace looked at Candice, her jaw set firmly.

Candice stared at the woman in disbelief. She shook her head. No, no. Impossible. This woman was saying that her great-great-grandfather cheated with a slave right under his wife's nose? "That . . . that doesn't make sense. I don't see how he could have managed that. I mean —"

"Well, from what I've learned, it wasn't all that uncommon. Although Mama used to say that after a while Andrew's wife refused to go to the plantation. She stayed in Richmond at the city home. So he kept Sara and her children on the plantation, and his wife and her daughters in Richmond, and he would travel back and forth."

Candice realized that she was sitting so far on the edge of her seat that she was damn near about to fall off. She sat back and chuckled, more from bad nerves than from anything funny. Certainly there was nothing remotely amusing about this. "That's quite a story," Candice said.

"I'm sorry," Grace said sympathetically. "You really didn't know about Sara, did you?"

Candice closed her eyes. "No. No, I didn't."

"I really am sorry you had to find out this way."

"I think I'll take something to drink now," Candice said with a deep sigh. "May I have a glass of water, please?"

"Certainly." Grace stood and left the room.

"Oh hell," Candice muttered. This story was so far-fetched, and yet all the missing pieces seemed to fall into place. What should she do now?

Grace returned with a tall glass of ice water, and Candice drank half of it. "Um, do . . . do you have any proof of all this? I don't mean to doubt you, it's just that I . . . I . . . this is so unexpected for me and —"

Grace held out her hand. "Wait here a minute. I have something I can show you."

She walked off and Candice held the cool glass up to her forehead. Right now she could use a real drink but this would have to do.

Grace returned with an envelope and sat in the armchair. She pulled out a photo and handed it to Candice. It was a black-and-white picture of a dark-complexioned black woman with her hair tied up in a scarf. She wore what looked like a long dress made of muslin or cotton. Her face was devoid of expression, but her eyes looked weary and wise.

"That's Sara," Grace said softly.

Candice nodded. Of course. She smiled thinly.

"Would you like a copy?" Grace asked. "It's the only one we have, but I'm sure I can get my daughter to have a copy made for you."

Candice looked down at the photo again. It was hard to believe that the woman in this photo was related to her. No, she had seen and heard enough. She didn't need the photo. She held it out toward Grace.

"No, thank you. But I do appreciate you showing it to me. Um, this is all so confusing, and I . . ." Candice's voice trailed off. What could she say? Nothing made sense anymore.

"May I get you another glass of water?" Grace asked. "All the color's drained out of your face."

"Yes, please." Candice watched Grace leave the room and wondered if she would ever be able to gather the strength to get up and walk out. Even if she did, it wouldn't be her, Candice Jones. It would be some other woman with some other life, some other past. It would be a black woman who looked white.

Grace returned with another tall glass of water, and Candice gulped it down.

"Are you feeling any better, dear?"

Hell, no, Candice wanted to shout. She felt lousy. But she nodded to reassure the woman.

"You know," Grace said thoughtfully, "we always wondered what happened to that side of the family after George moved up north. We knew that he had married and had children but we never met any of them. We suspected that George was passing and that maybe that was why he kept the two families apart."

Candice frowned. "Passing?"

"Passing for white."

"Oh. Right. But why would he do that? I don't understand."

"Maybe he thought it would let him lead a better life. It happened more than people realize."

"Do you think George's second wife, Marianne, believed that George was white?" Candice asked.

"Probably, since he never brought her back to visit his family in Virginia."

"Jesus," Candice murmured under her breath.

Grace stood and walked to a side table. She picked up a photo framed in silver and brought it to Candice. "This is my mother and father, Rose and Peter."

Candice took the photo. So this was Rose. It was a formal portrait of an attractive couple dressed for a special occasion. And if she hadn't been told otherwise, she would have assumed that the woman was white or ethnic. She handed it back to Grace. "Very nice."

"It was taken in the 1930s, I think. My father had retired by then."

"What kind of work did he do?" Candice asked.

"He was a physician," Grace said as she sat back down. "As was my husband. My mother was a teacher, and so was I."

"Oh? That's impressive."

"We are a family of high achievers," Grace said proudly. "You can see that although my mother could have passed, she chose not to. George hurt my mother deeply by doing that, and I don't think she ever really got over it."

Candice raised her eyebrows. How about what he had done to *her* family? What he was still doing to them from his grave. Her family had been living a lie all these years. "At least you knew who you were and where you came from. We didn't, apparently."

"My mother felt as if her brother was ashamed of her. They were very close before he left for Massachusetts, but he never talked much about his life up there whenever he came back to visit. So she assumed that he was passing and that we weren't good enough for him and his new life. Never mind that her husband was a doctor and she was a teacher. To have your own brother reject you for that . . . well, it really hurt Mother."

Candice nodded. It was strange to think how the horrors of slavery were still hanging over all of their lives even today. Or maybe not so strange. "I see how that would have hurt your mother."

Grace cleared her throat. "Well, I'm forgetting my manners, getting so emotional and running my mouth." She dabbed her face with her handkerchief. "This must all be extremely difficult for you."

"To tell you the truth, it is. Could you imagine waking up one day to find that you aren't really black? Nor your children? There are no words to describe how I'm feeling now."

"It must be terrible, what you're going through."

"It's going to take me a while to sort it out, but I thank you for your time. You've been very helpful." Candice stood up.

"I was glad to do it," Grace said as they walked to the front door. "You said you have daughters?"

Candice nodded. "Two."

"How old are they?"

"Fifteen and nineteen. How many children do you have?"

Grace smiled broadly. "Two children, five grandchildren and six great-grandchildren."

"You must be very proud."

"Oh, yes. One of my grandchildren is a very successful author. Two are doctors and another one is a lawyer. The youngest is in college at Stanford University. Yes, I'm very proud of all of them. Sometimes I think, If only George could see us now."

Candice smiled, and Grace opened the door.

"Thank you again for your time," Candice said.

"Oh, no problem at all. And if you have any more questions, feel free to call me any-time."

The smile disappeared from Candice's

face as soon as she stepped out onto the front porch. She pulled up the collar to her coat, popped her umbrella open and dashed out into a downpour. She jumped into her car and threw the umbrella onto the backseat, then sat and stared out the front window into the rain.

Grace had talked about her children with such pride and wished that George could see how they had turned out. Candice wished that he could see how he had turned *her* life upside down.

Candice walked down the aisle of CVS drugstore until she came upon boxes and boxes of do-it-yourself hair-coloring kits. Clairol, Revlon, L'Oréal. They all wanted to help her live a new life as a blonde.

She read the labels and studied the faces on some of the boxes, but that only confused her since she had never dyed her hair before. She finally just grabbed one and headed for the cashier.

She stood in line, looked down at the box in her hand and almost laughed out loud. This was totally insane. All her life she had been a natural brunette and happy for it. Did she really want to do something this crazy on the spur of the moment?

She looked back up with determination.

Yes, she wanted to do this. She *had* to do this. A dramatic change was exactly what she needed now, and what could be more dramatic than becoming a blonde?

Chapter 29

Barbara sat her handbag and luggage down in the foyer and picked up a pile of mail addressed to her. Bradford had never showed up at her aunt's house, and she'd had to do all the driving down to Smithfield and back herself. But that was fine. It had been good to get away from everything. She was tired after all the driving, but her mind was refreshed.

Most of the mail was junk, the usual promotions from American Express, Saks Jandel and the like. She tossed several of the envelopes out without even bothering to open them. Just as she put the mail down and picked up her suitcase, Bradford came in from his study. He kissed her on the cheek and took her Gucci bag. She smiled. It was good to be home.

"Aunt Gladys and Uncle Marvin missed you," she said.

Bradford shrugged. "Sorry I couldn't make it. But you understand how it is with work."

"I try to," she said as they headed up the back stairs to the master bedroom suite.

"How was the trip?" he asked. "How's Aunt Gladys? And your uncle?"

"They're fine. She's getting a bit forgetful, but a little arthritis is her only complaint. They said to tell you hello and that they'll look for you next year."

"Uh huh. Well, glad they're OK then."

"Yes, thank goodness," Barbara said as she dumped her purse on the bed and Bradford deposited the luggage in her walk-in closet. "I don't have to worry about her yet. So, where's Robin?"

"At the library studying."

Barbara nodded. "Did your meetings go well?"

He smiled. "They went just fine. I was wrapping up some things in the den just now."

"Good. I'm going to check my e-mail and take a nap. I'm really tired."

"I gave Phyllis the weekend off and Robin said she won't be home for dinner, so I'll order in some Chinese. How's that sound?"

"Perfect."

"I'll let you know when the food gets here," he said, and headed toward the door.

"Oh, I wanted to remind you that my class starts tomorrow night."

Bradford paused and frowned. "What class?"

She stared at him in disbelief. "The real estate class I'm taking. Remember?"

A flicker of recognition crossed his face. "Oh, that."

"Yes, *that*." She couldn't believe he had forgotten, especially since she had reminded him just before she left for Smithfield. "Honestly, Bradford."

"So you're really going through with it, then?"

"Yes, I told you that."

"Fine, fine. I'll be in my study."

She rolled her eyes to the ceiling and kicked off her heels, then entered her dressing room and unbuttoned her suit jacket. It was frustrating that Bradford could so easily forget something that was important to her. She had thought about the class all through the drive home. It would give her life new meaning. Yet he couldn't even remember she was taking it.

She sighed as she slipped into a floor-length robe and slippers, then strode into the sitting room adjoining the bedroom and sat at the small desk. Her e-mail always piled up when she was out of town, and it was one of the ways she stayed in touch with Rebecca.

While waiting for the mail to download, Barbara glanced up at a painting by Alix Baptiste that she and Bradford had picked up at the painter's gallery in Savannah,

Georgia, several years back. It was a Haitian scene in greens and yellows and oranges, and always brought back memories of their condo in Nassau. They hadn't been down there in ages, and it would be nice to get away with Bradford now that they were getting along so much better. Maybe she would suggest a trip together over dinner tonight.

Something coming across the laptop caught her eye and she looked down. The first message had a photograph attached, and she hoped that it was from Rebecca. She was always sending happy-looking pictures of Ralph and herself through e-mail. Barbara smiled in anticipation and scrolled down the screen.

Whoa. She frowned and leaned in more closely. This definitely wasn't from Rebecca. It was a photo of a man's white briefs and a woman's black bra and G-string sprawled across a king-size bed. A pair of faux animal print mules lay on the carpet. There were at least a half dozen similar photos to follow. Barbara twisted her lips in disgust.

Obviously, this was more of that ridiculous junk porn mail. It was getting out of hand. She moved the cursor up to the delete icon to get rid of the offensive trash, but just as she was about to press the mouse button, something dawned on her. She looked closer.

That was *her* king-size bed in the photo.

She leaned back in the chair, breathless. What on earth was going on here? How the hell did someone get a picture of her bedroom? And how did they get that underwear in with the picture? She covered her mouth with her hand. Oh my God. This was frightening.

She sat back up and scrolled quickly through each of the photos. Her bedroom was in all of them. Every one. She blew one up to twice the original size and looked at it closely. Yes, that was definitely her bed. Her nightstand. Her carpet. She could even see the Stuart Weitzman label in the animal print mules next to the bed.

She jumped up so suddenly her chair fell over backward and landed with a thud just as Robin passed by the sitting room. Robin doubled back and stuck her head in the door.

"What's wrong, Mama? I heard something fall."

Barbara quickly moved to block the monitor from Robin's view. "It's nothing. I . . . I just knocked the chair over. I thought you were at the library."

"I finished up early. Are you sure you're

all right? You have a funny expression on your face."

"I'm fine," Barbara said, trying to smile.

"Well, welcome back. What's for dinner?"

"Your father is ordering Chinese. Better go down and tell him you're back so he'll be sure to get enough."

Robin left and Barbara whirled around to face the monitor. This was scaring her. She had to tell Bradford. He would know what to do. Someone was spying on them and harassing them and . . . and . . .

Wait a minute. She leaned down toward the monitor. There was a copy of yesterday's *Washington Post* lying on the bed in all of the photos. How did that get there? What kind of trick was this?

Unless . . . unless someone was here yesterday and actually took these pictures. Was that possible? Could this be the work of another one of Bradford's mistresses? Or Sabrina again?

She picked the chair up and sat back down. She stared at the laptop monitor, her mouth hanging open. She didn't get it. She and Bradford seemed to be doing so much better. He had sworn to her that those days were over.

Maybe the photos had been doctored.

She'd bet that with the Internet and computers, it was a whole lot easier to do something like that these days. Someone could be trying to dupe her, to get her angry at her husband. It wouldn't be the first time that some woman who wanted Bradford had tried something wicked to get him. She'd had phone calls in the middle of the night, letters, G-strings in her bed. Now this.

Dammit. She did not want to deal with this anymore. Her husband said he had changed, and she was going to believe him, not some phony photos.

She pressed the delete button, again and again. Whoever sent her this filthy trash wasn't going to get away with it. She switched the computer off, slipped out of her robe and climbed into bed.

Thirty minutes later she was still tossing and turning.

Was he cheating on her? Again?

Was he up to his old tricks?

She sat up straight and pounded the bedcovers with her fists. She lit a cigarette. Damn that man. Even if he wasn't, it was his fault that she thought he might be. It was his fault for all the times when he really *was* cheating on her.

God, she couldn't take much more of this. She placed the cigarette in an ashtray on the nightstand, reached for the drawer and yanked it open.

"Ouch!" Dammit. She had broken a nail on the drawer handle. She yanked the nail off, then glanced down at the bottle of Belvedere vodka, half buried by all the clutter. It had been in that drawer for so long that it didn't usually register when she opened it. But it did just now, because she was looking for it.

She shoved aside paperback novels and stationery and grabbed the bottle. She held it up. Good old Mister Belvedere, her beloved companion on many lonely days and nights. She ran her fingers over the surface. She loved the satiny finish and elegant design.

One sip. One sip was all she needed, and then she would never take another one as long as she lived. She wanted to feel that burning sensation flowing through her veins just once more. It had been so long since she'd had a drink, almost three years now. One teeny-weeny taste couldn't hurt. She ran into the master bathroom and came back to the nightstand with a glass. She could use some ice but she didn't want to tip off Bradford or Robin.

She poured a shot and lifted the glass to her lips. Her tongue greeted the drink like a long-lost love. She closed her eyes and held on to the sensation as it flowed through her body. Then she went into the bathroom and washed out the glass.

She buried the bottle in the drawer and climbed back into bed. The telephone rang just as she dozed off. Dammit. She reached out and grabbed the receiver. "Hello?" she said curtly.

"Hi. It's me."

"Oh. Hi, Marilyn."

"I was checking to see if you got back OK."

"Yes, yes, I'm back."

"Did Bradford mention the big contract he helped James get? James is thrilled about it and he wants to get something special for Bradford. Any suggestions? We were thinking of a new golf bag or —"

"Not now, please, Marilyn." The last thing Barbara needed now was someone fawning over her husband. Bradford this, Bradford that. If only they knew what he put her through. "I'm really tired."

"Oh, sorry," Marilyn said. "I'll call back another time. Don't forget about class tomorrow night."

"Now how would I forget that?" Barbara snapped. "I'll be there."

Long silence. "Is everything all right, Barbara?"

Barbara checked herself. She couldn't believe she had just been so rude. Marilyn had helped her enroll in the real estate course and was only trying to be of help. "Everything is fine, Marilyn. I'm just tired from the trip." And tired of all the nonsense with Bradford.

Chapter 30

Pearl was still wearing the new black pantsuit she had bought for church to celebrate dropping fifteen pounds and flipping through the latest issue of *Essence* when Kenyatta strolled into the living room and sat next to her on the couch. It was a wonder he was up and dressed, even if it was in blue jeans and a Morehouse sweatshirt. Try as she might, it was impossible to talk him into going to church with her. He had this New Age belief that one could worship without going to Mass, and supposedly Ashley felt the same way. Pearl thought it was just an excuse to sleep in on Sundays.

"You should come over to BET with me for brunch," he suggested.

"You're not going with Ashley?" Pearl asked. Dare she hope that things were cooling off between those two?

"I'm going to run a few errands and then meet her there," he said. "You should join us."

Humph. So much for things cooling off between them. "Oh well. You go on. I don't think I feel like going back out. I baked cakes all day yesterday for a political reception, then got up early this morning for church. I'll just fix some bacon and eggs here."

He stood up. "You sure? Ashley would love to see you."

Sorry, son, but the feeling was not mutual. She was in no mood to sit around eating and trying to make conversation with that white child today. *I broke bread with her once to make you happy. And once is enough.* "Maybe another time."

"What is it, Ma?"

Pearl's lips tightened. "You already know how I feel. I don't need to tell you again."

"Damn, Ma. Why you gotta be like that?"

"Sorry. I guess I'm just too old to change my ways."

"That's crap. You're just too stubborn to change is more like it."

She shrugged. "Maybe."

He grabbed his Wizards cap from the coffee table. "Fine. We're going to hang out after we eat, so I won't be back until late tonight."

He walked out and slammed the door shut. Pearl smacked her lips. He was calling *her* stubborn? Look at him. He was determined to be with that girl no matter what. Pearl didn't understand it.

She found it even harder to believe she

was staying at home waiting for a phone call from some man, and a married man at that. She sighed. She had to admit to herself that was the *real* reason she didn't want to go out. And she was too ashamed to tell her son the truth.

She tossed the magazine on the coffee table and folded her arms. Patrick had phoned her every afternoon since their lunch meeting, but now that the political reception was over he had no reason to call her. She should have gone to brunch with Kenyatta. It wasn't every day that he asked her to go out with him, even if it was with Ashley.

Maybe there was still time to catch Kenyatta before he pulled out of the driveway. She stood up just as the phone rang. Oh shoot. She should try to catch Kenyatta and let the machine pick up. That would be the wise thing to do. But who said she was wise?

She ran into the kitchen and grabbed the cordless phone. She just wanted to hear his voice. If it was him.

"Hello?"

"Hi. It's Patrick."

Her breathing was heavy from running to catch the phone. *Calm down, girl.* "Hi."

"Are you OK, Pearl? You sound like

you're out of breath."

How embarrassing. "Um, I was in the other room, and I had to run to catch the phone."

"Oh, so, um, how are things going?"

She smiled. He seemed as unsure about this thing between them as she was. "Fine. Just got back from church. How was the reception last night?"

"A big hit, especially dessert. I'm just glad it's over. I've got a little more time now, at least until the next event. So, how about brunch? I'm at the office now but I could swing by and get you."

She sighed. She couldn't. Talking on the phone was one thing, meeting for brunch another. "I . . . I don't think so, Patrick. I may go and meet my son for brunch. He just left the house."

"Oh. Maybe another time then."

"Yes. Another time. Well, no, actually. Um, listen. I really don't feel right about this whole thing with us. So —"

"Why not? We're just getting to know each other. No harm in that."

"But there is," she protested. "In my book, at least. I mean, you're married and . . . and . . ." She stopped. There was nothing more to say.

He sighed deeply. "If that's the way you

feel, I'm disappointed but that's your right. I don't know if it makes much difference, but I doubt that I'll be married for long, anyway."

Her heart skipped a beat. "What do you mean?"

"Jolene and I don't exactly have the best relationship. In fact, we have a very bad relationship. And that's putting it mildly. We're nothing alike and never have been. Sooner or later one of us is going to walk. I would have done it years ago if it wasn't for Juliette. I'm trying to wait for her to go to college. And Jolene may decide to leave even before that. It wouldn't surprise me."

Oh Lordy. He wasn't making it easy for her to walk away. "Well, it surprises *me*. I had no idea and I'm sorry that it's not working out for you. But you're still married *now*."

"Right. And I understand your viewpoint, or I'm trying to."

"Good," she said. "If . . . if things don't work out between you two, you know, then give me a call."

"You bet."

She put the phone back in the cradle and stared at it. Talk about tough. That had to be one of the hardest things she'd ever had to do. It wasn't every day that a man she found attractive was attracted to her. She had never felt so miserable about doing the right thing.

Forget it, Pearl Jackson. Forget him. He is married, married, married. And it's wrong, wrong, wrong.

She decided not to try and catch Kenyatta. She would change into something comfortable, read a book and dive into that new box of Godiva chocolates. No, not that. The last thing these hips needed was chocolate. She had bought the box before a man started showing interest in her and when she wasn't so worried about the hips.

OK, she would just read and then start dinner. Alone. Watch some TV. Alone. Go to bed. Alone.

She picked up the phone and dialed Patrick's number. "Do you still want to get together? I can make breakfast here."

"Sounds perfect. I'm on my way."

She closed her eyes. How could a little breakfast and conversation be wrong?

The doorbell rang and Pearl jumped three feet, spilling eggs over the edge of the bowl. She covered her heart with her hand. Lordy. You would have thought someone had just kicked the front door in.

She quickly mopped the eggs up from the countertop, then buttoned the jacket to her pantsuit and pulled it down over her hips. She would give anything to weigh another thirty pounds less just now. But there wasn't a thing she could do about that. Thank the Lord, Patrick didn't seem to mind the extra weight. Bless his sweet soul.

She parted the curtain covering the window in the door and peeked out. He was standing there wearing a navy suit minus the necktie and holding a small bouquet of pink carnations. If that didn't beat all. It had been ages since a man had brought her flowers. Heck, it had been ages since a man had brought her *anything*. She crossed her heart and glanced up to the ceiling. Lord, help me keep this man in check. Help me keep *myself* in check.

She opened the door, and he smiled. She loved his smile. He stepped in and handed her the bouquet. "Good morning again."

"Good morning, and thank you. They're so pretty. Come on in and make yourself comfortable. I was in the kitchen starting breakfast. I'll just go and put these in some water. I really wasn't expecting flowers. That was so thoughtful of you. Do you like scrambled eggs and scrapple?" *Why don't you shut up, fool, or you'll scare him off.*

"Scrambled eggs and scrapple sounds perfect," he said.

She pointed to the couch. "Have a seat then. I'll go put these in water." *You already said that, you idiot.* "Um, I'll be right back."

Instead of sitting, he removed his suit jacket, laid it across the arm of the sofa and followed her into the hallway. "Can I help?"

"Oh no. I have it covered."

"You sure?" he asked, rolling up his shirt-sleeves. "I'm pretty handy around the kitchen. If you haven't put those eggs on yet, I make a pretty mean omelette."

"Really? Well, I —"

"You got some tuna, onions and peppers?"

"Of course, but . . . tuna? In an omelette?"

"Yup."

She frowned with doubt. "It sounds, uh, different."

He chuckled. "Trust me. You'll love it. Just point me to everything."

Forty minutes later she set her fork down on the table. She was tempted to lick her plate clean. "That had to be the best omelette I've ever had."

He smiled with appreciation. "Thanks."

"I mean it. I wish I had paid more attention when you were making it." *Instead of focusing on your butt, your biceps, your smile.*

She had been so thrilled to have a man cooking in her kitchen that she couldn't take her eyes off him. "You'll have to give me the recipe."

"Or you'll have to invite me over again to fix one for you."

She lifted her eyebrows and smiled. "Or that."

He reached across the table and placed his hand over hers. It was a big, masculine hand but his touch was soft and gentle. She expected him to say something, but he just smiled with those sexy lips and looked at her. She lowered her eyes and pulled her hand away slowly. This was moving way too fast.

"I'm making you uncomfortable," he said. He clasped his hands together above the table. "I don't mean to do that."

She stood up with her plate and placed it in the sink. "You don't have to apologize. It's just that I . . . I . . . ." Oh Lord. She wanted him to touch her hand and a whole lot more, and it was tearing her apart. She knew she shouldn't feel this way but she couldn't help it. She closed her eyes and said a quick, silent prayer. Then she opened them and turned to face him. "Would you like some more coffee?"

"Yes. But I can get it." He stood up.

"No," she said tersely, grabbing his cup and saucer from the table. "I'm up. I'll do it."

He sat back down. "Fine."

She turned to the stove to refill their cups, and when she turned back he was clearing the remaining breakfast dishes from the table. She couldn't help smiling. He reminded Pearl of herself. He just couldn't sit still when there was work to be done around the house. She hoped they could be friends and have a cup of coffee once in a while. No harm in that.

"You have a great house here, Pearl," he said as he placed the dishes in the sink. "Nice and cozy."

"Oh shoot," she said as she placed their coffee cups on the table. "It's not nearly as nice as yours. And aren't you building a bigger one nearby?"

He nodded. "Too big if you ask me. I prefer something like this. You've added some nice personal touches."

She chuckled. "I made a lot of things myself, if that's what you mean, like the curtains and these matching place mats. Only because I can't afford to buy them."

"It looks like you," he said as they sat back down at the table with fresh cups of coffee. "And by the way, you're looking real good since I last saw you, Pearl. You've lost some weight or something."

She smiled broadly. She was delighted that he had noticed. "Well, thank you. I have lost a few pounds and I'm hoping to lose more."

"Not too much more, I hope."

She shrugged. "As much as I can. You know what they say — you can never be too rich or too thin."

"I hope you don't believe that. I know that some brothers think a woman is only attractive if she's, well, a certain size."

"Humph. You mean, if she's skinny."

He nodded. "Well, yeah. But I happen to like a woman with some meat on her bones. And the older I get, the more I realize that it's much more important that a woman's heart is in the right place."

She couldn't stop smiling at this man. She was tempted to kiss him on the spot, and that shocked her. She stood up abruptly. It was getting warm in here. "Let's go sit in the living room," she suggested. "It will be cooler, er, more comfortable there."

He stood and followed her. She pulled her suit jacket down over her hips, certain he must be watching them every step of the way. She also put a little extra umph into her steps. If he liked a little meat on a woman's bones, he must love these bones on her.

She turned when they reached the couch, and that million-dollar smile was within inches of her face. Oh Lord. Before she could take a step back, his lips were on hers. Her heart was pounding so wildly she thought he must surely feel it beating against his chest. But she forgot all about her thumping heart as he wrapped his arms around her and pressed his body closer.

She was about to grab his shirt collar and pull him down to the couch when she heard the front door open. Oh Lord! If Patrick's lips hadn't been smothering hers, she would have screamed at the top of her lungs. Instead, she pushed him away and turned. Just as she feared. It was Kenyatta.

Kenyatta stood at the entrance to the living room and stared at them with his jaw hanging down to his knees. Pearl didn't know who was more stunned, Kenyatta or her.

"Ma, do you know who that was?" Kenyatta asked, his eyes big with surprise. His unexpected entrance had scared Patrick off, and Kenyatta was following Pearl around the kitchen like a puppy as she cleaned up.

"Of course I know who that was," Pearl replied curtly. "I'm not stupid. It was Patrick Brown."

"I know you know his name, Ma," Kenyatta said sarcastically. "I should hope so, the way you two were just getting it on. But do you know he's married?"

Pearl removed her suit jacket and draped it on the back of a chair. Then she rolled up the sleeves to her white blouse. She was trying to buy some time while she figured out how to talk her way out of this mess. Jesus. She was just slobbering all over a married man, and her son had walked in and caught her red-handed. Lord, have mercy.

"Yes, I know that," she mumbled, turning to the sink. "I don't know what came over me, but it won't happen again."

"Ma, you were kissing the brother. What the hell is going on?"

Pearl twisted her lips. "Nothing's going on. And stop cursing."

"Stop trying to change the subject. Ma, he's married."

"How many times are you going to say that? Like I said, I don't know what —"

"Holy shit. I can't believe this." He reached around and felt her forehead. "You been feeling OK?"

She smacked his hand away. "Stop that."

"But this is so unlike you. Is he still with his wife?"

"I . . . I don't want to talk about it anymore. So can you please drop it?"

Kenyatta lifted his hands and backed away. "Fine. But it's kinda hypocritical if you ask me, that's all."

There it was, Pearl thought. He was going to use it against her to justify his relationship with a white girl. She wiped her hands on the dish towel and turned to face him. "Exactly what do you mean by that?"

He scoffed. "You get on my case about Ashley and here you are necking with some married dude. What's with that?"

Pearl paused to compose herself. "You're right, Kenyatta. What I did was wrong, I admit it. But don't you dare compare that with dating outside your race. That's different. It's —"

"Yeah," Kenyatta said sarcastically. "Fooling around with a married man is sinful."

Pearl turned back to the sink and grabbed the edge tightly. Who was she fooling? Nobody but herself. What she had done *was* a sin in the eyes of God, and there was no way to defend it. "You're right. What can I say? You going to bug me about it the rest of my life?"

"Nope. Just for a couple of years."

"I bet you are. But can we drop it for now? You've made your point. And it's not going to happen again."

"Good. I should hope not. There are plenty of unmarried men out there who would be lucky to have you, Ma. I'm going on up."

"Wait. Why did you come home early, anyway? I thought you were going to have brunch with Ashley."

"She called me on my cell phone and said something came up at home. Her mom has some big news, and she wants the whole family there to hear it."

Just her luck, Pearl thought as he left the room. The one time he gets home early, she wishes he had kept his butt out. Well, maybe not. If Kenyatta hadn't showed up, there was no telling what might have happened with Patrick.

She wiped her hands and sat at the table. What had come over her? She had kissed a married man in their home after coming in from church, and loved every single minute of it. Well, that was it. They couldn't even be friends, since it was obvious that she had not one iota of control over herself around him. She was going to tell him this was as far as it went the very next time he called or came by the shop. *If* he called or came by. For all she knew, Kenyatta had scared him off for good. And it was just as well. Kenyatta was right. How could she criticize him about Ashley or anything else if she was sinning with a married man?

Chapter 31

Candice sat in the stuffed armchair and looked around the living room at her family. Caitlin was seated on the couch filing her fingernails, and Ashley sat next to her twisting a lock of her hair, her cell phone resting in her lap, no doubt in case Kenyatta called. Jim sat in a straight-backed chair with the Sunday sports page. Their lives were all about to change, and Candice wanted to remember this last innocent moment.

She couldn't be sure how they would react to the news that her great-grandfather was a slave. For all she knew, Jim could decide to split. He thought he had married a white woman, not a woman with slave ancestors. But they all had to know. It wasn't fair to go on deceiving them.

She wished she could tell them and then they could all put it aside and forget about it. She had gone over and over in her mind how that might work. But in the end she realized that was impossible. Sooner or later Ashley or Caitlin would tell someone and then it wouldn't take long for the news to spread through Silver Lake.

She was also going to have to tell her

folks, and that was really going to be tough. Mom would have to deal with the news about her ancestors and her racist husband's reaction to it. Candice wasn't even sure she would tell her dad. She might just leave that up to her mom.

She let out a big gust of air. Maybe this was a mistake. Maybe she should just keep her mouth shut and suffer in silence. This might be the one time when it would be better to hide the truth from her family.

"How long is this going to take?" Caitlin asked, not even looking up from her nails. "I have to call Sue Ellen back."

"And I had to cancel a date with Kenyatta," Ashley complained.

"I don't know how long it's going to take," Candice said, "but it's more important than a phone call or a date. Sue Ellen can wait. So can Kenyatta."

Ashley blinked at the sharp tone of her mother's voice.

Caitlin sighed impatiently.

"It must be pretty important for your mom to call us all in like this," Jim said.

"Caitlin, can you put that file down for five minutes?" Candice asked shortly. "It's getting on my nerves."

Caitlin rolled her eyes to the ceiling and dropped the file into her lap.

Candice set her eyeglasses on the coffee table and stood up. She tried to soften her tone of voice. "Um, you all know that I've been looking into the family background, right?"

"Yeah."

"Uh-huh."

"Well, I've come across some unexpected findings." Candice paused and looked down at her hands. She laughed nervously. "I hardly know where to start."

"At the beginning," Jim suggested.

Candice looked into the eager faces of her daughters — so young, so innocent. This would rock their little worlds. They should be dealing with hair and nails and boys and school, not this heavy race stuff. They were teenagers, for God's sake.

And what about her parents? It could ruin their relationship. She didn't want to be responsible for that.

She sat back down in the armchair. This was a big mistake.

"What is it, Mom?" Ashley asked with obvious concern.

"Well, I . . . I . . ." Candice paused and fumbled with her hands in her lap. She couldn't do it. She couldn't bring herself to say the words. "It's . . . it's about your great-great-grandfather George. It seems that he was, um, that he was married twice."

"And?" Caitlin asked impatiently.

Candice blinked. "And, well . . . everyone assumed Marianne was his only wife. But she wasn't."

"What about his father Andrew, the landowner?" Ashley asked. "Was he married twice, to Sara and that woman you found at the archives named Caroline?"

"Uh, yes. Yes, he was."

"Is that it?" Jim asked.

"Yes." *Coward. Liar.*

Ashley jumped up. "You mean you made me call off my date with Kenyatta for this?" she asked indignantly.

"I thought it was important for you to know," Candice murmured.

Caitlin stood and threw her hands in the air. "Like you couldn't have told us later. Honestly, Mom. I am *so* not believing you did this."

"Well, sorry," Candice said curtly. But she felt relieved, so she must be making the right decision. "You can go now." But they were both already halfway out of the room.

"Are you OK?" Jim asked. He was looking at her strangely.

Candice looked down at her hands. "Yes, I'm fine." Suddenly she didn't feel so relieved anymore. She felt guilty as hell. She had to get out of there. She picked her eyeglasses up and stood. "I'm going to do some reading."

"Wait. I thought we were going over to Home Depot to pick up some things to get the yard ready for spring."

"Oh, right." She frowned. "Maybe next weekend, Jim. I'm really tired." How the hell could she go shopping at a time like this?

"You're always tired lately," Jim complained. "Maybe you should get a checkup."

She didn't say anything. Maybe he was right.

"When are you going to tell me what's bothering you, Candice?"

Good question. And he had every right to ask. But not yet. "It's nothing, really. I'm fine."

He shoved his hand into his pocket. "Suit yourself."

She started for the stairs.

"No, wait," he said.

She turned back to face him.

"Look," he said. "If you don't want to tell me what's eating you, fine. But don't insult my intelligence by telling me there's nothing going on. We've been together long enough for me to know when something's not right. You act different. You look different. You even went so far as to dye your hair blond. What's that all about?"

"I thought you liked my hair like this."

"That's not the point," he snapped.

She nodded. If only he knew how right he was. She *was* a different woman from the one Jim thought he'd married. She was black, the great-granddaughter of a slave. But she couldn't tell him that yet. She looked down at the floor.

"Fine. I'm going out." He slapped the newspaper down on a chair and stalked out.

She dragged herself up the stairs, lay across the bed and stared up at the ceiling. Sometimes she thought she would take this to her grave with her, just as George had taken it to his. It would be better that way.

She realized that the television was on. She looked at the screen and was greeted by a cereal commercial. Happy family. Happy kids. All white. She changed the channel, and there was another family. Happy. White.

She sat up, grabbed the remote and threw it across the room. It hit the wall and fell apart. Just like her life, she thought bitterly.

Chapter 32

Patrick strolled into Pearl's shop on Saturday a week after that fateful Sunday looking as handsome as ever. But Pearl didn't care how good he looked. She knew exactly what she had to do. Their little affair was over before it had even gotten started. She pulled him back into her private office.

"Sorry to barge in on you like this," he said, "but why haven't you returned my calls?"

"I've been meaning to," she said, as she shut the door, "but, well, I've been trying to think how to tell you this."

"Tell me what?"

"I can't see you anymore, Patrick." There, she'd said it. It was over.

He shoved his hands into his pockets. "What brought this on?"

"You're married, Patrick. My son walking in on us like that drove the point home. I don't do that stuff. I never have and I don't intend to start now."

He nodded. "Believe it or not, it's a first for me, too. Well, not exactly. But that happened a long time ago. I felt bad about it and broke it off. I decided that if I was going to be married, I would do my best to make it work, and that meant no fooling around. Fortunately, I've never been tempted since. Until now."

He smiled awkwardly, and she looked down at her thumbs. She was embarrassed and flattered all at once. She liked so much about this man. But she had to let it go. "I'm sorry, Patrick."

"I understand if it makes you uncomfortable, Pearl, and I'll have to settle for us being friends."

She sighed. "No, not even that. I'm going to have to ask you to stop coming by the shop."

"Whoa." He yanked his hands out of his pockets. "Damn. Can I at least call you once in a while?"

"Patrick, please."

"Fine, fine. I get it. But just one question."

"Go ahead."

"What if I wasn't married? Would you still refuse to see me? Or is that just a convenient excuse because you're not interested in me?"

"No, it's not like that. If you were single, it would be different."

"That could happen any day, you know. I've just been putting it off because of Juliette."

"It's not me you need to be talking to. Sounds like a conversation you should be having with your wife."

He nodded. "Fair enough."

"Sorry to be so blunt."

He shrugged. "You're just being honest. It's one of the things I admire about you." He backed toward the door, then stopped. "Good-bye, Pearl." He turned, opened the door and quickly walked away.

She sat at her desk and put her head in her hands. Why did doing the right thing feel so wrong?

Jolene banged the phone down. She was absolutely thrilled. The architect she'd hired after breaking up with Terrence had just informed her that they could move into the new house in a week, no more delays this time.

She clenched both fists. "Yes!"

This was wonderful news. She had already contacted a mover, and all she had to do was call and confirm. She had packed most of her clothes and Juliette's, as well as the good dishes and silverware. Patrick was taking his sweet time about packing his things. Well, he'd have to get cracking now.

She was meeting Bradford later that afternoon at the Ritz and had just showered and slipped into a skimpy black bra and G-string for the date. She couldn't wait to tell him the good news, but first she needed to let Patrick know. Lately he had been out so much working on David Manley's campaign, so she'd better grab him while she had a chance. She threw on a bathrobe and slippers and ran down the stairs.

"Patrick," she yelled from the top of the basement stairs.

"Yeah."

"Can you come up? I have great news about the house."

"Can't it wait until after this movie is over?"

Jolene tapped her foot impatiently. What did she ever see in that man? He had no interest at all in the house these days, especially since getting involved in politics. You would think they were building a shed out back for all the interest he showed.

She skipped down the stairs two at a time, ran into the media room and switched off the television set. It had a 42-inch plasma screen and took up half of the room, but not for long. In the new recreation room, they would have enough space for the TV as well as pool and Ping-Pong tables. She had wanted to install a home theater but Patrick refused.

"What the hell is wrong with you?" Patrick yelled as he sat up on the leather couch. "I'm watching that."

She turned to face him. "Patrick, that was Sean on the phone. We can move in next weekend."

"What?"

"The house, silly. We can move into the new house on Saturday."

"Fine. *You* can move in. I won't be joining you. I've been meaning to tell you that."

She frowned and put her hand on her hip. "Excuse me? What the hell are you saying?"

"I'm not moving into that monstrosity. We can't afford it, and I don't want to be there when your butt gets evicted."

"But . . . but you have to move in with us."

"Why? We haven't gotten along in years, Jolene. We hardly talk to each other anymore. And you screw every man who comes along, looking for a better deal."

Her eyes grew big. He knew about her affairs? Impossible. She had been so careful, and he never said a word.

"That's right." He smirked. "Don't think

I'm in the dark about it. You think I'm an idiot, don't you? Well, I've known for a while that you can't keep your skirt down. So has everyone else in Silver Lake."

Deny, deny, deny. What else could she do? "I . . . I don't know what you're talking about."

"Fine. Play dumb. I kept quiet about the architect and the others before him because I really didn't give a damn. But this latest thing with Bradford, that's the last straw. It's cold, tacky and thoughtless."

Jolene gulped. It felt like someone had stuck her head in a hot oven. She was speechless for the first time in her life.

"Cat got your tongue?"

She licked her lips. "What . . . what? How . . . ?"

"I just found some of the e-mail you sent to his office. Some pretty hot and heavy stuff there."

Jolene stomped her foot. "You had no right snooping around in my e-mail."

"Oh? And you have the right to screw my boss? Get some perspective here."

Jolene was furious, mainly with herself. How could she have been stupid enough to leave all that on the computer? Well, it didn't matter now. She wasn't even going to try to deny it anymore. Why should she? She was a vibrant, healthy woman, and he hadn't lit her flame in years. "Don't you dare scold *me*. Hell, you've never done bullshit to get us anywhere. Now you're putting all your time into this silly politics obsession of yours."

"I happen to like politics. What's wrong with that?"

"Everything, when you're neglecting your family. You're never home anymore. You're always running off to some political event in Annapolis or Upper Marlboro or God knows where else."

"Look. Don't try to twist this all up and make it look like *I've* done something wrong. *You're* the one who's been screwing around. Are you still seeing Bradford?"

Jolene didn't answer. She pulled the belt to her robe tighter. Now was not the time for him to see the G-string.

"Fine. Go right ahead and have your little affair. The sad thing is, I don't even care anymore. I just wish you'd do it with someone besides my boss. But I realized a long time ago that I'd never be good enough for you 'cause you never got over Jonathan Parker or the lifestyle you think you would have had with him or someone like him."

"I don't have to listen to this."

"No, you don't. But this is it for me. I'm not moving."

Shit, Jolene thought. She'd always known they would break up sooner or later. She just preferred later, and on *her* initiative. Not his. This was terrible timing. She needed him to help her get settled in the new house.

There was one thing that might get him to change his mind. "What about Juliette?"

He looked at her sharply. "What about her?"

"This is going to kill her," she said. "She adores you."

For the first time, his face softened. "Not if we handle it right. I'll break it to her, but I need you to cooperate. Don't make me look bad in front of her, and give me joint custody."

"Fine, if you agree to move into the new house just long enough to help us get settled. Then you can do whatever you want, and I'll cooperate when it comes to Juliette."

He glanced away and thought for a moment. She was tugging on his weak spot with all this concern about Juliette, and he knew it.

"How long do you think it will take you to get settled?" he asked.

"Well, after the housewarming party next month might be a good time for you to move out."

"Housewarming party? What house-warming party?"

"For the neighbors in Silver Lake. I've already hired a caterer and arranged for the decorations. And I plan to invite the governor and lieutenant governor."

"Wait a minute. And you didn't even tell me?"

"Don't get me started. You're just now telling me you never planned to move in with us."

"All right. But after the party, I'm gone."

Damn. How had this happened without her suspecting anything? "Is it another woman?"

"What?"

"Why are you doing this now? Are you seeing someone else?"

He sneered. "I wish."

"Well, where will you stay after you move out?"

"I'll stay here."

"That's impossible. We have to put this house on the market. We can't afford to keep two mortgages if you stay here."

"It will only be until I can get something smaller, a town house or condo. Until then we'll do whatever it takes to make ends meet."

She sighed. He had obviously been thinking about this for a while. Now she knew why he hadn't started packing his clothes. "Fine."

She stormed out of the room and climbed the stairs. He had really socked her between the eyes with that one. She always assumed that *she* would be the one to make the first move and that she would have another man lined up at the gate when she did.

She flopped down on the bed. This was definitely a setback, with Patrick wanting out and Bradford not yet in. Patrick was right. If word of her affair with Bradford got out before she was his woman, she would be shunned by everyone in Silver Lake who mattered. But if she was married or even engaged to Bradford Bentley, no one would dare treat her badly. She was going to have to come up with something to get her man. And fast.

Chapter 33

Barbara was having trouble getting her eyeliner to go on straight. She couldn't hold her hand steady to save herself. Darn. She grabbed a tissue and tried to rub the crooked black line off, then leaned closer to the mirror over the bathroom vanity.

She couldn't help giggling at what she saw. She had smeared the black stuff all over her eyelid. It looked like Bradford had socked her. Oh gosh. They were due at a black-tie charity dinner in thirty minutes, and this would never do. She searched through dozens of cosmetics bottles on the marble vanity top for her makeup remover. Where the hell had she put it? She knew she had some in here somewhere.

"Barbara, what's taking you so long?"

She jumped at the sound of Bradford's voice and knocked a bottle of astringent to the floor. Bradford, dressed in his black Armani tuxedo, was standing in the bathroom doorway tapping his foot. Barbara put her hand over her heart to steady it. "Shit, Bradford. You scared me."

Bradford pointed at his watch. "We should be pulling out of the driveway now, and you're still in your bathrobe and hair rollers."

"I'm coming, I'm coming. I'm almost ready." She bent over to pick the bottle up off the carpet, then stood up and nearly toppled over backward. She hiccuped and covered her lips with her hand. Oops. Did that come from her mouth?

Bradford narrowed his eyes at her. He sneered. "You're drunk. I don't believe this shit."

"I am not drunk."

"Yes you are. You're stone drunk."

"I had one drink and that was hours ago." She hiccuped again. "Maybe two."

"Dammit, Barbara. You're in no condition to go out tonight. When did you start drinking again?"

"What do you mean? I'm . . . I'm not drinking again. I just —"

He frowned. "Can't you do anything right? I give you the moon and the stars and you can't even keep your ass sober."

She calmly picked her cigarette up from the ashtray on the vanity and took a deep drag. "Maybe if you could keep your dick in your pants I could stay sober."

"What did you say?"

She smashed the cigarette out. "Nothing."

He stepped into the bathroom and grabbed her arm. "What did you just say?"

She yanked herself free. "I *said,* Nothing."

"You know what? I'll go alone. You're too much of an embarrassment in this condition." He turned and stormed out of the bathroom.

"Go ahead then," she yelled after him. "I hate going to these stupid affairs with you anyway. It's all so damn phony. Pretending to be Mr. and Mrs. Perfect. Mr. and Mrs. Happy Couple. Put on a happy fucking face. Pfft. We're anything but."

She stopped yelling when she realized that she was all alone. Fine. Go without her. He was probably running off to screw another one of his whores anyway, the one who sent the photos by e-mail. What did he take her for? A damn fool?

She had better company in mind for tonight anyway than a no-good, lying, cheating husband. Good old Mr. Belvedere was always there for her. And on Monday she would start the real estate class. Didn't need him. Nope. She blinked. Wait. Didn't the class start *last* Monday? Or the one before that? Gosh, she had forgotten all about it. She should call Marilyn to check.

She turned toward the door but realized

that she was still holding the bottle of astringent. She set it down on the countertop, then looked up and got a glimpse of herself in the mirror. Oh hell. Look at this mess. Mascara smeared all over her face, rollers in her hair. No wonder Bradford didn't want her. His new mistress probably never looked this bad. She never wore curlers and probably had boobs that stretched to California and back. And no doubt she had a big important career.

She sobbed, grabbed two tissues and stumbled into the bedroom. She flopped down on the bed, opened her nightstand and removed the bottle of vodka. Mr. Belvedere never cheated on her. He didn't play golf on rainy mornings and never worked late at night. He didn't care about her size 34A boobs and lack of talent. He was always right there when she needed him.

She stood up to get a glass from the bedroom, then changed her mind. Why bother? No one was here but her. She lifted the bottle to her lips and tilted her head back.

Chapter 34

Coward. Liar. The way she was deceiving her own family was utterly disgusting. Why, she was no better than George himself. Candice Jones, passing for white. Candice Jones, living a fat lie.

No, no, no. That was the wrong way to think about it. Things were better this way. Absolutely. Why destroy her daughters' lives simply to satisfy her own need to get this secret off her chest? Her parents' lives. Her husband's. They were all much better off not knowing the truth, and she would be better off forgetting.

She stared at the web page on the computer monitor in front of her. Lately that was all she'd done. Stare at it. She was weeks behind, and if she didn't get moving on this web site design now, she was going to find herself out of a job.

She sighed. One more bathroom break and then she would get down to business. She stood up and walked out of her office and down the hall, past the desk of her assistant, past Bradford's suite and past Brenda's desk with her eyes glued to the floor. She found it hard to look them in the face these days. When they saw her they saw a white woman. Ha. What a joke.

She turned a corner, opened the door to the rest room and stepped into a room full of men, all staring at her. She froze. What the hell were a bunch of men doing standing at urinals in the ladies' room?

Keith, a young web developer, had a big grin on his brown face as he zipped his fly. "Wrong room, Candice."

Holy Toledo. A wave of heat rose through her body. She backed out of the room and looked up at the sign on the door. "Men," it said in bold letters as big as you please. Damn. She had walked straight into the men's room. How utterly embarrassing.

She turned and fled into the women's room next door, walked into a stall and slammed the door shut. She sat down on the toilet and some of the faces she'd seen in the men's room started to come to her.

"Wrong room, Candice."

She shook her head. Ha. How about "Wrong life"? It was all a lie, starting with the color of her skin.

She exited the stall, walked to the sink and splashed cold water on her face. She dried it with a brown paper towel and stared at her reflection in the mirror.

How did her great-grandfather do it? How did he manage to live a lie day after day without losing his mind?

Chapter 35

Lee climbed out of the car of one of her regular customers and lit a joint. She walked to the corner, stood next to a building and watched the headlights floating up and down the rain-slicked street. God, she hated this life. If it wasn't for this stuff, she didn't know how she would get through the nights.

One of her roommates walked up, and Lee passed the joint to her. Andrea was as close to a friend as Lee had out on the streets of Baltimore. She was Latina and probably in her early thirties, since she claimed to have a daughter living in New York who was about Lee's age. Andrea's face was starting to show the years, but her body was still in top shape.

"Hey, what's crackin'?" Lee asked.

Andrea took a puff and handed the joint back to Lee. "Tony was out here looking for you, girl. And he was pissed."

"Shit." Lee stomped the ground and took a drag. "He say what it was about?"

"No. Said to tell you to get your ass over to his place as soon as you got back. What's with that?"

Lee shrugged. "He's probably mad 'cause

I been slackin'. Didn't even work last night. I'm so fucking sick of this shit."

Andrea shook her head. "Then you better take your ass on over there now. You got it coming, girl, but if he got to come out here to find you, it's gonna be much worse. For real."

"Let the nigga come find me. Shit. Last time he beat me, I was sore for days."

Andrea shrugged. "Hey, don't shoot the messenger. I'm just telling you what he told me."

"Yeah. Thanks."

"So, what you gonna do?"

"Damn if I know. I'm thinking of getting the hell on out of here."

Andrea's eyes popped open wide. "And going where? Shit. Anywhere you go, he's gonna find your ass."

"Maybe not. I got connections."

Andrea looked at her doubtfully. "Yeah, right. This that daddy of yours you always bragging about?"

Lee was silent.

Andrea chuckled. "If your pop's so rich, why the hell is your ass out here?"

"I won't be for long. Just got to find out where Silver Lake, Maryland, is." Although Lee didn't have the slightest notion how to go about it.

Andrea's eyes narrowed. "Did you say Silver Lake? That's right down there in P. G. County."

Lee blinked. "How do you know?"

"Don't you read the paper, girl? There was an article about Silver Lake in the *Washington Post* just the other day. Big spread with pictures and all. For real."

Lee smiled. Her heart was racing. "Get out of here, girl. You lying."

"Why would I lie? Ever heard of Mitchellville?"

Lee's eyes lit up. "Shit, yeah. Some rich niggas live over there."

"This Silver Lake is in that same area, from what I read. Anyway, I gotta get back." Andrea took a deep drag off the joint and gave it to Lee. "You better get your ass on over to see Tony. Don't go do nothin' stupid, girl."

Sometimes Lee thought walking away from all this would be the smartest thing she'd ever done. But Andrea was right. If she walked and Tony ever found her, she'd be in worse trouble than she was now. Last time, he busted her upside the head, using a phone book to keep her from bruising.

But she might know where her daddy lived now, and it wasn't all that far from Baltimore. It felt like Andrea had just dropped a ten-karat diamond into the palm of her hand. Maybe it was time to change the game.

She flicked the butt on the ground and stomped it out. She looked up and down the street to make sure Tony wasn't nearby, then rounded the corner and walked away. She never looked back.

Chapter 36

Pearl felt so odd coming to Jolene Brown's housewarming party after what happened between her and Patrick, not to mention the fact that she and Jolene weren't exactly friends. But Patrick had called out of the blue and convinced her to stop by.

She had to admit that she was curious to see the inside of the mini-mansion that had been shaping up on the hillside in Silver Lake, North. It had the whole neighborhood buzzing.

As soon as she stepped through the double doors and into the soaring two-story foyer, all she could think was, Wow. There were marble columns and gleaming hardwood floors and lots of crown molding. A huge chandelier dangled from way up above.

A butler took her coat and pointed her in the direction of the "great room." It was one of the biggest rooms Pearl had ever seen. She could practically fit her entire town house into it. One wall was made almost entirely of glass and it looked out over a huge lawn with flower beds and a deck.

Patrick said he didn't like the new house, that it was over the top. She agreed with him on that. It was beautiful, but she wouldn't feel comfortable living in a place like this either. She couldn't see herself plodding down the elaborate staircase early in the morning in her dingy old bathrobe and slippers.

A waiter bearing a tray of champagne flutes walked up to her. She shook her head at first, then thought, Why not? She took a glass and looked around. A lot of the neighbors were there but no one else from the town houses. She shouldn't have been surprised, given that this was Jolene's shindig.

If Candice had her way, they would all have stayed at home. But Jim and the girls wanted to come to the housewarming party, and Candice had to admit to herself that she needed to get out and focus on something besides her problems.

She looked up at the soaring ceiling. This must be how an ant felt standing on the floor of my kitchen, she thought. Frankly, she liked her own house on the southern side of Silver Lake just fine, thank you.

"Candice, you made it." She turned to see Jolene holding out her arms. They hugged and kissed, and Jolene greeted Jim and the girls.

"Yes," Candice said. "We wouldn't have

missed it for anything."

"So, what do you think?" Jolene asked.

"Um, you mean the house? It's lovely."

"Yes," Jim added. "It's beautiful."

"But I think you're going to miss the old neighborhood living over here in all this house," Candice teased.

Jolene chuckled. "Yes. Like a fork in my ass."

Ashley and Caitlin giggled as Jolene blew a kiss and moved on to the next group of guests.

That Jolene was a piece of work, Candice thought. There were probably no others like her. Thank goodness. One was enough.

Barbara noticed the faux animal print mules on Jolene's feet right away. Now where had she seen them? She blinked, trying to clear her head of the two shots of vodka she'd had before leaving the house.

And then she remembered. They looked just like the Stuart Weitzman mules in the photos of her bedroom that someone had sent her over the Internet. Barbara couldn't believe her eyes. Bradford and Jolene? She needed another drink.

"How are you, darlings?" Jolene asked as she kissed first Barbara, then Bradford, on the cheeks.

"Fine," Barbara muttered tersely. *Don't be silly, you idiot. You're imagining things.* Lots of women wore animal print mules.

"Your house is lovely," Barbara said sweetly. What a lie. It was the biggest, most ostentatious piece of tawdry junk she had ever been forced to step foot in. But so like Jolene Brown.

"You've outdone yourself," Bradford said.

"Thanks," Jolene said. "Have you had any champagne yet?"

"Not yet," Bradford said.

"Which way?" Barbara asked.

"The waiters should be by with some shortly. If not, go on down to the bar in the rec room. Enjoy yourselves, darlings." She blew kisses in their direction and sauntered off to the next batch of guests.

Barbara looked around for a waiter. "I'm going to mingle."

Bradford grabbed her by the elbow before she could take a step. He squeezed. "You don't need to drink anything here but water."

She pulled her arm away discreetly. "I'll drink whatever I damn well please," Barbara whispered tartly. "Just like you screw whatever you please."

Bradford cleared his throat. "Don't embarrass me, Barbara. A lot of my employees and business associates are here."

"I'm shaking in my boots. The day you start worrying about humiliating me with all your carrying on is when I'll start worrying about embarrassing you." She walked away from him and found a waiter. She grabbed a glass of champagne and took a big gulp. There. That was much better. She downed the rest and grabbed another.

Bradford and Jolene? Was it possible? She shook her head. No, no. Patrick worked for Bradford, and Bradford had always been careful not to mix business with his personal life. Still, there was a first time for everything and she would give anything to see the label inside those mules.

Jolene chuckled at the naughty thoughts dancing through her head. Had Barbara noticed the mules? She had worn them on purpose, hoping Barbara would recognize them from the photos she'd sent over the Internet. For the life of her, Jolene didn't understand why Barbara didn't leave Bradford right after getting the pics. Maybe the woman had convinced herself that they were fake or something. Fine. She would just have to convince Barbara that the photos were real, even if it meant shoving the mules up the woman's nose. Anything that might hasten a breakup in the Bentley marriage was on her to-do list.

Jolene was loving everything about this gathering. It was fabulous. A smashing success. This was the biggest, most elegant house in all of Silver Lake, North. OK, so maybe not as big as the Bentley place. But it was damn close. And it was brand spanking new.

She had worked her ass off the past month getting the house ready, but it was worth every late night, every aching bone, every spat with Patrick.

Some of her guests had insinuated that the house was too big and pretentious. Like Candice — that white bitch with her smart-ass mouth. *I'm afraid you're going to miss the old neighborhood living in this big house, Jolene.* Puh-leeze. Fat fucking chance. Candice was just jealous, plain and simple. They were *all* jealous — black, white — every last one of them. Some of them were so ungrateful it was disgusting. She would be sure to scratch them off her guest list for the next party. See how they liked *that*.

She couldn't really tell what Barbara thought about the house. Barbara was so clever at disguising her real feelings. But she didn't see why Barbara wouldn't like the place. Barbara was used to nice big things. Like Bradford and his dick. As much as she had come to despise Barbara, the woman knew a good thing when she saw it.

She didn't know why Patrick insisted on inviting that town-house trash Pearl Jackson and her nappy-headed son. Pearl did hair, for goodness' sakes. How working class. How like her husband.

Jolene shrugged. She didn't have time to think about that now. She mingled and smiled proudly as she watched Juliette chatting graciously with the guests. Her daughter had class. She fit in this house like it was custom-made just for her. The girl did her mama proud. And she had only recently turned fifteen. Jolene wondered if Bradford had noticed how delightful Juliette was.

Come to think of it, where was he? She excused herself from her guests and looked around for him. She had promised him a private tour of the house, starting with the master bedroom. And hopefully ending there, too.

Pearl was so glad to see Kenyatta and Ashley arrive that she ran up and kissed them both on the cheek.

"What do you think of the house?" Pearl asked.

"Big," Ashley replied. "Too big for me. I prefer smaller rooms. They're so much cozier."

"I kinda like it," Kenyatta said. "The rooms are nice and airy."

Pearl was with Ashley on this. The house was too showy for her. But she said nothing. She had kissed the girl, hadn't she? That was enough for now.

"It's got Jolene written all over it, that's for sure," Ashley said. "We lived next door to her before they moved, and this is her. Totally."

"Really?" Pearl said. "That's funny. 'Cause it's nothing like Patrick. He's much simpler and more down to earth than this."

"Uh-huh," Kenyatta said, frowning at Pearl in disapproval. "Is he now?"

"I mean, based on the little I know about him," Pearl added quickly. She was going to have to watch her mouth. Better yet, she shouldn't say anything about Patrick around Kenyatta, period.

"Oh, Bradford!" Jolene was sprawled out on the floor of her giant walk-in closet, christening the master bedroom of her new house. She and Patrick hadn't had sex in it. So somebody had to help her christen it.

She moaned and he clamped his hand

over her mouth. She shook it away. What the hell was that all about? It was a soft moan. She wasn't stupid. She knew she had to keep her voice down, that she had a houseful of guests downstairs.

He seemed to be in such a hurry. He hadn't even kissed her once. He had locked the door so he didn't have to worry about getting caught. But he was so totally focused on getting through this, it felt like he had forgotten she was even there. Maybe he was uncomfortable. He *was* lying on top of her on the floor with his bare butt exposed and half of his staff right downstairs. Not to mention his wife.

Personally, she wouldn't give a damn if the whole world heard them. She was living in a fabulous house and making love to the man of her dreams. Her man. Or soon to be. As soon as Barbara put two and two together, she'd *have* to leave him.

"Oh, baby," she whispered.

Chapter 37

Lee and Mookie rolled up to the entrance to Silver Lake in an early 1980s BMW sedan, courtesy of the Landover Mall parking lot.

"Holy shit." Mookie whistled. "You said your pops lives here?"

"That's what I'm hoping," Lee said.

"Damn, he must be making a lot of paper. They even got a gate to keep niggas like you and me out."

Lee giggled. It was hard to believe there were places like this in Prince George's. It was a world away from her old neighborhood in Seat Pleasant, that was for sure.

The guard, a black woman probably in her late thirties and wearing a uniform, stepped out of the gatehouse. Mookie rolled the window down and stared straight ahead. They had agreed that he would do the driving and she the talking. Lee smiled and held up the snapshot of her folks.

"I'm looking for my uncle," she said. "I was here visiting him a couple of months ago but I can't remember exactly where the house was."

The guard glanced at the photo, then at Mookie and back at Lee. She narrowed her eyes suspiciously. "That's an old photo, but I recognize him. Is he expecting you?"

"Uh, no," Lee said, clearing her throat. "We're driving through on our way home from . . . from Hampton University. We're students there. We're on our way back home to New York, and I thought I'd stop by and say hello."

The guard leaned down and looked in the backseat of the BMW. Then she took another close look at Lee. Thank God Mookie had picked out a fancy car to hot-wire this time, even if it was kind of ancient.

The guard stood back up. "OK. It's straight up this way. Take the second left. It's the last house on the right."

Lee smiled. She was in. "Thanks."

"And by the way," the guard added with a smile, "you look just like your uncle."

Whew! That was scary, Lee thought as they pulled away. But they had made it through the gate, and the guard recognized her daddy. She was getting close. She could feel it.

As soon as the car was out of the guard's sight she and Mookie slapped each other with a high-five. "You was cool," Mookie said, laughing. He turned up his nose and mocked her. "We go to Hampton University and we're up here lookin' for my uncle."

Lee cracked up and clapped her hands.

But they both grew silent as they drove deeper into Silver Lake, past Tudors and colonials with three-car garages and huge landscaped lawns. Some of the estates had swimming pools and tennis courts right in the backyards. There was a lake, a community golf course and a clubhouse. And Lee had never seen so many big new Benzes and Lexuses.

"Damn," Lee finally exclaimed as Mookie turned left. "My daddy lived here while I was fighting off fucking rats and roaches? And a rapist."

Mookie just shook his head and stared. By the time he pulled up in front of the house and shut off the engine, they were both thoroughly pissed.

"All I can say is, if this is the right house, your pops been living large while you been out there hustling."

"No shit." Lee frowned. He was up in there living in luxury, probably with a wife and kids, while she and her mama scraped and suffered. His life here was so grand, he probably wouldn't want to have anything to do with her.

"You sure you want to do this?" Mookie asked.

Lee bit her bottom lip. What the hell did

she care what he wanted or didn't want? He was some fake-ass sucker who knocked her mama up, then fled back to his castle. She had gotten this far in life without him. If he didn't want her, so be it. She would walk away. But he was going to know that he had a daughter living on the other side of the tracks who knew all about him.

"Hell, yeah," she said. "Wait here for me."

"You better take this," Mookie said, reaching in the glove compartment for the gun. "In case this is the wrong house. This look like one of them neighborhoods where white folks get out the rifle when they see a nigga coming to the door."

She took the gun and tucked it into her shoulder bag. Then she walked up and rang the bell. She waited a minute and rang again. Damn. Just her luck. No one was home. Or they peeked out the window and saw her black face.

She turned and walked back toward the car just as a middle-aged black woman strolled by with a poodle on a leash. The woman slowed down and stared, and Lee looked at the pavement. What the hell was that bitch looking at? Lee stuck her hand in her bag and felt for the gun. Just in case. She was obviously a stranger in these parts, and there was no telling what this uppity black bitch would do.

"Can I help you, young lady?" the woman asked.

Mind your own fucking business. "Um, I was just looking for my uncle. I'm from out of town."

"Ah," the woman said. "They're probably over at the housewarming party. Most of the neighbors are there."

Lee looked up. "Housewarming party?"

"If you drive up here a few blocks and turn right at the fork, you'll come to it. It's a big new contemporary-style house on the right. You can't miss it. There will be a lot of cars parked out front."

"Thanks." Lee smiled and hopped into the car with Mookie.

"Where are you coming from?" the woman asked.

Mookie sped away before Lee could answer.

As they followed the woman's directions, the houses became grander and the lawns bigger and Lee's jaw dropped to her chest.

A black family in a BMW SUV glided away from the curb, and Mookie pulled in behind them. Lee leaned forward and looked out the front window. She could hardly believe what she was seeing. A goddamn black Beverly Hills.

"I don't have to tell you I don't like this place, Lee. I'm thinking we should take our butts on back to Seat Pleasant. This the kind of place where even the niggas will turn your ass in if you don't look a certain way."

Lee shook her head. "No," she said firmly. "Not till I find him." She was gonna go up there and look around for the man in the picture. But her plan had changed. Now she wanted to tell this dude a thing or two.

Chapter 38

Barbara downed her second glass of champagne and licked her lips. Now she was ready to confront Jolene and get to the bottom of this mule business.

She walked from one crowded room to the other. The place was packed with people, but there was no sign of Jolene. Come to think of it, she didn't see Bradford either. Dammit. All sorts of dirty little thoughts about what they were up to danced through her head.

Then she spotted Jolene coming down the stairs and Bradford out on the patio talking to a small group of Digitech employees. Barbara shook her head. She was letting her imagination run wild.

"Jolene," Barbara called. "I want to talk to you."

Jolene turned and saw Barbara approaching her. Oh hell. There was something different about Barbara's tone, something about the expression on her face. Had Barbara seen something between her and Bradford? Jolene smiled. "Yes, Barbara?"

"Um, how have you been, Jolene?"

"Actually I've never been better, Barbara."

"Well, I don't know how you managed all of this so quickly, with all the work that goes into moving."

"Well, like an idiot, I insisted on having this party a month after moving in. But I'm so glad we did. Now it's out of the way. Everyone knows we're here, and I can focus on other things." Like your husband.

"I know what you mean," Barbara said. She had barely heard what Jolene was saying, she was so busy trying to figure out how to get to that label. She glanced down at Jolene's feet. "I love your shoes, Jolene."

Jolene blinked. "Oh, thanks." Was Barbara onto her little gimmick with the photos? She certainly hoped so.

"Um, which designer is that?" Barbara asked.

Jolene smiled. "You know, I can never remember which designer I'm wearing, unless it's Manolo Blahnik." She slipped the mule off, and they both looked down. "Ah, this one is Stuart Weitzman," Jolene said nonchalantly. "Not an incredibly expensive shoe but a nice one for a casual affair like this. And I haven't seen this particular style on anyone else since I got them." In other words, yes, *I* sent the pics to you, bitch. Yes,

I was in your bedroom with your man. "Do you wear mules, Barbara?"

Barbara froze. So those *were* Jolene's Stuart Weitzman mules in the photo. And Jolene's funky underwear. And obviously, Jolene wanted her to know it. Barbara felt hot rage swelling up in her throat. She ought to throw this drink in her hands right in Jolene's face. But she was a guest in Jolene's home and would never do that.

Instead she took short, deep breaths of air. She was surprised at how easy it was to control her anger, probably because she had seen it coming. And she'd had a lot of practice over the years with these women. The booze also helped.

"Do you wear mules, Barbara?" Jolene asked again.

Barbara blinked and stared at her. "What?"

"I *said,* Do you wear mules?"

"No, I don't," Barbara finally replied. God, she hated this woman. The sneaky, conniving little tramp. She despised Jolene more than all the rest of Bradford's women. Their husbands worked together. They socialized in some of the same circles. They had visited each other's homes. Barbara felt she had been deceived not only by Bradford this time but by Jolene, too.

"I always thought mules were inappropriate outside the bedroom." Barbara smiled wickedly. She couldn't resist getting that little dig in.

Jolene's eyes popped open. "Excuse me. Are you trying to tell me that I look tacky? Is that what you're saying?"

"It's what I'm trying *not* to say," Barbara said coolly.

"Oh!" Jolene could barely catch her breath. She couldn't believe that Barbara Bentley would insult her to her face. If anyone else dared talk to her that way in her own home, Jolene would have had them thrown out on their derrieres in a minute. But she couldn't possibly throw Bradford Bentley's wife out. Patrick worked for Bradford, along with half her other guests.

It had to be the alcohol making Barbara behave so outrageously. Everyone in Silver Lake knew she couldn't control her drinking and she'd been nursing a flute of champagne ever since she arrived.

Jolene tossed her weave over her shoulder and stalked off. Drunken country bitch.

Barbara glared at Jolene as she walked away. Cheap tramp.

Candice noticed Ashley standing across the room chatting with Kenyatta and his mom. She had assumed that Ashley would eventually bring Kenyatta over to speak to her. But it didn't look like that was going to happen anytime soon. Candice supposed she shouldn't be surprised. She hadn't exactly given Ashley the impression that she was delighted about the two of them as a couple.

She twirled her glass of red wine between her fingers. Maybe she should walk over there and say hello. It would be a nice gesture. She had nothing personal against Kenyatta or his mom. In fact, she had a few things in common with Pearl. From what Ashley had said, Pearl's ex-husband had been fooling around when they were married. And they both ended up raising their children as single moms.

And if this ancestry stuff had taught her anything, it was that Kenyatta and Pearl didn't choose their heritage. It had chosen them. And now her. And there wasn't a damn thing anyone could do to change that.

Candice sighed. Everything — every thought, every look, every gesture — led her back to this black-white thing these days. Enough of that for now. She was going to go over and say hello to Pearl and Kenyatta simply because she knew them and they were nice people.

★ ★ ★

Oh Lordy, Pearl thought. Here she comes — that Candice Jones. What on earth would she say to her? Pearl smiled and did the French double-cheek kissy thing with Candice. Kenyatta nodded politely in Candice's direction. Ashley smiled faintly.

"You look great, Pearl," Candice said with a smile. "How have you been?"

"Oh, I'm fine. And you?"

"I'm well."

"Good." Pearl cleared her throat and folded her arms and the four of them stood silently with smiles plastered on their faces. Pearl tried to steal a closer look at Candice without appearing obvious. What on earth did one say to a white woman wearing a flowered dress and those hippie-like sandals? Not to mention that weird crystal around her neck.

Candice shifted on her feet. Now what? She used to be so comfortable around black people. She worked with them. She lived next door to them. So why the hell did she feel so damn awkward now? *The secret.* This damn secret was ruining her life. She ought to yell right this minute and tell everyone.

"How do you like the house?" Pearl asked.

410

"Oh, it's lovely," Candice said. Perhaps if you were Jolene, that would be the truth, but it was too flamboyant for her. Still, it would be rude to say that. Everyone would think she was being the snotty white bitch. "What do you think of it?"

"Actually, it's a bit much for me," Pearl said. "Although it has some beautiful things in it."

Candice blinked. Well, this woman obviously spoke her mind. Candice liked that. Then again, it was easier to get away with saying something like that if you were black. No one assumed you were racist.

Stop it, Candice Jones. Stop thinking that way. She could say what she thought as long as she was tactful about it. "Actually, I agree with you, Pearl. It's beautifully done but not for everyone."

"Yes," Pearl said. "That's exactly what I mean."

"Ma," Kenyatta said, "we're going to mingle."

"See you around," Ashley said.

"Just a minute," Candice said. "When are you going to come to our house for dinner, Kenyatta?"

Kenyatta blinked. Ashley's jaw dropped.

"Whenever you'd like," Kenyatta replied. "I'm just waiting for the invitation."

"You and Ashley talk it over. We'd be glad to have you."

"Thanks," Kenyatta said, still looking stunned.

Ashley reached up and kissed Candice on the cheek. "Thanks, Mom," she said softly.

"Kenyatta is a nice young man," Candice said after he and Ashley walked off. "I know from experience that it isn't easy raising a child on your own."

"Tell me about it," Pearl said. "Does your ex-husband help out much?"

"Please." Candice waved her hand. "He sends a check now and then and they visit him a couple of times a year, but he's into his new life with a new wife. I did most of it myself."

"Same here. But personally, I preferred it that way. The man could move to Alaska for all I care."

Candice chuckled. "I know what you mean."

"Although it was tough on Kenyatta not spending much time with his daddy while he was growing up, and I regret that."

Candice nodded with understanding. "I imagine it must be harder with a son."

"In some ways. The temptations out there — gangs, drugs — seem to entice boys more." Pearl shook her head. "Girl, the things I went through to keep him out of all that could fill a book."

"Those things entice girls, too," Candice said. "Although with girls, the problem is more about the kind of boys they bring home."

"And to think you had two girls to deal with. Umph."

"Well, we both got through it. And we did all right, didn't we?"

"Amen to that," Pearl said, clasping her hands together.

"Maybe we should get together sometime and swap stories, Pearl. Lunch?"

Pearl hesitated for a second. Lunch? With Miss Hippie? Well, why not? It was obvious that she and Candice had a lot in common, if they could just look past the race thing. If Candice was willing to give it a go, how could she say no?

"I'd like that, Candice."

Jolene couldn't believe her eyes. Patrick and Bradford were out on the patio together and it looked as if they were having harsh words. All Jolene could think was that they'd damn well better be arguing about work. Of course they were. Patrick would never tell Bradford that he found the e-mail about their affair. Or would he?

As if to answer her question, Patrick took a swing at Bradford. Jolene gasped as the two of them went at each other like high school kids out on the playground. Grown men didn't fight like this about business. How dare Patrick behave this way at her party.

She banged her champagne flute down on a side table and ran out to the patio. Everyone had stopped what they were doing and stared at the commotion. Just as Jolene approached the scene, four men grabbed Patrick and Bradford and held them back.

"You ought to be ashamed of yourself, man," Patrick yelled as two of the men held on to him.

Bradford didn't say a word. He just jerked his arms, freed himself and glared at Patrick.

"Stop it!" Jolene screamed. She turned to Patrick. "What the hell is wrong with you? Fighting with our guests."

Patrick wriggled free of his captors and straightened his suit. He gave Jolene a dirty look, then turned back to Bradford. "And don't bother to fire me," he snapped. "I quit."

Jolene gasped. Was Patrick losing his mind? How the hell would they pay their mortgages? "Patrick, no." She turned to

Bradford. "He didn't really mean that."

"The hell I didn't," Patrick snapped. He stormed past Jolene and headed inside.

"Fine with me," Bradford said, wiping blood off his lip with his handkerchief.

Jolene tried to stay calm. She smiled nervously. "Everyone, please go on and enjoy yourselves. We'll work this out."

The crowd began to disperse, and Jolene walked up to Bradford. "Are you all right?" she asked.

Bradford ignored her question. "What the hell is this about you sending some pictures of my bedroom with your things in it to Barbara?" he whispered as he dabbed his lip.

Jolene swallowed hard. Sweat popped out on her forehead. Patrick found the photos on the computer, too? She had been so careful about hiding them. After she sent them to Barbara she gave the file a business-like name and buried it deep inside two other folders. And still he found the photos. The little sneak. "Uh, I'm . . . I'm not sure what you mean. What did Patrick say?"

"He said he found them in an e-mail addressed to Barbara. Is that true?"

Jolene's mouth felt like *it* was the one that had just been socked. She avoided his eyes.

Bradford gave her a withering look and

turned to walk inside.

"Bradford, wait. I can explain. I . . ."

He ignored her and kept walking.

Oh hell, Jolene thought. This was turning into a nightmare. First she had a spat with the doyenne of Silver Lake — but she had engineered that. Then her husband attacks Bradford and tells him about the photos. It couldn't get any worse than this.

Barbara lifted her glass to Patrick as he flew past her. "Good for you."

Patrick glanced at Barbara, then shook his head as he walked upstairs.

Barbara giggled and took another sip of champagne as Bradford walked in from the patio holding a bloodied handkerchief to his lips. As he approached Barbara, she could see that he was raving mad. Good. He had gotten exactly what he deserved.

"Come on," he barked at her. "We're leaving."

"No. *You're* leaving," she said curtly. "I'm not going anywhere."

"Barbara, I said we were leaving."

"*Bradford,* I said I'm not going anywhere." She rolled her eyes and lifted her glass to her lips.

He took her arm. "You're too drunk to stay here."

She yanked herself free just as Jolene walked up to them. Now what the hell did that bitch want?

"Bradford, please," Jolene pleaded softly. "Can I speak to you in private for a moment?"

Barbara's eyes opened wide. Of all the nerve. After what had just happened, this whore had the audacity to walk up to them and ask to speak to Bradford in private?

"Hell, no!" Barbara shouted before Bradford could respond. "Who the hell do you think you —"

"Barbara," Bradford hissed. "Will you please calm down? You're really embarrassing me."

Barbara turned on him. "*I'm* embarrassing *you?*" she shouted. "Well, that's a new one. You've been embarrassing me for thirty damn years, Bradford Bentley, with all your screwing around. So don't you talk to me about embarrassment." A few people turned and stared at them, but in that moment, Barbara was beyond caring what anyone thought.

Bradford lowered his head and walked away. So did Jolene, in the opposite direction.

Chapter 39

A tall, clean-shaven black man wearing a dark suit answered the door. He had closely cropped hair and a ready smile. But the smile disappeared when he saw Lee standing on the front porch. He looked over her jean-clad body with obvious disapproval. "May I help you?" he murmured.

"Um, I'm lookin' for Smokey."

"There's no one here by that name."

Now how could he be so damn sure of that, Lee wondered. There must be a hundred cars parked along the driveway and the curb outside this pad.

"You sure about that?" Lee asked, trying to peek around him. "Can I come in and look?"

"I'm afraid not, miss," the man answered indignantly as he moved deliberately to block her view. "This is a gathering for the residents of Silver Lake only."

"And who are you?" Lee asked.

The man looked down his nose with an air of superiority. "I am the butler for the evening. And you are?"

"Uh, never mind." She backed away and fled down the long driveway. She reached the car and turned to see the snobby butler standing in the doorway watching her every step. She got in, and finally the butler closed the door.

"What the hell happened?" Mookie asked.

"Punk-ass butler won't let me in."

"Well, that's that." Mookie started the car.

"Wait. I'm going to try around back."

"Are you tripping?" Mookie shouted. "Someone will stop your ass before you get anywhere near that place. In case you forgot, this isn't my car. And I can't afford to have the police coming around asking questions."

"You don't have to wait for me."

"What the hell are you saying? How you planning to get back to Seat Pleasant?"

"I'll find a way. It ain't all that far."

Mookie shook his head as Lee opened the car door. "Be careful out there."

She dashed off into the bushes at the end of the driveway as Mookie drove off. She wove her way through a wooded area surrounding the house until she came to the rear. A few people were mingling on the patio, holding drinks and talking. Lee walked out of the bushes and straight toward the house.

A white woman looked at her and smiled.

The woman opened her mouth to say something, but Lee dashed toward the house. She reached the French doors and tried one. It opened and she stepped in.

Whoa. Talk about fancy. This pad was the bomb. The room she was in was bigger than any apartment she'd ever lived in. The ceiling must be two floors high. She looked up, craning her neck to see to the top. For a second she thought it must be the wrong house. No way black folks could live here. Then she realized that most of the people in the room were black, and that there must be two hundred of them.

Sweet Jesus. Every black person on the face of the earth who didn't live in the hood was here. Light ones, dark ones, fat and skinny ones. They were tall and short and everything in between. And they were all dressed in the finest clothes. There were a few whites, and they looked good, too.

Lee was so taken with the place that she forgot why she was there. She wandered around from room to room, admiring the pretty surroundings with her mouth hanging open. There were chandeliers and sconces, arches and columns, and lots of big gold-framed paintings on the walls. It felt like she was visiting a museum.

She strolled up the stairs and saw closets

bigger than most bedrooms, a bathroom with two sinks, two toilets and two showers, and a bathtub big enough for two sitting up high on a pedestal. So rich folks got to have two of everything. It figured. Why share when you didn't have to?

She walked back down the stairs. She wanted to see the kitchen. They probably had two stoves and two sinks. Hell, maybe even two refrigerators. She was making her way back through the big room with all the people when she noticed a long table piled high with enough food to fill a grocery store. She stopped and stared. There was beef and ham, shrimp and chicken. And all kinds of salads and desserts. Lee hadn't seen this much food in months.

She grabbed a plate and filled it with some of everything, then stood off in a corner away from most of the guests. She realized that she had forgotten to get a fork but never mind. She was hungry as hell.

She stuck a piece of shrimp in her mouth with her fingers and closed her eyes. Man. It had been so long since she'd tasted anything this good. She was shoving a handful of carved beef into her mouth when she noticed a woman wearing mules approaching her. Shit. Lee chewed quickly and stuffed another handful of beef between her lips while she could.

"Young lady," the woman called.

Lee swallowed and looked up. Who the hell was this?

"Who are you here with?" the woman asked, eyeing Lee suspiciously.

Lee set the plate down on a nearby table. What had gotten into her? She was walking around like she belonged here. She didn't come to party or sightsee. Or even to eat. She came to find her daddy. "Um, no one in particular."

The woman's lips tightened. "Do you live in Silver Lake?"

Lee wiped her mouth with the back of her hand and glanced around, trying to decide what to do. Should she run toward the front door or the back patio? No. She wasn't going to leave before she found her daddy. Not after all she had been through to get here. She looked at the lady in the mules and reached down and touched her purse until she felt the hardness of the gun. "No ma'am."

"Then I'll have to ask you to leave."

"Um, yes ma'am." Lee started to walk back toward the patio door.

"This way," the woman snapped, pointing toward the front door and the snooty butler.

Lee went that way, with the lady following close behind, and now others had noticed. They stopped talking and drinking and stared as she passed by with her hand clutching her purse.

This wasn't going at all as she had hoped. Her daddy could be in here, and she was being marched back out. And back to what? The police were looking for her ass in P. G. County, and Tony was probably all over Baltimore asking for her. Sweat broke out on her forehead.

As she approached a young white woman standing alone in the foyer, she slipped her hand inside her purse and sized the young woman up quickly. She looked to be about twenty and was not much bigger than Lee herself. Lee knew what she had to do.

She grabbed the young woman and pulled the gun out of her purse all in one smooth motion. She wrapped her arm around the woman tightly and held the gun to her head. The woman screamed, and a gasp ran through the crowd. The woman in the animal-print mules dropped her flute on the marble floor of the foyer. It shattered. Then all went silent.

"What are you doing?" the young woman yelled. "Let me go." She struggled, but Lee held on. Her heart was racing, but she couldn't let these people know she was scared.

"Shut up, bitch," Lee screamed. She tightened her grip on the woman and pulled her back toward the wall. She didn't want anybody sneaking up behind her. She would have pulled the woman back further, but the bitch was wiggling so much and dragging her feet.

"Who are you?" the woman in the mules asked. "What do you want with her?"

A crowd of people gathered behind the woman in the mules. Lee knew she had to keep anyone from coming any closer.

"Don't anybody move," Lee demanded. "Or . . . or I'll shoot her. I swear."

Everyone froze except a woman in a long flower-print dress. She broke through the crowd, followed by a young man wearing dreadlocks.

Lee pointed the gun at the woman in the flowered dress, then back at the young woman's head. "Stop, dammit, or I'll shoot her."

The woman stopped and held up her hands. "I'm her mother. Please. Don't hurt her."

"I won't hurt nobody if you just stay the hell away from us."

"All right," a man said with practiced

calm. He made his way to the front and held his hands out. "Everybody stay back." He looked at Lee. "What is it you want?"

"Please," the woman Lee was holding said softly. "Let me go."

"Shut up, white bitch. And keep still. Don't make me have to shoot you."

"Ashley, stay calm," the mother said. "Do as she says."

"For God's sake, Patrick, do something," the woman in the mules pleaded. "Don't just stand there."

"Jolene, please," Patrick said. "Listen, young lady, we don't want anybody to get hurt here. Just tell us what you want. Is it money? Let her go and we'll get it for you."

"I don't want your damn money," Lee spat. "I'm looking for somebody."

"Who?" Patrick asked.

"My daddy."

Patrick frowned. "And you think he's here?"

Lee nodded. "His name is Smokey and he lives here in Silver Lake."

"There's no one here by that name," Jolene said.

"He's here," Lee shouted. "I know it. Find him or I'll shoot her."

"OK, OK," the mother said. "We'll do

our best. Just don't hurt her."

"Smokey sounds like a nickname," the young man wearing dreads said. "What's his real name?"

Lee hesitated. "I . . . I don't know. I mean, I ain't never seen him. I just know his name is Smokey."

"Well, he's not here," Jolene insisted.

"Look," the young man said. "Don't hurt her. She doesn't know anything about your daddy. Let her go. You can take me instead. My name is Kenyatta."

"Oh my God," a plump woman shouted from the rear. She made her way to the front and stood next to Kenyatta. "Please, let the girl go," she pleaded with Lee. "And we'll help you find your daddy. But we can't do it with you holding a gun to her head. Nobody can think —"

"Shut up, bitch," Lee shouted. "And everybody, y'all just . . . just keep still. Or I'll shoot her. I ain't kidding."

Ashley suddenly bit Lee on the arm.

"Ouch!" Lee smacked the gun upside Ashley's head and grabbed her tighter.

"Oh God," the mother whined. "Ashley, please. Stay still."

Ashley whimpered and rubbed her head.

Lee stuck the gun in Ashley's ear. "Stupid-ass white bitch," she shouted. "Shit. I ought to waste your ass just for the hell of it."

"Please, no," the mother cried. The woman was in tears. "She's not . . . she's not white. Her great-great-grandfather was a slave."

The room fell silent. Everyone turned and stared at Candice.

Chapter 40

"Yeah, right," Lee said. "And my great-great-granddaddy was the king of England."

Good God, Jolene thought. Her party was completely ruined. Fights. Hostages and guns. And now Candice was declaring herself black. What was next? People would talk about this party for years to come but for all the wrong reasons. And why the hell didn't that lame husband of hers do something instead of standing there looking like he'd just seen a ghost?

Barbara drained her glass of champagne. This was too much. Where on earth did that comment about Candice's ancestors being slaves come from? And where the hell was Bradford? She hadn't seen him since this wild child pulled the gun.

An awful thought crossed Barbara's mind. Could Bradford be this girl's father? He had never used the name Smokey to her knowledge. But she didn't put anything past that horny man.

Pearl blinked. Uh-huh. She knew it. She knew there was something strange about that Jones family. Candice, Ashley, Caitlin — all of them were weird. Poor Ashley.

But as bad as Pearl felt for Ashley, she didn't want her son exchanging himself for anybody. He didn't need to be anybody's hero. What good would that do? What he needed to do was stay calm. Everybody had to stay calm. The young girl talked tough, but Pearl would bet her last dollar that she was more frightened than anyone in this room.

Candice felt all eyes on her, and tears flowed down her cheeks. "It's . . . it's true. I recently found that out. So please, stop calling her a white bitch."

"OK, then," Lee said. She pressed the gun into Ashley's temple. "Black bitch, shut up."

"Look, we're not getting anywhere this way," Patrick said gently. "What's your name?"

"What's it to you?" Lee retorted. "You think I'm stupid?"

"No, not at all," Patrick replied calmly. "But if we knew your name, maybe it would help find your daddy."

Lee hesitated. "The name's Lee."

"How old are you, Lee?" Patrick asked.

"Sixteen. And that's all you need to know."

"Fine," Patrick said. "Lee, why don't you give me the gun? And we'll talk about finding your daddy."

"You really do think I'm stupid, don't you? You'll just haul my ass off to jail if I do that. Hell, you going to do that any damn way, so I'm not giving up this gun or the girl until somebody tells me where my daddy is first. I got myself into some real bad trouble and . . . and . . . he's the only one that can help me."

"Trouble?" Patrick asked. "What kind of trouble?"

Lee stomped her foot. If only they knew. This stuff she was doing now was nothing compared with what she'd done to Uncle Clive. Why didn't these people find her daddy? She was so scared, she wasn't even mad at him anymore. All she wanted was to find him.

"It's pretty bad," Lee said softly. "Please, just help me find him. I don't want to have to hurt nobody."

"I'll . . . I'll help you," Patrick said in almost a whisper. "Just give me the gun."

Lee whimpered. She wanted more than anything to get rid of this thing. It seemed to be causing more harm than good. But she couldn't. "No," she said stubbornly. "I . . . I can't. Not before I find my daddy."

"I . . . I think I'm your daddy," Patrick said softly.

Everyone gasped.

Lee blinked. "Huh?"

Patrick nodded. "A long time ago, I used the nickname Smokey. And you're about the right age."

Jolene's mouth dropped open. She stared at Patrick. What the hell?

Lee looked at Patrick with doubt. "You're lying. You just trying to get me to give up the gun."

"Your mother's name is Blanche," Patrick said. "Am I right?"

Now Lee was crying. She quickly wiped the tears from her eyes with the hand holding the gun. She was tired of being so mean to the girl Ashley, so she pointed the gun at the floor instead. But she held on to Ashley.

"How . . . how did you know my mama's name?"

" 'Cause I met her about sixteen, seventeen years ago at a conference in D.C. She worked for the government. But I only knew her for a short while, and I didn't know anything about you. She never told me she had a child."

"What's she look like?" Lee spat out.

"A lot like you, now that I think back," Patrick said. "Only she was a little plump, at least back then. She was very pretty."

Lee swallowed hard. So it was really him. Now what should she do? She could run and hold the woman as a hostage until she got out of the house. But she was tired of all the running.

She took a deep breath and let Ashley go. She was about to place the gun on the floor when a man grabbed her from behind and wrestled it from her. He was tall and had a bloody lip. She didn't know how he had gotten back there without her seeing him, but she didn't really care. Not anymore. She was tired. She sank down onto the floor.

"Thank you, Bradford," Candice said, still weeping as she held on to Ashley.

"We've got to call the police," Jolene said breathlessly.

"I already called them on my cell phone," Bradford said. "They're on their way."

"Thanks a lot," Patrick snapped. "I would have handled it. This is my house."

Bradford held his hands out in mock surrender. "Sorry. I was trying to be helpful."

"The last thing she needs now is the police," Patrick said.

"But Patrick!" Jolene protested. "She just broke into our home and held one of our guests hostage. It has to be reported."

"I know that, but I want to talk to a lawyer first and get her some protection."

Jolene folded her arms and glared at Patrick as he helped Lee up from the floor and pocketed the gun.

"I'm going to take her to the den and calm her down," Patrick said. "Then I'm going to call a lawyer." He led Lee into another room and shut the door.

Jolene stood near the front door and fumed in silence as the crowd dispersed. They barely looked at her as they rushed to get out before the police arrived.

This had turned into the worst day of her life. Barbara had insulted her. Bradford was mad at her. Patrick had cheated on her and produced a child — a trashy thing who looked and sounded like she was from the hood. And worse, the little thug had the nerve to come into her brand-new house and hold a gun to the head of one of her neighbors.

Now her guests were tripping over themselves in their rush to get out of her house. She would never live this down. She felt a lump in her throat and turned and fled up the stairs, ignoring the stares of the few guests still lingering in the foyer.

Chapter 41

Barbara didn't say a word to Bradford. Not during the drive home from the party, not Sunday morning at breakfast. And he seemed to know better than to say anything to her.

That evening she removed the tuna casserole that Phyllis had prepared the day before from the refrigerator and dumped a can of Alpo dog food in it. The family dog had died shortly before Rebecca's wedding, and the food was almost a year old. This was as good a way to get rid of it as any, Barbara figured.

She stirred it in carefully, reheated it at 350 degrees for twenty minutes and served it to Bradford on their best china. She fixed a small tuna salad for herself, then sat down to watch him eat his dinner.

"What kind of casserole is this?" he asked, his brow furrowed in contemplation as he chewed slowly.

"Oh, a little tuna, a little pasta, a lot of dog food." Barbara smiled with exaggerated cheerfulness. "Do you like it, darling?"

Bradford dropped his fork on the floor and spit his food out across the kitchen table. "What?" he yelled.

"I said a little —"

"I heard what you said," he interrupted with indignation. "What the hell is wrong with you, serving me dog food for dinner?"

Barbara stood and smiled. "If the shoe fits . . ." She shrugged. "And tomorrow you'll have to get your own dinner. I start my real estate course and then I'm having dinner with Marilyn. I won't be home until after eleven." She strolled out of the kitchen, ignoring the string of obscenities that Bradford hurled at her.

She entered the family room, marched to the bar and filled her arms with every bottle of liquor she could find. She carried them all into the laundry room and dumped the contents down the drain, one by one, then threw the bottles into the wastebasket. She grabbed her pack of cigarettes off the coffee table in the family room and cut it up with scissors.

She knew it was going to take more than this to quit all of her vices. She'd had this drinking problem off and on for years. The cigarette habit, too. She had to get her head together if she was going to succeed.

As soon as she got her real estate license, she was going to find herself a nice luxurious clinic where she could relax and dry out in private and in style. She was going to straighten herself up and get stronger. And then she was going to become the best damn real estate agent in Prince George's County.

She might not ever actually leave Bradford. A part of her still loved him and always would. But if she stayed, it would only be because she wanted to, not because she needed him to feel important.

She entered the kitchen. Bradford had obviously left the room in haste. His uneaten plate of food still sat on the table, his fork on the floor. Barbara walked right past it and put on a strong pot of Jamaica Blue Mountain coffee. Then she went into the den and picked up one of the books about real estate that Marilyn had given her. Her first instinct was to reach out to the coffee table for her cigarettes. Then she remembered that she was trying to quit. She sat back, curled her feet up on the couch and opened the book to Chapter One.

Jolene couldn't get out of bed. It was just as well. Juliette had stayed overnight at a friend's. Patrick had moved out. And Bradford wasn't speaking to her. She was the laughingstock of Silver Lake, so she had no reason to get out of bed. Ever.

Why did she have such rotten luck with men, starting with Jonathan? The ones she really wanted never seemed to want her. Patrick was the only man who ever genuinely cared about her, the only man who liked her for who she really was. But she hadn't wanted him, and now even he wanted out.

Last night, after everyone had hastily departed, Patrick and Lee went to the police station, where they met an attorney who advised Lee while she was questioned. When they returned to Silver Lake, Patrick put Lee to bed in the guest room.

Then he quietly told Jolene that he had an interview for a position as director of information technology in the Prince George's County government. If he got it, he would have a staff and be paid a lot more than what Bradford had paid him. He even hinted that there was a new woman in his life. He slept on the couch in the family room, got up early the next morning and packed a few bags, and left the house, taking Lee with him.

Jolene couldn't believe all this was happening to her. She snatched a tissue from the nightstand and dabbed her eyes. She was already starting to miss him. Imagine that. It was too damn quiet in this big house.

And obviously, Patrick wasn't the wimp he seemed to be. Or maybe he had changed. Whatever. She had been chasing all over town after these no-good married men, and the best man for her was right under her own roof.

She threw the bedcovers back and jumped up. She was going to pay Patrick a visit at the old house and tell him she would be willing to forgive his infidelities if he would forgive hers. She would suggest that they try to make a fresh start in their new house.

But first she was going to take a long hot bath, then put on her favorite St. John suit and her new pair of Chanel two-toned pumps. There was no telling who she would run into, and she had a lot of ground to make up in the image department, especially if Patrick landed a new position as a director in the county government. She had to look the part of the boss's wife.

Pearl shook her head as she stood over the sink in her bathrobe and washed the dinner dishes. She still couldn't get Lee out of her mind. That poor child had to be desperate to find her daddy to pull a stunt like that one last night. And to think that Patrick was the daddy.

And Ashley. Lord have mercy. Just when she was coming around to liking the girl, this stuff comes out about her not even really being white. Humph. She looked white, but thanks to the one-drop rule in America she was black. Pearl shook her head again. Poor child. It must be awfully tough to wake up one day and learn that you aren't really who you think you are.

It just went to show you, life was tough. But she had gotten through the rough times, and so would Lee and Ashley. If there was one thing Pearl had learned, it was that you couldn't let these setbacks keep you down. You had to get up and keep on moving. Heck, she was still learning, because crazy stuff was always happening.

She just hoped Kenyatta could deal with this news about Ashley. He thought he had a white girlfriend and now he learns she's black.

As if on cue, Kenyatta entered the kitchen, came up from behind and kissed her on the cheek. The fresh scent of a recent shower lingered around him, and he was dressed in a new pair of blue jeans and a crisp white cotton shirt that Pearl had ironed just that morning.

"Where are you off to?" she asked.

"Over to Ashley's."

Pearl nodded. "I've been meaning to ask you something."

"Yeah?"

"How are you with all this about her family?"

He sighed deeply. "It's mind-blowing. She's trying to be cool about it, but I can tell that it's rough on her."

"Oh, no doubt. But my question was, how are *you* handling it?"

He shrugged. "It doesn't really faze me. I mean, I worry how it's hurting her. But you know, I'm not seeing Ashley because I thought she was white. She's kindhearted and thoughtful. She's good to me. *That's* why I'm with her."

Pearl smiled. She was so proud of this boy. "Good for you. Obviously, I didn't raise no dummy."

They both laughed. Pearl wiped her hands and turned and hugged him warmly. Then she looked into his face. "You know something? You're a much better person than I am. But I'm working on it." She was always worried about teaching and showing him what was right. Now she realized that he might have a thing or two to teach *her.*

"You do OK, Ma. I just wish you'd relax and not take everything so seriously. Go have some fun. Get yourself a man."

Pearl chuckled wryly and turned back toward the sink. "Yeah, yeah. I hear you."

"Well, I'm off."

"Tell Ashley I said hello. You know, I'm having lunch with Candice this week."

"For real?" Kenyatta asked, clearly surprised.

"Yeah, baby, but I'm a little nervous about it now, after what happened at the party. What do you say to a woman who's just discovered she's black?"

Kenyatta shrugged, then his eyes lit up. "Hey, sista!"

Pearl cracked up over the sink. "Oh, you. Go on."

She was still chuckling when Kenyatta shut the door and the phone rang. She wiped her hands on a towel and picked up her cordless phone.

"Pearl. Hi, it's me."

Pearl sank down in a chair at the kitchen table. This was the last voice she expected to hear. "Patrick?"

He chuckled at the obvious surprise in her voice. "I wanted to apologize for all the confusion last night," he said softly. "I guess you must think I'm a jerk after what happened."

He should be having this discussion with

his wife, Pearl thought. "It's no business of mine."

"I figured you would say something like that. Well, I also wanted to tell you that Lee is still with me. I'm going to keep her for the time being."

Pearl nodded into the phone with approval. "And the girl's mother? Where is she?"

"In Baltimore. We got in touch with Blanche late last night. It turns out that Lee had run away from home several months ago. Her mother was worried sick about her."

Pearl gasped. "Well, why did Lee run away?"

"Oh man. It was a bad situation with her mother's boyfriend. I still haven't gotten the whole story out of Lee, but it seems that he attacked her and she shot him. She thought she had killed him, so she ran."

Pearl closed her eyes. This story was getting more unbelievable by the minute. "Oh my Lord."

"The guy was badly wounded but he survived. We found that out last night when we talked to Blanche."

"Well, thank goodness, but it sounds like a mess. How is Lee holding up?"

"She's doing all right considering the circumstances. I knew nothing about her until now. The relationship with her mother was brief, at a real bad time in my marriage. But I'm going to do whatever it takes to help Lee."

"That's so good of you, Patrick. It sounds like that girl really needs you. How is Jolene with all of this?"

"That's the other thing I wanted to tell you. I left Jolene. I'm back at the old house with Lee now."

Pearl's mouth dropped open. "I . . . I'm sorry to hear that," she mumbled.

"Don't be. It's been a long time coming. I told you that."

"Well, if you think it's for the best."

"I *know* it is," he said firmly.

"Then I wish you the best of luck, Patrick, especially with Lee."

He chuckled. "You don't have to sound so final. There's one more thing I wanted to tell you."

Goodness, Pearl thought. How much more could there be? "And what is it?"

"I'm standing outside your front door."

Pearl jumped up. Good Lord. He couldn't be serious. "I hope you're joking."

"Nope. Can I come in for a minute?"

Pearl looked down at her robe and slippers.

"I don't care what you look like or whether the house needs cleaning or any of that," he added as if reading her mind. "I just want to see you."

She chuckled. "I hope you mean that, 'cause I'm not even dressed yet. And the kitchen really is a mess since I was just doing the dishes."

"You gonna let me in or not?"

She opened the front door. "Hello, Mr. Brown," she said into the phone. Then she reached out and pulled him through the doorway.

They sat at the dinner table in silence, each deep in thought.

"Well," Jim said, "looks like I'm the only white person around here now."

Caitlin grunted and Ashley smiled faintly. Candice shoved her peas around on her plate. If that was an effort to ease the tension, it had flopped miserably. She took a deep breath. "I'm sorry about what happened at Jolene's last night."

Ashley looked up from the table. "You apologized once, Mom. It's not your fault what that girl did. I still get to shaking every time I think about it, but it's not your fault."

"Maybe it wouldn't have happened if I had been more open about us from the start," Candice said.

"Well, that girl . . ." Ashley paused and frowned. "What was her name?"

"Lee," all three of them said at once.

"Right," Ashley continued. "I was so scared it's all like a blur to me now. But she wouldn't have known the difference anyway. We look white."

"You're right," Candice said. "But I still should have told you sooner. The way it came out last night was horrible."

"Why didn't you tell us before, Mom?" Caitlin asked.

"I . . . I was frightened and angry about it."

"Angry?" Jim said. "With whom?"

Candice shook her head. "I don't know. With the world, I guess, but mostly with my great-grandfather for being dishonest about his background and deceiving all of us, all of his descendants."

"Why do you think he did it?" Ashley asked softly.

Candice sighed. "I understand it now. I mean, even today, with slavery behind us, I had a hard time admitting that one of our ancestors was black. I didn't want that stigma on us. And it was a hundred times worse back then. So I have a sense of what motivated him. I'm not saying that what he did was right. But I understand it."

Caitlin frowned. "It feels different from what I would have thought. What do I tell all my friends?"

"Kenyatta didn't believe it was true at first," Ashley said. "He thought you just said that to get Lee to let me go. I told him there was no way you would have said that unless it was true."

"How's he taking it?" Candice asked.

Ashley smiled. "He's being very supportive, just like I knew he would be. He's a real sweetheart. But I don't know how some of my white friends will react."

"I'm not going to tell anybody," Caitlin said stubbornly. She shoved her food around on her plate, and Candice realized that Caitlin hadn't taken a bite since she sat down at the table.

"I think you have to tell your closest friends," Candice said gently. "You know how word gets around in Silver Lake. They'll hear it sooner or later, and it's better that they hear it from you."

"You don't need any friends who have a problem with it, anyway," Jim added.

Candice nodded and smiled at Jim. She had completely misjudged him. They had stayed up practically all night talking about how they would handle it with the rest of the family, their friends and neighbors. He promised to help her get through this, and she hoped he meant it. She really needed him now.

"What if they *all* have a problem with it," Caitlin cried out suddenly. "I won't *have* any friends."

Candice was surprised at the outburst. Caitlin had always seemed so open-minded about things like this. She had supported Ashley when her mom raised objections about Kenyatta. "I doubt that, honey. What about Sue Ellen? Didn't she date a black guy once?"

"Some of our friends bad-mouthed her behind her back and they broke up," Caitlin retorted. "And her mom didn't like it any more than you did."

Candice cleared her throat. "Well, I've changed about that," she said firmly. "I was wrong. Look, honey, nobody said this was going to be easy. But you can make new friends who will like you for who you are, not your background."

Caitlin moaned. "Do you have any idea how hard it is to make friends, Mom? Why couldn't you have told us in private. You didn't have to blab about it in front of all of Silver Lake."

"Again, I apologize for how I did it. But

the secrecy stops here. I tried to keep it a secret, and it was awful."

"Your mom's right," Jim said. "People have to know the truth."

Caitlin jumped up. "Why? And what is the truth? We look white, and as far as I'm concerned I *am* white. You can't change that."

"Caitlin, sit down," Candice said firmly.

Caitlin ignored her mother. "We're already the joke of Silver Lake. Now this."

"What do you mean?" Candice asked, frowning.

"Look around you, Mom. Just about everyone else drives big new Mercedes-Benzes and Jaguars. We drive a tired old Ford Taurus. And we live in one of the smallest houses around here. Now we find out we're niggers."

Candice stood up and slapped her daughter firmly on the cheek. "Don't you ever let me hear you use that word again."

Caitlin winced and grabbed her cheek. She gave her mother an icy stare, then turned and fled the room.

Candice flopped back down in her seat. She couldn't believe she had just smacked Caitlin. More than that, she couldn't believe Caitlin's harsh words. But maybe she shouldn't be surprised. Caitlin had no

doubt heard much worse from her grandfather's lips. And she herself had behaved
like an idiot about Ashley and Kenyatta.

"Do you want me to go and talk with
her?" Jim asked.

"I'll go if you want," Ashley offered.

"No, I'll do it," Candice said as she stood
up.

It seemed only right, since she was the
reason her daughter was behaving this way.
She couldn't do anything about the past,
about George or even her dad. But she
could do a lot about the future by setting a
better example for her children. Starting
now.

Lee was the happiest she had ever been.
No doubt she was in trouble for shooting
Clive. But her daddy was sticking by her,
and the lawyer thought it was a good case of
self-defense. Mama had left Clive after
learning what he had done to her, and the
authorities hauled him off to jail.

Every morning Lee woke up, went
straight to her bedroom window and looked
out over the estates of Silver Lake. She
loved to see the tulips blooming and to
smell the scent of freshly mowed lawns. She
had everything she had ever wanted and so
much more. She was living with her daddy

in a big, pretty house. And there was plenty of food, clothes, cars and money.

She was living the American Dream.